INHUMAN ACTS

A NOVEL

BROOKE L. FRENCH

Black Rose Writing | Texas

ISBN: 978-1-68513-035-0
PUBLISHED BY BLACK ROSE WRITING
www.blackrosewriting.com

Printed in the United States of America
Suggested Retail Price (SRP) $21.95

Inhuman Acts is printed in Baskerville

*As a planet-friendly publisher, Black Rose Writing does its best to eliminate unnecessary waste to reduce paper usage and energy costs, while never compromising the reading experience. As a result, the final word count vs. page count may not meet common expectations.

For my mother, who has always had big dreams
and the courage to make them come true.
Thank you for showing me how.

INHUMAN ACTS

CHAPTER 1

April 7, 2017

A week at sea produced a lot of laundry. It fluttered above Jessa Duquesne as she lay on the foredeck of her parents' sailboat, soaking up the morning sun. The air smelled of salt, waves splooshed against the hull, and seabirds cried out in the distance. It was everything she loved about a life lived outdoors.

Jessa lifted her head, searching the water for Mark. The ocean glittered, and the Nápali coast rose in the distance. Razor-sharp crags, each peak edged with green. Beautiful but empty. Just like the sea. No Mark.

She twisted to check their port side and spotted him beneath the surface. His body slid through a seemingly endless expanse of water, all sun-kissed skin and muscle.

Yum.

She'd never planned to marry, never had any interest in men that a one-night stand couldn't fix. At least, not until she'd met Mark. He surfaced for a breath, then slipped back under the waves. Something moved behind him, further out. A dark shape, getting closer. Thick body, elongated dorsal fin, maybe eight feet long.

Jessa rolled onto her stomach and undid the shoulder ties of her bikini.

The sandbar shark was probably a female, given the size, and harmless as sharks went. Odd it was out this far from shore, though. Poor thing would probably be lunch for a bigger predator.

A great white or a tiger shark. And it shouldn't have been so close to the surface. Sandbar sharks usually hugged the bottom.

She should go get her camera. Maybe make a note of when she'd spotted it so she could have the data point. She could look up any other odd behavioral patterns when—

Stop it, Jessa.

There would be plenty of opportunities to study marine life when she got back to her office at the university. What she needed to do now was focus on all the wedding planning still left undone. She'd been putting off the worst of it — seating charts and table linens and all the other things she didn't actually care about — hoping she could pawn them off on her sister. Or, at least, that she and Letty could handle them together this week, powered by a steady rotation of caffeine and wine.

Jessa sighed and shifted on her towel. It couldn't be helped. Letty wasn't the type to say no when work called, and it wasn't like Jessa was sorry to be here. A little get-away with Mark was the perfect use for the week she'd already taken off work. But still…

Seating charts and table linens.

Yuck.

The minutiae danced through her mind, conspiring with the warm press of the sun to lull her into a near-doze…

Ice-cold water dripped onto the small of Jessa's back, and she jumped with a yelp. "What the—?"

Mark stood over her, a grin on his face, dark hair dripping onto the deck. And her.

"Asshole." She laughed, using the edge of her towel to wipe the water away while she admired the broad stretch of his chest, the V of his abdomen where it disappeared into the top of his swim trunks. "How was your swim?"

"Lonely." He pulled a T-shirt from the rigging, where she'd hung it to dry. "Want to go below for a bit?"

She shook her head with a smile. "We're out of condoms." They'd used the last one the night before, and the memory brought heat to her cheeks. Even in the cramped confines of the cabin, he was a remarkable lover.

Mark shrugged. "The wedding's in a month. You wouldn't even be showing by then."

His dark eyes sparked with mischief.

"You're so bad." Jessa retied the straps of her suit. "I'll meet you down there. I need to hop in and cool off first."

Mark helped her to her feet and pulled her close. "Don't be long." He pressed a kiss to her lips that tasted like salt water. "We've got to return the boat to your dad by four."

She stepped back, winked at him, and dove off the side.

"Show-off!" he called down after her.

Jessa slipped into the water with barely a splash, like the lifelong swimmer she was. The water brushed a cool relief against her hot skin. Moored as far from land as they were, there was nothing to swim to. So she settled for circuits around the boat. After a dozen, she turned onto her back and floated, giving her shoulders a break. The sky was a bright, almost unnatural blue. It made a wide crescent against the darker indigo of the sea where the two met at the horizon.

Something brushed her foot.

Jessa stilled her legs, paddling with her arms to keep herself afloat as she searched for the culprit. A light-blue mass swirled below her.

Oh shit.

Ghostly strands reached up, inches from her skin.

Jellies.

And not just any jellyfish — box jellyfish. Large, square bodies with tentacles trailing below. Lots of them. Some as long as ten feet. Each tentacle had as many as five thousand stinging cells. Each one capable of causing excruciating pain and even death.

Don't panic.

She had to stay calm, keep her wits. Which would be easier if she didn't know their venom was deadlier than a cobra's. Her mouth went dry. She turned in a slow circle, her breath tightening with each new jelly she spotted. They pulsed through the water underneath her. A writhing, growing mass.

She shifted the direction of her strokes, pulling herself away from them. How many were there? And why were they out now? Box jellyfish were always in the ocean, but Hawaii's jellyfish tended to come and go with the cycle of the moon. And they weren't due for weeks, especially not here. She and Mark had dropped anchor off Kauai, nowhere near the beaches of Oahu where box jellyfish were usually spotted.

"Mark?" She called out, but there was no sign of him.

Must be below deck.

She judged the distance to the boat. Maybe fifty yards. It would be easier and faster if she could kick. But she didn't want to accidentally make contact with the jellyfish. Even one sting could send her into cardiac arrest. Her mouth was so dry, she could hardly swallow. The world shrunk to nothing more than the distance between her and the boat. She treaded water using only her arms, her muscles protesting, tired from the laps she'd done.

Just get to the ladder.

If you get stung, you'll find the vinegar and douse yourself.

Jessa kept swimming, trying not to move her legs, gliding over the still-growing mass of jellies. Her heart pounded, and she struggled to keep herself from hyperventilating. Forty yards, thirty, twenty-five. This was taking forever.

A lightning bolt of pain shot up from her ankle, a radiating, burning sting. "Shit."

Fuck this.

She kicked off, powering toward the boat. Her ankle burning, her jaw clenched tight against the pain.

Another strike, this one on the other leg and higher near her thigh. Like a thousand wasps stinging at once. Sweat broke out on her forehead, and she gasped at the sudden shock of pain, then another struck. And another. Her body seized, her arms freezing in place as the jellyfish wrapped themselves around her. Delicate strands weaving bands of fire across her body. Her heart thundered. The sear of agony blotting out the rest of the world, until it was the one true certain thing left.

Not the only thing.

"Mark!" Jessa forced out the word as her head slipped under the water, a sharp pain slicing her chest. She willed herself to push toward the surface, not to breathe in the saltwater around her. Except it wasn't water. The jellyfish were everywhere.

A few feet below the surface, she opened her mouth and screamed.

CHAPTER 2

April 6, 2018

Letty Duquesne stepped inside the Flying Dawg, the bar's tinted windows turning it from early afternoon to "five o'clock somewhere" in an instant. She blinked, her eyes adjusting to the darkness as she scanned behind the bar. No familiar faces appeared. But the televisions lining the walls played half a dozen versions of ESPN and indie rock boomed in the background, which told her enough that she could guess who was on shift.

She moved through a sea of twenty-somethings, most wearing the University of Georgia's red and black, and wrinkled her nose. As usual, the place stank of greasy chicken wings and stale beer. The dive bar reek didn't normally bother her. But she'd woken that morning with a low simmer of nausea. Her stomach a constant reminder of the date.

Letty found an empty booth near the back. It would be a tight squeeze when the rest of the lab team showed up, but they could make it work. She slid into the bench seat facing the door and pulled a menu from a metal holder near the wall. The laminated surface was sticky and the offerings as unappealing as she remembered. Everything fried except the potato skins.

Maybe she'd go with a liquid diet. Her anxiety had been building all week, and she needed to take the edge off. Especially now that Bill had dropped his bomb. According to her boss, she was overdue for a professorship, and he'd as much as said she was either going up or out.

"For her own good."

Letty scowled. The fact that it made objective sense for her to keep climbing the academic ladder didn't make it any more appealing. She spotted their usual server and waved, her need for a drink out-weighing any etiquette that said she should wait for her friends to arrive. But the waitress turned the opposite direction, focused on the over-loaded tray of half-empty glasses and plates covered in congealed ketchup she carried toward the kitchen.

Shit.

Letty put the menu back, wiping her hands on her jeans. She'd done countless papers and presentations, even been a co-investigator on a grant from the National Science Foundation, all in the hopes of being the principal investigator on her own research. She'd worked for years for the chance to expand the research she'd done with Bill into something that might make a difference.

Might change things.

And, in the end, all it had earned her was an opportunity she wouldn't wish on anyone. By next fall, she'd be teaching hordes of undergrads. And no amount of money was worth that noise. No matter how good it was for her career. Why didn't good things just stay good?

The bar's front door swung open. Priya came in first, walking several feet in front of their other lab-mate. As if she and Chris hadn't in come together. Letty waved to get their attention and scooted over to make room as the two negotiated the growing crowd.

"Thanks for coming early to get seats, Let." Priya slid her tiny frame in next to Letty. She wore leggings and the oversized t-shirt she'd bought the last time they'd gone for retail therapy. The outfit made her look more like a freshman than a woman on the edge of a PhD.

Chris took the opposite side of the booth. Ever since their not-at-all-subtle secret romance had begun, Priya and Chris never sat next to one another and seldom made eye contact. It would have been easier to wear signs — we're not sleeping together, really.

"Like you'd have to drag Letty to the bar." Chris grinned at her.

She shrugged as she handed Priya one of the sticky menus. He wasn't wrong.

Priya ran a finger down the laminated sheet, a line of concentration running down her forehead. She stopped on the nachos. Same as she always did.

Chris tucked a strand of surfer-blonde hair behind one ear. "Whose turn is it to buy? I got last week."

"Bill's," Priya answered, and Letty and Chris moaned in unison. Professor Bill McTigue was a man upon whom good alcohol was wasted. "Five bucks he buys pitchers of PBR again."

"I'll take that money. He's buying us Coors Light, no question." Chris's foot nudged hers under the table and then shifted quickly in Priya's direction.

"Definitely Coors Light." Letty had seen the Lean Cuisine boxes in his office trash can when she was getting her marching orders. Bill was dieting again.

Priya nodded. "You're on." She raised a hand and shouted to be heard above the rising din in the room. "Bill, over here!"

The head of their research team waved back, then twirled one finger in the air. Did they want a round? Letty's tablemates responded with cheers and thumbs-ups. They'd all happily drink anything offered, even if it was the cheapest beer-water the bar had on tap. Given what graduate students got paid, her friends rarely turned down free drinks. And Letty's stipend as a post-doc research fellow wasn't much better.

"Did you read the Zika articles I left on your desk? The ones for Bill's lecture on Monday?" Priya asked Chris as she gathered up her long, black hair, tying it into a knot high on the back of her head.

Chris watched her, nothing subtle about the hungry look on his face. His gaze flicked to Letty, and he cleared his throat. "Yeah.

Although I think we need to cover the CDC report that came out yesterday, too. Did you see the copy I emailed you?"

Priya shook her head.

He leaned closer. "CDC says the spillover rate is up twenty-five percent from last year."

"It's what?" Letty leaned in, too, eyebrows raised. The transfer of viral infections from animals to humans already accounted for three of every four new human diseases. What would a jump that big in one year mean going forward? Some of the new diseases would result in isolated infections, like anthrax or histoplasmosis. But others, the ones that could be transmitted human to human, would be a much bigger problem. Maybe the world's next Ebola.

"No shit." Chris punctuated each word with a tap on the table. "Twenty-five percent."

Letty shook her head. "I don't see how that's possible. That would be—"

"Fucked is what it is. It's like I keep saying, the more we disrupt natural habitats, the deeper we're going to get into parts of the virosphere we wish we hadn't discovered." He gave a slow shake of the head. "I mean, you know how many microorganisms are out there."

Letty nodded. There were at least as many on Earth as there were stars in the sky.

Chris looked around the table, as if to make sure he had all of their attention. "What're the chances the rest are gonna be friendly?"

"Didn't you guys get enough shop talk at the lab?" Priya rolled her eyes. "We're here to drink."

As if on cue, Bill appeared with two over-filled plastic pitchers of beer. It sloshed onto the table as he sat them down. "Here we go, campers." He wiped up the spill with the hem of an old concert t-shirt, too faded for her to tell which band. Then he disappeared back to a bar strung with Christmas lights, chatting with a waitress while he loaded his arms with pint glasses.

Chris picked up where he'd left off. "What's gonna happen when we slash and burn our way through to whatever's hiding in the rainforests of Brazil, Panama, Ecuador, or Peru? Or Jesus, Central Africa. Ebola, Zika, Chikungunya, AIDS. Just imagine what else is waiting."

Bill slid in next to Chris, handing a glass to each of them.

Priya took hers. "Ugh, not the rainforest again."

"Said the disease ecology grad student." Bill shook his head in mock disappointment, but Letty had no doubt he agreed with Priya's assessment. The one summer Chris spent volunteering with a research team in the Brazilian rainforest had given him an insatiable appetite for discussing its ruin.

Letty poured for everyone, then raised her glass for a sip. One whiff of the foam, and she knew. She owed Priya a fiver. The alcohol hit her empty stomach with an acid burn that would only go away if she kept drinking. She downed half the pint.

Chris spun the glass in his hand. "I'm serious, though, man. It's not just zoonotic illnesses either. As we start encroaching on the space they need to live, animals are gonna start fighting back."

Letty stiffened, images that usually only emerged from the murk of her nightmares bobbing up to the surface. Jessa's head slipping under the waves. Bright blue eyes staring at her through murky water. Bubbles slithering out of her sister's mouth where the words "help me" should've been.

Priya put a hand on Letty's arm and glanced her way. Her eyes held a silent "are you okay?"

Letty pretended not to notice the look of concern on her or Bill's face. She stared up at the closest TV screen instead, the back of her throat burning. The television replayed a golf tournament, but all Letty could see were silvery tentacles wrapping around Jessa's body. Squeezing, stinging.

Letty drained her glass, but it didn't dull the pain any more than the last hundred times she'd tried.

Chris finished his pint. "You'd think there'd be alarms going off all over the place. If we could just get the general public to give a shit, maybe we could keep what happened to Jessa from—"

"Chris!" Priya leaned over the table and smacked his arm. But it was too late. Grief settled over Letty like a cold, wet blanket. Smothering, sticking to her skin as it pressed down, blocking her airways.

"Don't worry about it." Letty choked out, forcing a smile. *Keep it together.*

Bill stared at Chris, his mouth a hard, flat line. And Priya pulled her closer, wrapping an arm over Letty's shoulder. "Don't mind him. You know he's an idiot."

Letty didn't trust herself to speak. She nodded and grabbed her purse from under the table with shaking hands. She would not cry in front of them again. The last thing she needed was more of the awkward walking-on-egg-shells silence that had followed her around in the months after Jessa's death. "It's not a big deal. I just... I have a, um... I have a date." She tilted her head toward the aisle, gesturing for Priya to let her pass. "Would you guys mind?"

"Of course, yeah." Priya slid out of her way, her face a mask of hesitation and worry. She lifted a hand, as if to stop Letty from going but then, let it drop. "Will you call me later? Let me know if you need anything?"

Letty nodded again, and Chris finally spoke up, his face red. "Sorry, Letty. I— "

"Don't worry about it. Really. I just forgot I'm supposed to meet someone." She held her bag tight to her chest. It sounded like a lie, even to her ears. "I'll get the first-round next week."

Bill stood up from the table. "Do you want me to... walk you out, or anything? You could come by our house for coffee later tonight. You know you're always welcome." The creases of his already sun-weathered face deepened with worry. She'd seen the expression less and less in the last year but still recognized it.

"No, I'm okay." Letty tried harder to sell the smile. She'd leaned enough on his kindness over the past year. Right now, all she wanted was to be alone. "Thanks, Bill."

Priya's voice drifted after Letty as she left. "Chris, what the fuck? You know tomorrow's the anniversary..." Letty didn't hear the last bit, but she knew how the sentence ended.

She held it together as long as she could. But by the time her feet hit the sidewalk, tears wet her face. She would have given anything for solitude. Instead, the streets teemed with University of Georgia undergrads, staff, and faculty out enjoying the warmth of the early evening. Probably celebrating the nearing end of the semester. She kept her face down as she moved through the crowd, not wanting her tears to draw notice. She scuttled past young families strolling together with ice cream cones and co-eds at outdoor tables, drinking and laughing. The Flying Dawg aside, Athens was a place filled with good food and even better music. A place to enjoy life. The way her sister had done.

The way Letty couldn't anymore.

She swallowed hard, trying to push down a lump of guilt that wouldn't budge.

CHAPTER 3

April 7, 2018
Detective Andrew Marsh popped open his glove box and rummaged around until he found the Tylenol. He shook two pills into his palm and swallowed them dry. The clock on the dash read 3:55 a.m.

A halogen flood light cast an eerie blue-white hue over the still smoldering low-slung structure just west of where he'd parked. The building hunched beneath a thick growth of trees, half overtaken by kudzu. A sign at the undamaged end read "East Appalachia Animal Research Facility, No Visitors Allowed."

Of all the nights to get a call.

He wasn't sure which he missed more. The bed he'd just crawled out of or the willing woman still wrapped up in his sheets. Ronnie? Renee? Something with a "R." His head pounded, and his mouth tasted like cheap bourbon and cigarettes.

Maybe the bed.

Andrew climbed out of the car. The night was cool for spring, but the air held the acrid smell of smoke, and it was still damp from a downpour they'd had the day before. Which was probably a good thing. Might've helped stop the fire's spread.

He'd expected the scene to be busier, but only the city fire investigator's truck remained. Between coaxing himself out of bed, and the half hour it'd taken him to convince his partner she didn't need to find a babysitter so she could come with him — as if that

13

was even possible in the middle of the night — he was definitely late.

As far as he could tell, there was no reason either of them needed to be there until morning anyway. Jeanie Ann Littler was as good a fire investigator as Chattanooga had ever had. He'd never been to a scene that told him anything her report hadn't already. Andrew called out toward the truck. "Jeanie?"

"Over here." Her muffled voice came from the blackened end of the building.

He stepped over a pair of muddy ruts probably left behind by the firetruck. Then went for drier ground near the edge of the woods. The bright white sneakers he'd worn out to the pool hall the night before had not been the best choice for a fire scene. Brush snarled out from under the pine trees, catching at his shirt sleeve. And it was harder going outside the beam of the flood light, but at least the ground was dry.

A branch cracked in the forest, and Andrew stopped. Another noise, a rustling from the darkness. Something moving. Twigs snapped, this time deeper in the overgrowth off to his left. More than one something. He peered into the woods but couldn't see a thing. The night sky was heavy with clouds, a murky gray above the trees. In the hint of moonlight filtering through, he could only make things out a few yards away. Andrew doubled-back to the car and got his Maglite from the trunk. He eased the lid into place and crept back to the trees, keeping his footfalls soft.

Andrew held the flashlight palm up at his shoulder but didn't turn it on. Not yet. He cocked his head and listened. Crickets, a frog, a train whistle in the distance. The shifting of branches came again to his right. He flicked on the light, aiming the beam toward the noise.

Nothing but trees. He panned side to side, a window of light playing over leaves, brush, and saplings. Andrew looked for anything out of place. But nothing moved except for a few of the smaller tree limbs swaying in the wind. He waited, listening again.

The wind carried only the usual sounds of night creatures singing to themselves or each other.

Andrew rounded the corner of the building. Jeanie stood half-in a side door to the facility. She had a clipboard under one arm and her flashlight pointed at something on the far wall. "What took you so long?" she asked, without turning.

He cleared his throat. "Police business."

"Is that her name?" Jeanie chuckled, sweeping the flashlight beam up toward the ceiling.

Andrew put a little extra sugar in his voice. "You know you're my favorite, Jean."

"Mm-hmm. Tall, bald, and easy's not my type." Jeanie was a fifty-something woman who carried her weight around her middle. She wore a badge on a lanyard and her usual high-waisted polyester slacks, covered in cat hair. She shared her small apartment with five rescued tabbies and a girlfriend.

"See that?" Jeanie pointed to the line between burned and unburned space on what was left of the drywall. It made a broad V, growing wider toward the top. Near the bottom, the sheetrock had scorched away, revealing the studs underneath. The exposed wood was singed and covered in blisters that looked like alligator skin. Her flashlight tracked the edge of the V down to the floor. Debris scattered the blackened, faux-hardwood.

"Point of origin?"

She pursed her lips. "One of them."

"Crap." He puffed his cheeks out with a long exhale. That's why he'd been called in. More than one point of origin almost certainly meant arson. And that made it a police matter — one more case added to his already overloaded plate. Even so... "Couldn't we have done a walk through tomorrow morning? Easier to tell what we're doing in the daylight."

"You'll see." Jeanie jerked her head toward the open door. "Structural engineer just left. He says we're safe to go in. I finished my walk through, but I can show you the highlights before I start the paperwork."

"After you." He followed her inside, inspecting the door and the surrounding jamb as they passed. No sign of forced entry. Jeanie sloshed down a narrow hallway that was one long puddle. After a moment's hesitation, he followed. So much for the sneakers. "Anybody here when the fire started?"

"Not so far as we can tell. Anonymous tipster called it in."

"I'd expect a facility housing animals to have someone on site overnight, or at least on-call." He waded through a particularly deep part of the puddle. The wet seeped through his shoes and into his socks.

"I would, too." She shook her head.

"Were your guys able to get the animals out?"

Please don't let it be dogs...

He could handle mice in cages, but he'd spent half his childhood riding his family's Mastiffs around their yard. The idea of someone sticking needles into a dog made him squeamish, and the thought of them trapped in a blaze was worse.

Jeanie led him into a large, square room, lit by another floodlight. "Looks like most were already gone when the fire started."

He blinked spots from his eyes, his vision adjusting slowly to the glare of bright, white light. A series of metal racks lined one wall, each filled with row upon row of clear rectangular bins about half the size of a bread box. Many had melted, the perforated metal tops collapsed down to the plastic base. In each rack, there were maybe ten rows down and at least that many across. Five racks that he could see. He stepped closer, peering into the unmelted containers. They were some sort of cages. All empty.

On the bottom row, the metal lids had been cast off. They lay in a scattered mess on the floor. Small oblong pellets and shavings remained in a few of the areas not touched by the fire. Here and there, he picked out the singed carcass of some sort of rodent among the debris. But there weren't nearly enough bodies to fill that number of containers. Maybe the containers had been empty to begin with?

Or the fact that the animals were already gone could mean a good Samaritan had beaten them to the scene. Saved as many as they could before the fire took over. Maybe their anonymous tipster? Could be the arsonist had been there to free the animals to begin with. There were lots of crazy animal nuts out there. But, if that were the case, why would they have left some behind? Surely some hippie-dippie animal freak wouldn't be on board with burning them to death. Even rats.

"Looks like rodents to me, maybe mice? Or guinea pigs?" Jeanie pointed to a row of slightly larger containers at the far end. She turned toward the interior of the building, and Andrew followed her down another narrow hallway.

"There are fish in this one." She gestured to the first room on her left. A similar rack system lined the wall opposite the door and to his right. But these containers appeared to be intact, and each was filled with what looked like water. "They seem okay from what I can tell."

She pushed open the next door, the interior pitch black. "Not sure what was in here." She shone her flashlight inside, and he did the same. Instead of a rack system, this room held a series of cells. Solid metal to waist-height, with thin, closely spaced bars above that. All the doors stood open, but he couldn't see inside the stalls.

Andrew stared into the space, trying to find some indication of what it had housed. Whatever had been there, the charred stench in the air held an undertone of bleach. He sensed Jeanie move again and followed, his mind still caught in questions he couldn't answer. He turned to find her stopped in his path and jerked to a halt.

Jeanie pointed toward the far wall, which was marked with another blackened V. "Second point of origin's here." A pile of ash and debris surrounded the base, just as it had by the first. A fire extinguisher lay a few feet away, its surface discolored and peeling.

INHUMAN ACTS

Andrew dropped to his haunches for a closer look at the charred remains of whatever had probably been used to start the blaze. "Looks the same as what we saw by the door. Maybe newspaper?"

She grunted, the noise noncommittal. "What else do you see?"

He scanned the area, but, other than the fire extinguisher, it didn't look materially different from—

A series of irregular, dark spots spattered the floor near the pile of debris. "Is that...?"

"Dunno. But I thought I should call it in."

"Right." Because, if it was human blood, this might be more than an arson scene. And if he worked it right — got a solve on something major — it could be his ticket out of the property crimes division. Whatever bourbon-induced fog had clouded his thoughts evaporated. Andrew nodded toward the fire extinguisher as he got back to his feet. "You think someone tried to put out the fire before the cavalry arrived?"

"Possibly. Maybe the same person who let the animals out. Or could be the supports holding it to the wall burned free." She shined the flashlight up to a hunk of melted plastic on the wall midway up the burn mark. "I haven't been able to reach the facility manager." Jeanie crossed her arms over her chest. "Guy named Richardson."

Andrew rubbed at one temple, willing the Tylenol to kick in. Could be Richardson's blood. Maybe they had a missing person to go with the arson case.

"I'm tempted to go ahead and call animal control. Somebody's gonna have to deal with the fish." She jerked the flashlight beam further down the hall. "Let's keep moving. I need a coffee." Jeanie led him to the end of the hall and went right where it split. "This side of the building was spared, other than some water damage. It's all labs and office space."

Andrew followed, and they moved quickly through the undamaged rooms. Each space was clean and neat. Stainless steel tables, laboratory equipment or offices that could have been anywhere — computers, desks, chairs. Nothing out of place.

Jeanie stopped in a small reception area. Sofa, potted plant, bad artwork, and the glass door he'd seen from the outside. Jeanie tilted her head toward the door. "This was unlocked when we got here. No sign of forced entry."

"Well that's interesting, isn't it?" The door had a deadbolt, and a security keypad hung from the wall to its right. It didn't make sense to go through the effort and expense of securing the lab, only to leave the front door open.

Jeanie nodded. "Figured you'd think so." She turned back, leading him out the way they'd come in.

He aimed his flashlight into the corners of each room they passed. No security cameras. "Any sign of where the animals went?"

"Not a thing." She stepped back outside.

Andrew followed, clicking his flashlight back on to light their path.

"Hello?" A voice called out from the front of the facility.

Jeanie looked back at him with a nod. "What do you want to bet that's Richardson now?"

"Let's hope." Andrew lengthened his stride. With any luck, he could get an interview done quickly — if it was Richardson. That would give him time to run home, make sure last night's friend wasn't making herself too comfortable at his place, and grab a can of Red Bull before he had to head to the department. He was going to need it. Andrew rounded the side of the building.

A big man, stooped and paunchy, stood a few yards behind Jeanie's truck. His khakis were rumpled, and his glasses sat crooked on a pug nose.

Andrew approached. "Evening. Can I help you?"

"I'm Stuart Richardson, the facility manager here." He stared off toward the damaged side of the building and ran a hand over the back of his neck, where sweat dampened the collar of his shirt. "What happened?"

Andrew held out a hand. "Detective Marsh, Chattanooga PD."

"Police?" Richardson shifted on his feet, then gave Andrew's hand a limp shake before taking a step backward. "I guess, when I got the message, I was expecting the fire department. Are the animals okay?"

Andrew eyed the man, trying to decide if Richardson was the normal sort of nervous people got when they talked to the police. Or the kind that meant something more. "From what we can tell, there were only a few present at the time of the fire."

Richardson shook his head. "We have three hundred house mice, two hundred brown rats, a dozen New Zealand White rabbits, a thousand zebrafish." He pulled off his glasses and rubbed at his eyes. "Are they dead?"

Please don't cry.

Maybe the fear coming off Richardson had nothing to do with him. Andrew softened his voice. Him trying to comfort anyone — let alone a full-grown man — would be an absolute shit show. He didn't do warm and fuzzy. "A few of the rodents didn't make it. But I think the fish are okay. And it looks like most of the other animals were gone before the fire started."

"Gone?" Richardson replaced his glasses, which were still crooked, and shook his head again. "That doesn't make any sense. Can I go in?" His voice thickened, and his eyes got shiny. "I need to make sure none of them are suffering."

Andrew swept his hand forward. "Of course." If it meant he could avoid a heartfelt moment with Richardson, he was in.

They trudged past Jeanie, who sat filling out paperwork under the dome light in her truck. She didn't look up.

Andrew aimed for the side door, talking to Richardson over his shoulder. "Unless it's necessary so you can care for the animals, don't touch anything."

Richardson's footsteps slowed. "Is it still dangerous? The fire's out, right?"

"This is a crime scene."

The footsteps behind him stopped, and Andrew turned.

Richardson gaped at him.

"We believe someone may have started the fire intentionally." Andrew studied Richardson, waiting for a reaction that might tell him something — surprise, recognition, guilt.

But Richardson's face remained blank, his voice flat. "I can't imagine anyone would want to do something like that."

"It happens." Andrew led him inside, through the puddled hallway, and back into the bright light of the rodent room. The fact that Richardson wasn't more upset, didn't seem angry about what had happened to his facility or about the loss of all the research that had probably been underway there, possibly even the loss of his job — that told Andrew plenty.

Richardson rushed forward to the melted bins. He started at the rack closest to where they'd come in and inspected the plastic cages one by one. He paused at the middle rack, where a small body lay on the floor. He bent, as if to pick it up. Then stopped, maybe remembering what Andrew had told him outside. Richardson's voice was thick. "Rats get a bad rap, you know. They're actually really smart."

Andrew wasn't sure how to respond to that.

Richardson kept moving, checking the remainder of the cages. "I don't get it. The place was locked up tight when I left last night. And I looked at the cameras before I went to bed. Everything was normal. Just as— "

"There's camera surveillance?" Andrew looked again into the corners of the room, then across the ceiling. Nothing but your average drop ceiling, some of the tiles destroyed by fire. Wet insulation hanging down through the gaps.

Richardson pointed toward the stainless steel counter on the opposite wall. A lump of melted plastic sat on one end of the table, something reflective at the center. Maybe a lens. "There. Every containment room has one." He finished peering into the last row of plastic cages and hurried off toward the room with the fish tanks.

Andrew followed. He'd missed the camera because it wasn't one set up for surveillance. It was lower, directed toward the animals. Apparently, a means for monitoring them remotely, rather than surveilling the facility. Even so, there was a good chance one of the cameras might've caught an image of their arsonist. "Is the video recorded?"

Richardson didn't turn from the fish tanks. "Why would we need that?" And then, perhaps realizing the stupidity of his question under the circumstances, he answered. "No, it's just a live feed. So we can make sure nothing's amiss overnight."

Well, shit.

Richardson pulled a cell phone from his pocket and carried it over to Andrew. He tapped an app, and the screen showed four black squares, each marked at the bottom right-hand corner: Rear 1, Rear 2, Aquatic, and Canine. "Of course. They wouldn't be working, would they? Not after this." Richardson stepped back toward the hall. "I'll need to take a look at the rest of the facility and then make some calls, find a place for the fish, let corporate and our insurer know what's happened."

The fire explained why the cameras in the rear rooms of the facility wouldn't be working, but what about the others? Why would the video feed for the rooms undamaged by fire be out? Surely the cameras would have a battery back-up. As often as the power went out this far out of town, they'd need it. And something else was off about what the man had said.

But what?

He followed Richardson through the facility, his mind running back over Richardson's words.

Canine.

Richardson had been so specific about the other animals — a dozen New Zealand White rabbits, a thousand zebrafish — why wouldn't he have mentioned the dogs? Either there hadn't been any housed at the facility at the time of the fire, or Richardson already knew they were missing. Andrew eyed the man. "Does the facility house dogs?"

"Not recently." Richardson step faltered, but he kept moving and words tumbled over-eager out of his mouth. "Used to have a dozen Beagles, but that project ended more than a year ago." He cleared his throat. "This is the diagnostics lab, and this one is my office, right here..."

The answer was plausible, but instinct told Andrew there was more to it than that.

Richardson rounded the corner, still chattering about the facility's capabilities and staff. They neared the second point of origin, and Andrew sped up, reaching out to tap Richardson's shoulder so he wouldn't contaminate the scene.

But Richardson hugged the opposite wall before Andrew could reach him, going silent as he gave the burned area wide berth.

Andrew's gaze narrowed on Richardson's back.

Inside job could explain the unlocked front door.

Except what motivation would Richardson have to torch the place? He was just the facility manager, not the owner, so it wouldn't be financial. The insurance wouldn't go to him. And there were easier ways to quit a job. Andrew frowned. What was he missing? Richardson didn't look injured. Not that a gash couldn't be hidden under a sleeve or a pant leg.

Had someone besides Richardson been there?

Either way, a bunch of research animals had been released into the wild.

Into the woods.

Could that have been what he'd heard lurking beyond the tree line on the way in? Andrew rubbed his hand over the stubble on his chin and forced a nonchalance he didn't feel into his voice. "Exactly what sort of testing do you do here?"

CHAPTER 4

May 2, 2018

The alarm system beeped, insistent and waiting. Letty kicked the door to her apartment closed, phone pressed to her ear with one shoulder. "Hang on." She punched her code into the panel, and the room went quiet except for the hum of the air conditioner.

Better.

She slid her purse onto one of the bar stools at the kitchen counter. "I moved the RV into the long-term lot. Hangtag's on the rearview, and the keys are in your top desk drawer."

"You shouldn't have done that." Bill's protest sounded more like gratitude. "I was planning to take care of it tomorrow before we left." A parrot screeched in the background. One of three African Greys his youngest daughter had left at home when she went to college. Which had been about the time Bill had become her major professor, and, as he liked to say, she'd become his "academic daughter."

"I know you were," Letty said, even though experience told her he'd actually have let it sit outside his office until the university administration called to complain. Their mobile research lab had every piece of cutting-edge equipment the ecology department could need for field work — but, at forty-five feet, the RV that held it all was a beast. Bill struggled to drive it.

Thanks to the fact that Letty had lived in one about the same size for two years of high school, for her, it was second nature. She tossed her keys next to her purse. "You and Marcia have a great time with the grandkids. Give everybody my love, okay?"

"Mm-hmm, okay." Bill's voice grew muffled as he yelled something about swim trunks, probably to his wife. He came back on the line as Letty was about to disconnect the call. "I know I said this a bunch of times already, but you're welcome to come with us. Marcia says it won't be the same without you there. And I can't imagine why you'd want to spend the summer bartending." He stopped and snorted a laugh. "No, scrap that. Of course I can. But even if you don't want to head to St. Simon's with us, there are plenty of things you could do at the university that would help build your CV. Shoot, Letty, with that big brain of yours, there's no limit to what you could do. If you'd let yourself embrace the opportunities."

"I have to teach next semester." She said the word "teach" like it was a synonym for "eat monkey shit." Even though she knew it wasn't an argument she was going to win. Bill was determined for her to move up through the university ranks, whether she wanted to or not. "Until then, just let me pickle my big brain in peace."

He laughed again. "You can do that anywhere. And I'm serious about you coming with us." Another parrot screeched. Bill's voice was softer when he continued. "I don't like the idea of leaving you here on your own all summer. Not with everything you've been going through."

Not with her freaking out yesterday. That's what he meant. Letty cringed.

Bill tried again. "Are you sure you won't come with us?"

"It was just a rough day. That's all. I'm fine now."

"I'm sorry I didn't realize it was the anniversary of Jessa's death earlier. If I had, I would have waited to bring up the promotion, and I could've hog-tied Chris." His smile came through in his voice. "You okay now?"

"I'm good." And she was, or at least, as close to it as she got anymore. Letty glanced up at the clock. "I need to hop off. I'm supposed to meet Priya for one last end-of-year hurrah."

Bill's answer came slow, probably as he was trying to decide whether to let her off the hook that easy. "Okay. Just make sure you check in with us here and there."

"I will, I promise." Letty said her goodbyes, dumped a can of white bean soup into a bowl, and left it heating in the microwave. She needed to hurry up and make herself presentable. Priya would be waiting for her at the bar in half an hour.

Letty poured a glass of rosé to sip while she got ready, clicked on the TV, and carried the wine into her closet. Neat rows of sensible shoes lined the floor. Above that, work pants, jeans, and tops hung by type and color. She slipped off the flats she'd worn to the lab and lined them up with her other work shoes.

What would Jessa say about that?

"How did this family produce someone so anal?"

Letty choked out a laugh. They'd grown up with no stability, no real home, and no friends but each other. A family of free spirits, and her. Letty hated it, and Jessa thrived.

Is that what you call it?

Lying dead somewhere on the ocean floor wasn't exactly living the good life.

All because of me.

Letty pushed the first in a row of hangers, and they screeched against the rod. The clothes shifted, then settled into place. She pushed again. Harder. Hangers tilted up on one side, jeans slipping toward the back wall. One knocked into a pair of boots that fell over, taking several others with them. In the swirl of fabric, two of her shirts fell free, landing in a soft puddle on the carpet. She left them there.

Letty ignored the beeping from the microwave and went in search of her phone. Going out was too much effort, too much pretending everything was okay. She dug through her bag.

Shit.

She had been doing so well, kicking ass at work, enjoying her friends, even gone on a few dates. And then, with the anniversary of Jessa's death, all the grief came crashing back.

Because you haven't dealt with it.

She shook her head. Either way, right now, the weight of a smile was too much to carry. Even if it meant she couldn't properly send Priya off before she left for her summer project. Letty texted her friend a raincheck, downed half her glass, and went back to her bedroom in search of pajamas.

The television news played on in the living room, just loud enough for her to hear through the wall. "In the early hours of Tuesday morning, a young woman identified as Emma Canning arrived at CHI Memorial Hospital in Chattanooga, Tennessee. She presented with symptoms consistent with severe influenza, persistent vomiting and fatigue."

Letty stripped out of her work clothes and flipped through her t-shirt drawer until she found the one she wanted. Tattered and teal green with a realtor's logo across the front and holes in the armpits. It was soft as butter. She pulled it over her head, her work brain re-engaging as the news anchor continued. "It wasn't until Ms. Canning began to lose muscle control and salivate profusely that doctors suspected they might be dealing with rabies. Our sister station's Samira Bell-Vargas met with one of those doctors earlier today."

Holy shit.

Letty left the drawer standing open and padded back to the living room in her t-shirt and undies. On the television, a small woman in a headscarf stood in what looked like a hospital hallway. She nodded, one hand holding an earpiece in place, her face earnest. "Thanks, Carol. I'm here with Dr. Sue Ellen Hendrick, one of Ms. Canning's treating physicians. Dr. Hendrick, what can you tell us?" She tilted a microphone toward a thirty-something woman with bright red hair, cheekbones that would cut glass, and curves barely contained by a lab coat.

Worry lined the doctor's face. "I cannot comment on Ms. Canning's case. But I can confirm that we have a local case of rabies. This is highly unusual in the United States, where rabies vaccination among the susceptible animal population is widespread." She paused, as if choosing her words carefully. "And I am particularly troubled that we've been unable to determine how the patient contracted the disease. Without the ability to identify and contain the source animal, I'm concerned we may see more cases." She crossed her arms over her chest, and her face grew hard. "Worse, the health department appears either unable or unwilling to take any material steps to protect, or even inform, the public of the risk."

Letty lowered herself to the couch. The image on screen changed back to two anchors behind a desk. A young woman with a short, neat afro turned to face the camera. "We reached out to the Tennessee and Hamilton County health departments to follow up on Dr. Hendrick's concerns. Both refused to comment. We'll keep you updated as..."

Letty turned down the volume. Maybe Bill was right. Maybe she should be using her brain for something useful.

And it wouldn't hurt to have a distraction.

If she had to guess, the rabies infection had come from a bat. Most rabies cases in the U.S. did. And that would make sense with the doctor not being able to identify the source animal. Bats were so small, their bites could go undetected. A person might notice the animal fly close by, realize later that they had some small abrasion, and never connect the two. She'd read of one guy who'd awakened to find a bat in his room. He'd been bitten and slept right through it.

She went to get the wine she'd abandoned in the bedroom, her mind turning over the few details they'd given on the news. The doctor's worried expression. The health departments' refusal to comment. She settled back on the couch with her glass. The disease's spillover into the human population was almost certainly an isolated incident. She took a sip. But what if it wasn't? What if identifying the reservoir animal early was the difference between one case and multiple? With her training, she was more than qualified to do it. And she could be in Chattanooga in three hours.

Plus, she'd be able to use the time to catch up with Caroline. Letty had only seen her former partner in tequila-related crime a handful of times since they'd graduated college. Caroline got wrapped up in internships and politics, while Letty had been knee deep in a wetland or tromping through pine forests doing fieldwork. But, if she remembered right, Caroline's current position was in the Chattanooga mayor's office. She'd probably be willing to make a few introductions for her, or at least share a cocktail.

She could almost see Jessa, perched on the other end of the couch. Legs tucked under her butt, eyebrows raised in the same "let's do it" expression Letty had never been able to resist. The same one that had gotten them grounded a dozen times and nearly arrested twice. Totally out of character for her? Yes. Worth it? Every time.

She put down the wine, pulled her laptop from the coffee table, and logged in to the Bank of America website. She had $132.57 left in her checking account after paying this month's bills, and her next check wouldn't deposit until the fifteenth. She grimaced, her finger hovering above the computer's touchpad.

She tabbed over to the other account, the one she never accessed. The one she tried to forget existed. The balance hadn't changed, except for the few hundred dollars in interest she'd earned since making the deposit after her sister died. Just under twenty thousand dollars. Her dad hadn't been able to stand the sight of the boat after what happened, and the money from its sale was just as bad. So her parents had given it to her. Never mind how broke they were. Again.

Letty rolled her eyes.

Never met a bad decision they didn't want to make.

She blew out a slow breath. Hadn't she done exactly the same thing, just by different means? Living on a shoestring while the money sat untouched, like a shrine. As if refusing to acknowledge it made Jessa any less gone.

Made it any less her fault.

Pain tightened the back of her throat and still, she heard Jessa's voice. Just as if she was there.

"Let's do it."

Letty transferred half the money into her checking account. She retrieved her phone from her purse and looked up the number for the Flying Dawg. They were going to be short a bartender.

CHAPTER 5

May 3, 2018

Andrew honked the horn. A curtain in a front window of Mary Washington's split-level ranch swept back, and her scowling face appeared behind the glass. She held up a finger — the pointer, she was too church-going for the middle one — and mouthed "one minute." The curtain slid back into place.

He tapped the horn again and grinned. Irritating the hell out of his partner might be the best part of his day. Andrew pulled a still blazing hot cup of McDonald's coffee out of the center console and popped open the plastic flap on the lid. He considered the steam rising from the sugary black brew and took a sip anyway.

"Shit, that's hot." He rubbed a now numb tongue across the roof of his mouth and glanced back at the house. Mary was probably packing lunches or searching for one of her kids' lost school shoes. Kaylie and Marcus rode in the back of an unmarked car to school about as often as they managed to catch the bus. Andrew reached behind his seat, searching inside the messenger bag he'd left on the floorboard. He found his notepad and pen by touch then propped the pad on the steering wheel. At least he could be productive while he waited.

He ran his pen down the to-do list he'd made for their arson case, touching the tip to each item as he went. They still needed the particulars of the facility's remote video surveillance system. He'd spent some time researching surveillance apps that morning while shoveling Frosted Flakes into his mouth. With the system the facility was using, there was at least some chance footage would be in the cloud or saved to email. He'd read that some apps sent images to the user's email on a schedule or when motion was detected. If any existed, he wanted them.

Andrew moved his pen down to the next line. He needed to follow up again on their request to the facility's corporate parent regarding contact from animal rights groups. He'd already tried twice and been told someone would look into it and get back to him. They hadn't. He tapped the pen on the page, each strike leaving a tiny dot behind. Could be they were busy. Or that they didn't want the PR that sort of break-in would cause. A trip down to their headquarters in Atlanta might be in order. It was harder to ignore someone who had a badge in your face.

He skipped over the could-be blood splatter. He'd be lucky to have something back from the lab on that before the end of next week. He went to the next item on the list. They needed to better nail down Richardson's story. Find out why it took him so long to arrive at the scene. Andrew took a cautious sip of coffee, which was still too damn hot to drink. Then gave another tap on the horn. At this point, he was pretty sure Mary was messing with him. Which he had earned, but still. They had shit to do. He eyed the house. No movement in the curtains. Nothing to see but Mary's neatly trimmed yard, a hanging basket filled with dangling pink flowers on the front stoop, and her tired Chrysler LeBaron parked in the drive.

The screech of tires and a distant thump drew his attention to the far end of the street. Andrew opened the car window and listened, hoping nothing else would follow. He'd been thinking maybe, for once, he would make it to work on time.

Yelling echoed down the block, but he couldn't make out what was said. Multiple voices, at least one woman and a man. No, two men.

So much for an easy morning.

Movement from Mary's house caught his eye. She stepped onto her front porch with Kaylie and Marcus on her heels. Both kids wore oversized backpacks, and all three of them stared off in the direction of the commotion. With the curve of the road and all the shade trees in the way, he doubted they could see any more than he did.

He called up to Mary. "I'm gonna go down and check it out. Sounded like maybe a fender bender."

She nodded but didn't look convinced. "Call if you need me."

Andrew turned the key in the ignition. The dash lights flashed on, but the engine didn't turn over. "Shit, shit, shit." He stepped out of the car and slammed the door.

"Starter busted again?" Mary rolled her eyes. "If you're going on foot, I'm coming with you." She turned to the kids. "I need to go help Uncle Andrew with something. You guys head inside. I'll be right back." Marcus held out a fist. His sister met it with her own, and they flicked their fingers open in simulated explosions, no doubt stoked for whatever delay this might mean for the start of the school day. Mary shooed them back through the door. "Go on now. Inside, I said. And lock it behind me."

More unintelligible yelling came from down the street. The words muffled by other, morning sounds. The faint beep-beep-beep of a garbage truck, the rustle of wind through trees.

Then, a woman's scream.

· · ·

Traffic spread out in front of Letty as far as she could see. A wall of taillights glowing red on all six lanes northbound toward Chattanooga. She smacked her palm against the top of the steering wheel.

Ouch.

She'd been okay with the thousand stoplights on Highway 316, sat through forty-five minutes of traffic on I-85, even held it together through the gridlock on I-285. But her fourth traffic jam of the morning was one too many. How had she not factored rush hour into her planning? Or, for that matter, common sense?

No part of this trip was a good idea. She could be sitting in a cool dark bar getting paid to play on her phone and chat with the regulars. Instead, she had at least another hour planted in traffic. And then what? Walk into the health department and offer her services?

"Hi, I drove up from UGA because I thought I'd be able to do your job better than you."

She shifted in her seat, forcing her shoulders to relax. It wasn't quite that bad, and it wasn't like she didn't have a plan. Caroline had promised to do what she could to connect Letty with the right people. And, even if that didn't work out, the doctor on television had as much as asked for someone to come help. She'd wanted it badly enough to go to the media. Letty would start there. If it looked like she could do something useful, she would. If not, she'd spend the time catching up with Caroline. It'd be a vacation. A change of scenery for the weekend.

Because nothing says vacation like rabid bats.

Her phone buzzed in the cupholder. A text from her mother. "Heading to Mexico for the month. Don't worry if you can't reach us." A heart emoji, then "Have you talked to Mark? He has exciting news." Letty reached for the phone, then put her hand back on the wheel. She couldn't deal with that. Not now. Maybe not ever. Another buzz came from the cupholder. She ignored it, willing the car in front of her to move.

It buzzed a third time. She steeled herself and checked the phone. The two new messages were from Bill. "I got your message. Call me." The one under that said, "ASAP."

Crap.

Letty grimaced, knowing what was coming. She'd tried to downplay the trip on the voicemail she left for him, but Bill was no idiot. He'd have heard the same news out of Chattanooga she had. For a disease ecologist, it would be hard to miss. They saw what, maybe one or two cases of human rabies a year in the U.S.? And this one was basically in their backyard.

She connected the call. No reason to delay the inevitable.

He didn't bother with a hello. "Are you out of your mind?"

"Probably." It would explain why she was racing off to Chattanooga to butt in where she hadn't been invited. Sirens came from somewhere behind her, and she twisted in her seat. An ambulance raced up the shoulder, the noise growing louder as it got closer. "Hang on." She waited until the first responders flew past. The ambulance disappeared behind an eighteen-wheeler a few cars ahead of her, and the sirens faded. "Okay, that's better."

After a long pause, he spoke. "What exactly are you planning to do up there?"

"I dunno. Maybe go to the aquarium."

The line went silent. Apparently, he didn't think that was funny. She tried again. "I just thought I'd take a look around, see if anything stands out to me. Nothing intrusive. If I pick up on something useful, I'll pass it along to the authorities. If not, I'll spend the weekend at a cute spot I found near the river, do some hiking, and I'm back home next week. It's just curiosity and too much time on my hands. That's it."

Another long pause. "That's it?"

"Of course, Bill. It's not like I'm planning to start collecting specimens on my own." She glanced at the gear piled into the back of her Subaru.

"No. No, of course not." He sounded relieved. "Just promise me you'll be careful, and try not to ruffle any feathers. The locals might not like you stepping in."

"I'm always careful. And it's just a long weekend in Chattanooga. I'll be fine."

■   ■   ■

Emptied trash cans littered the sidewalk, apparently discarded at random by the trash collectors. Andrew dodged them as he ran, cursing each one. Other than the noise of whatever was happening ahead and the tut-tut-tut of a sprinkler here and there, the neighborhood was quiet. Most of Mary's neighbors were probably out of their houses already, on their way to work or school.

Mary caught up to him, running in the street.

He veered down a driveway and sped up to keep pace. It didn't work. She pulled ahead, leaving him two steps behind. Then she glanced back over her shoulder with a smirk. Once a track star, always a show off.

By the time they reached the corner, Andrew had sweat through his shirt and his breath came out in wheezes. Probably thanks to all the cigarettes he "only smoked when he was drinking." It was a long block, but still. He needed to get back to the gym. Rounding the bend in the road, he slowed to a stop a few feet behind Mary.

A heavy-set man with a full beard staggered from one side of the street to the other. His movements were jerky and erratic, his clothes disheveled. Shirt half-buttoned, one shoe missing. There was no telling what the guy was on. The bearded man shook his fists at everything and nothing as he bellowed out garbled nonsense. His words — if they were words — rose and fell in angry bursts.

Behind him, a car idled at an angle in the street. Both doors hung open, and a man-sized dent creased the hood. Two teenagers in dark green private school uniforms stood on a lawn nearby. A boy, beanpole tall with a face full of acne, and a girl with curly brown hair and tear-streaks of mascara down her face. Neither looked injured. The girl held a cell phone out in front of her. She tilted it toward Andrew and Mary.

Great.

The boy had at least put his cell to better use. He held it pressed to his ear.

Andrew held up his badge and called out to them. "Did you call 911?"

The boy nodded, lowering his phone. "He came out of nowhere and then just went crazy."

"Okay. Stay back." Andrew pocketed the badge.

Both kids moved a few feet further away, but the girl's camera didn't waver.

Andrew turned his attention back to the bearded man, still lumbering side to side down the road. Given what looked like an accident, maybe it wasn't drugs? Maybe a head injury? Whatever the cause, it seemed safe to assume he wasn't in his right mind and to proceed accordingly. Thank God the kids had thought to call for help. The man obviously needed it.

As Andrew drew closer, he got a better look at the guy's face. He'd seen it before. Eight foot images of Randy Bullard and his wife were plastered on billboards all over town. Smiling with righteous benevolence, arms spread wide. A flock of doves taking flight behind them and an invitation to Sunday services at the Chesapeake Hill Baptist Church underneath. Come one, come all. Andrew had never been inclined to accept.

The minister looked nothing like that today. Skin slick with sweat. Eyes wide and flicking left to right. The man's mouth hung open, globs of saliva clinging to his beard.

What the hell would cause that?

Andrew couldn't see any head wounds. Maybe a stroke or dementia? Whatever it was, the man needed help. "Pastor Bullard?"

The minister didn't acknowledge his name. He changed paths, careening up a driveway to a ranch house with calico-colored brick.

At the top of a short front stoop, an elderly woman in over-sized glasses and a purple bathrobe watched the show from behind a storm door. She had a newspaper tucked under one arm and a "World's Best Nana" coffee mug in her hand.

Bullard made a bee-line for her.

The old lady's eyes bugged behind her glasses, and she disappeared inside, slamming the door.

Bullard's yelling grew louder, and he lurched from the driveway up the woman's front walk. He grabbed hold of the rusted porch rail, planted his feet, and shook until one end came loose. Bullard went quiet, staring down at the handrail as if satisfied by its submission. He rubbed at his face and turned back toward the street, wiping the froth from his mouth on a sleeve.

Andrew rested his hand on the butt of his service pistol and checked Mary's position. She approached slowly, fanning out to the left and up the driveway. Her hand went to her hip, same as Andrew's. But there was no gun there. She met Andrew's gaze with a small shake of the head. She'd probably meant to put her gun belt on after she walked the kids to the bus.

Andrew jerked his head in her direction, a silent signal for her to hang back. She raised one eyebrow but slowed. Which was more than he'd expected her to do.

He kept going, moving with slow, careful steps through the patchy grass of the yard. "Sir?"

Bullard didn't respond. He stood almost unnaturally still, except for the movement of his eyes as he tracked Andrew's progress. Something about the man's sudden calm wasn't right. Every instinct Andrew had flared with warning. The second sense that came from a dozen years on the force screamed at him — this is about to go sideways. A prickle on the back of his neck, a stone in his stomach. The same feeling he'd gotten as a rookie, right before a dime bag carrying soon-to-be three strikes loser tried to stab him with a spork.

And however bad this situation might be, it was going to be worse because of the two teens looking on. The girl was probably live-streaming them already. Not that it changed a damn thing about what he was going to do. The process was simple enough, at least in concept — ask, tell, order, make. If asking for compliance didn't do the trick, they moved on to the next step. And, if necessary, the next. And the next. Camera or no camera.

He tried to engage the man again. "Pastor Bullard? It looks like you may've had an accident. Why don't you sit down? Maybe here on the step." He gestured behind Bullard to the cracked steps leading up to the old woman's front stoop.

Bullard cried out as if startled from sleep. A sharp, guttural protest. Followed by another and another, each one louder than the last. His body convulsed with every outburst, his eyes flicking left to right and back again.

"You seem like a reasonable guy." Andrew moved closer, keeping his body turned just enough so that Mary was still in view. She gave him some side-eye, but said nothing. Andrew kept going, keeping his voice low and even. "I understand you're upset. We're here to help."

Mary moved in from the other side, closing Bullard between them.

Andrew shot her a look. Bullard wasn't a large man, five foot nine at most, and soft. His bulk more burrito than muscle. But he still had five inches and at least fifty pounds on Andrew's unarmed partner. Not that he'd had any real expectation she'd stay out of it. Mary wasn't one to back down.

She kept going, closing the distance, her voice low and even. "Sir, please calm down. If you would take a seat, I'm sure we can talk things out."

The minister's face went slack, and his posture changed, relaxed. And, in that moment, he almost looked like himself.

A car horn blared from somewhere down the street.

Bullard lunged toward Mary, snarling.

She widened her stance, her voice pure authority. "On the ground. Now."

Bullard's next lunge knocked Mary backward to the driveway, his body landing on top of hers. She struggled underneath him as Andrew closed the distance.

Bullard wrapped a hand around her neck, and Mary punched him hard in each side. Blows which should have put Bullard into the fetal position. She might have been small, but Mary was no joke. Andrew had seen her take down guys three times her size in training. She landed a solid shot to the side of his head. Bullard didn't flinch.

Mary tore at the man's grip, still tight on her neck. Andrew grabbed Bullard from behind and pulled as hard as he could. But Bullard held tight, jaws snapping. Saliva spattered Mary's face, leaving dark splotches on her blouse. Mary looked at Andrew over Bullard's shoulder, eyes wide, mouth gasping for the air that couldn't reach her lungs.

Bullard twisted and sunk his teeth into the soft skin between Andrew's thumb and finger. Andrew hissed in pain. He jerked his hand back, tearing the flesh beneath Bullard's teeth. Bullard roared at Andrew over his shoulder. Blood mixing with the saliva on his face. But he still didn't let go of Mary's throat.

Andrew reached for him again, but he was too slow. Bullard lifted Mary's head from the pavement. Then slammed it back to the ground. The thunk of her skull against concrete a sickening dropped melon sound.

Andrew drew his weapon, adrenaline pounding in his ears. "Let her go, or I'll shoot."

What if he hit Mary?

He tightened his grip on the gun.

What if the shot hit Bullard, but it passed through him and into her?

Bullard lifted Mary's head again, and time stopped.

Andrew fired.

CHAPTER 6

Andrew sat on the edge of a hard plastic chair, his leg bouncing with nervous energy. He'd been waiting in hospital limbo for forty-five minutes, and it was getting old.

A half-open green curtain partitioned him from the rest of triage. Nurses hurried past, sensible shoes squeaking on linoleum. Alarms sounded and then silenced in the distance, and a kid somewhere nearby played Elmo's birthday song on loop. He barely heard any of it. His mind echoed with the sound of his partner's head thwacking against the concrete. Could he have done more? Moved faster? Would things be different if he hadn't let go of Bullard's shoulder? If he'd drawn his weapon sooner?

Dr. Sue Ellen Hendrick pulled open the curtain. "Sorry to keep— "

"Is Mary back from the MRI?" Andrew interrupted, his leg bouncing faster.

"She wasn't when I came in." Sue Ellen sat on a short stool and wheeled it closer, glancing down at his leg. "Try not to worry too much. She's as hard-headed now as she was in high school." Sue Ellen smiled at him, and for a second, she looked just the same as she had more than a decade ago, when she'd been the cheer captain and Andrew had been a chubby freshman spray painting graffiti under the bleachers.

"I went to see her when I heard she'd been admitted." Sue Ellen smoothed the pleats of her skirt into place. "If I had to guess, Mary's looking at a mild concussion. Nothing worse than that."

Andrew forced his leg to be still. The pressure in his chest eased a bit, but it didn't go away. He doubted it would until he saw for himself that Mary was okay.

A nurse carried in a metal tray with several large syringes, a hypodermic needle, a roll of gauze, medical tape, and a small pair of scissors. He slid it onto a table to Andrew's right and slipped back out of the room.

Andrew eyed the needle. "They already took blood for my tox screen."

"Mmm-hm." She gestured for his injured hand. "May I?"

Andrew held it out, and she leaned over, inspecting the crescent-shaped gash between his thumb and pointer finger. "I don't think you need stitches, which is good. Better not to suture in these cases." She picked up one of the bigger syringes from the tray. "First, we'll irrigate the wound. Wash out what we can, then we'll flush it again with an iodine solution." Holding a folded piece of gauze underneath his hand to catch the overflow, she washed the wound.

A cold gush of water left his hand dripping.

She moved to the next syringe and did the same. "Given the circumstances of your injury, I'd also like to treat you for rabies exposure."

Andrew blinked up at her. "Rabies?" Even as he asked the question, things clicked into place. The man he'd heard about on the news. Randy Bullard's irrational violence, the foam around his mouth. And something else. It itched at the back of his mind. Something he couldn't quite put his finger on. "You think— "

"We're waiting to hear back from the CDC, but we should have confirmation on whether Mr. Bullard had rabies by tomorrow. We can hold off treatment until we know for sure, if you'd like. The rabies vaccine is expensive. It could be three to seven thousand dollars to complete the treatment, depending on your insurance. And it's very unlikely you'd become symptomatic before then." She leaned back on the stool, tucking one ankle behind the other. "The incubation period for rabies is highly unpredictable. Could be a week, could be a decade. But I've never heard of anyone becoming symptomatic in less than five days."

He raised his eyebrows. "That's quite a range."

"It is." She nodded. "With a bite to the hand or face, it tends to be on the faster end." She smoothed her skirt again, picking off a piece of lint. "And you do need to know that if you develop symptoms, there's very little we can do to help. There is no cure for rabies, no real treatment for patients once they've become symptomatic. Of course, it's possible Mr. Bullard's test will come back negative." It didn't take a detective to read her expression. As far as she was concerned, the chances of that were slim to none. Sue Ellen went on. "If you want to wait and check with your insurance or— "

"No." Andrew had looked into Bullard's eyes and found nothing human left in them. He could deal with more bills, but not what he'd seen outside that old lady's house today. "Just do it."

She nodded and picked up the third syringe. "I thought you might feel that way. This is human rabies immune globulin, or HRIG. It'll supply your body with rabies antibodies until the vaccine has time to take effect. We'll apply some at the site of the bite, and the remainder intramuscularly."

He blinked at her again.

Sue Ellen smiled, but it felt like it was at his expense. "As a shot." She covered the bite mark in what she'd called HRIG and applied a bandage over the top. "The nurse will be back in a moment to take care of the rest. You'll get the remainder of the HRIG and the first dose of the rabies vaccine today." She pulled her gloves off, tucked one into the other, and tossed them into a plastic trash can. "You'll need to come back for three more doses. It'll all be detailed in your discharge paperwork, but the subsequent shots need to be administered on the third, seventh, and fourteenth days after the first."

Super.

Sue Ellen turned to go. "Call if you have any pain or swelling around the wound."

"Doc?"

She stopped, one hand on the curtain.

"Any idea where they got it from? Pastor Bullard and..." He trailed off, unsure of the other victim's name. He'd heard it on the news, but at the time, it had been just one more random detail. Nothing to do with him.

Man, how things can change in just a few days.

"Emma Canning." She shook her head. "Ms. Canning had no idea how she might have been exposed." She paused, as if deciding whether to go on. When she did, her voice was lower. "Ms. Canning died this morning. And, of course, we weren't able to speak to Randy Bullard, so..." She cleared her throat and turned away again. "I'll go see if Mary's back."

The weight of what she hadn't said settled heavy in his chest. They weren't able to speak to Bullard because Andrew had killed him. In more than a dozen years on the force, it was the first time he'd fired his weapon in the line of duty. Randy Bullard's was the only life he'd ever taken. The heaviness turned into an ache. Where had he gone wrong? What could he have done differently?

Not a damn thing.

He didn't have a choice. He knew that. And if he had to do it over again, he would do the same. He would choose his partner's life every time.

Let's just hope the DA agrees.

He hadn't gotten the call putting him on admin leave yet, but it was just a matter of time. The department would do an investigation of the shoot, and DA Nguyen would do her own. A separate, independent assessment of whether — in that split second — he'd made the right decision. He leaned back in the chair, turning his hand up and down, as if to inspect the bandage. But he didn't register what he was seeing.

Knowing what he did now, that Bullard had been sick. Not in his right mind. Did that change things? Would it change how the brass saw them? Yeah, maybe so. Andrew closed his eyes and said a short prayer — for Bullard, for Mary, for forgiveness.

Voices came from beyond the curtain.

He opened his eyes, willing Sue Ellen to come back with news of Mary. But no one appeared.

Shit.

Andrew went back to his thoughts. He'd never heard of anyone getting rabies. And now there were two cases in a town the size of Chattanooga? How did something like that happen? He rubbed a hand over the back of his head. He had no fucking idea. The only things he knew about rabies he'd learned from Old Yeller. He stopped, hand still pressed against his scalp.

Dogs.

He leaned back in his chair, the thought he'd been grasping at earlier finally within reach. What if Richardson's facility hadn't "phased out" their canine research? What if that research hadn't been focused on macular degeneration like he'd said in their second interview? If they'd been doing some sort of rabies research and the dogs escaped or were let out during the fire, would Richardson really say so? Risk the consequences? The liability? The fact that he hadn't gotten a call back from the facility where Richardson claimed the "retired" Beagles had been sent might mean more than Andrew had realized.

That's a lot of "what ifs."

He rolled his head side to side, stretching the kinks from his neck. Even if he was way off in left field. Even if it was nothing. Even if it was someone else's case now. All those "ifs" needed answers.

Sue Ellen's voice rose in the distance, polite but tense. "You should have called first. I'd have saved you the trouble of coming all this way."

Another voice. "It's no trouble."

Andrew pulled back the curtain, leaning out so he could see.

Sue Ellen stood near a bank of elevators with a woman he didn't recognize. A few inches shorter than the doctor, she had an athletic build, with sunglasses holding wavy brown hair off a heart-shaped face. Not his type, too fresh-faced, but he wouldn't kick her out of bed either.

The woman shifted on her feet. "Thanks for seeing me. I heard you on the news and thought, if I could help, I should try." She dug through a cross-body bag. "Let me give you my number."

Sue Ellen put a hand on her elbow. "I'll walk you out. With what we..."

Andrew stepped into the hall, straining to hear. But they were too far away for him to catch the rest. Whoever she was, the woman seemed to be trying to make herself a part of the excitement surrounding the rabies cases. Like any other public tragedy, there would be people drawn to the spectacle — reporters, fame-seekers, or just folks with too much time and curiosity on their hands.

"Mr. Marsh?" The nurse who'd delivered the tray to Sue Ellen appeared behind him, another syringe in his hand. "Ready?"

Andrew nodded.

God, he hated needles. He tried not to look at it as he followed the nurse back inside and settled in his chair. "Any chance you've got word on Mary Washington?" Andrew rolled up his sleeves. "They took her for an MRI an hour ago."

"Sorry." He smiled at Andrew and tore open an alcohol prep pad.

"No worries," Andrew said and looked away.

But that wasn't even close to true.

CHAPTER 7

The hospital doors whooshed open. Letty stepped outside, carrying a cup of cafeteria chai tea by the rim. Sunlight glared off the hospital's green glass exterior and into her eyes. She squinted, sat the cup on a short stone wall beyond the entrance, and pulled her sunglasses into place.

She should be happy. With the second rabies case, there'd be no shortage of qualified people on the ground. The local health department, the state health department, and probably the CDC, too. Which meant she didn't need to get involved. She could go back to Athens. Settle into a lazy summer routine. Work, drink, repeat. No higher reasoning required. She bobbed the tea bag in the water.

So why wasn't she relieved?

Letty stared off into the parking lot. In the trees dotting the median, squirrels chittered to each other, jumping branch to branch. One stopped, as if sensing her eyes on him, and stared in her direction, tail twitching.

What're you looking at?

She went back to her tea. Part of her had been dying to get back in the field since her lab finished their last project. Six weeks in the far reaches of Georgia's Tray Mountain Wilderness studying parasite transmission in wild turkeys, while she bunked in the RV with three other people — one of them Chris. It should have driven her away from fieldwork for good. Especially because, unlike their fattened-up domesticated cousins, wild turkeys were assholes. Even when they didn't have parasites.

But, if anything, it had confirmed what she already knew. She was happiest with her boots in the dirt. Collecting data, doing the everyday hard work of science. Which made the prospect of the semester ahead — teaching ecology to a bunch of bored undergrads — all the more depressing.

She dug around in her bag, sorting past keys, a half-eaten protein bar, and an extra pair of socks, before she found her cell phone. She'd missed a call from Priya, which gave her a quick pang of guilt. For not making it out to say goodbye before Priya left, and for not checking in sooner to make sure Priya'd made it onto her flight. Letty wouldn't even see her for the month or more she'd be away. Letty cringed.

She'd been so wrapped up in her own nonsense, she hadn't been a very good friend. She sent Priya a quick text. "FaceTime me when you get there. I need to see the amazingness of your summer digs for myself."

Nothing more she could do about that now. She double-checked her texts and voicemails, but there was still nothing from Caroline, who was probably at work with her ringer off.

What now?

Letty threw the used tea bag into a trash can. Maybe Caroline being out of touch since she'd arrived was a good thing? It would be easier to cut the trip short if she didn't have a crazy night, followed by one of Caroline's infamous recovery brunches, which would lead to God knew what else.

If she left now, she might be able to pick up a shift at The Flying Dawg tomorrow night. She flipped through emails looking for the confirmation she'd gotten from the Inn she booked. Fingers-crossed, they'd still let her cancel.

A voice drifted over from the distance. "For someone who just got their head cracked open, you sure are bossy..."

A beefy, bald guy in a rumpled button-down and blue jeans charged out of the hospital's front entrance with a phone pressed to his ear. He had a square jaw, a five o'clock shadow, and the look of someone who'd been up all night. "The kids are at your mom's. I'll go by after I pick up the food and—" He grimaced as he stepped into the bright light of the sun. "Yeah, I know. No onions. Same as usual." He met Letty's gaze and stopped walking. "Let me call— " He rolled his eyes. "Extra crispy, got it."

The man hung up and tucked the cell into his back pocket, but he kept looking at Letty.

Great.

She stared down at her phone and turned the other way, projecting "not interested" with every pore. She scrolled through email until she found the one she was after and took a sip of the now lukewarm tea.

"Afternoon."

Letty choked.

She turned, coughing spiced tea into the crook of an elbow. The bald guy had crept up behind her, like a fucking ninja. He held a badge in a hand wrapped with gauze.

What the hell?

"Sorry," she said, her voice strangled. "Hi."

Amusement crossed his face. "Detective Andrew Marsh. And you are?"

She cleared her throat. "Letty Duquesne. Nice to meet you." Should she offer a handshake? Is that what you did with the police? Her high school exploits with Jessa had hardly been a user's guide for how to properly interact with law enforcement. She opted against it. Especially not if he was about to give her a parking ticket.

"What brings you to the hospital today?" His eyes were bright blue and shrewd.

Even for a policeman, that question seemed a little over the line. What business was it of his? She could have been there because of something personal, something embarrassing.

Hi. My name's Letty, and I have syphilis.

Seeing no other option, she answered. "I came to see Dr. Hendrick."

He nodded, but didn't speak, the silence quickly becoming awkward.

She'd seen enough TV to recognize the technique. Letty raised an eyebrow and waited.

A flicker of a smile crossed his face.

She stayed silent.

Two orderlies breezed past in a cloud of cigarette smoke. Still, she let the silence hang.

The cop tucked a thumb into his belt loop and leaned back against the stone wall, as if settling in for a long chat. His gaze never broke hers.

Letty relented. "I'm a disease ecologist with the University of Georgia. I saw the statement Dr. Hendrick made on the news, and thought I might be able to help with the..." She waved a hand around. "Rabies."

Well, that didn't sound shady.

"I see." He pursed his lips, as if she'd confirmed some suspicion. "While I'm sure Dr. Hendrick appreciates your offer..." He sounded sure of no such thing. "We've got all the resources we need. From what I hear, the CDC is already on the way." He gave her a smile she suspected he thought was charming, then turned to go. "You have a good day now." He swaggered down the sidewalk toward the parking lot.

Letty's cheeks burned and several things came to mind that she had the foresight not to yell at someone with a badge and probably a gun. But what sort of misogynistic bullshit was that? He might as well have told her to let the men-folk take care of it.

The hell I will.

■ ■ ■

Letty piled a small plastic plate with an assortment of cheese cubes and water crackers. She balanced it on top of a glass of what was probably terrible Merlot. Then, with her free hand, snagged the second glass. This one, she'd filled from a ceramic carafe sitting in a mostly melted bucket of ice water. It was labeled only as "white."

Not the healthiest dinner. But when an ill-advised, non-refundable overnight stay comes with a free happy hour, who was she to say no?

She nodded hello to a young couple heading down to the spread she'd just left and headed for the stairs. The inn was spotless, if a little shabby in places. Heavy carpets, worn down the middle. Floral drapes on every window, and the faint smell of potpourri in the common rooms downstairs. Dated, but cute.

The stairs creaked with each step up to her room on the second floor. And her calf muscles protested at least as much. The hike she'd taken after she checked in had been a two mile climb straight up. The first mile, she'd done double-time. Each step pounding the dirt, while she worked off her frustration over what she wished she'd said to deputy doofus.

Near the top of the trail, a small wooden staircase had led to a bluff with unobstructed views of the North Chickamauga Creek Gorge. A soft, pine-scented wind cooled her skin and her temper. It ruffled the leaves of lush, green treetops extending out as far as she could see. The only break in the broad expanse of green was a river winding through the middle. None of it had been spoiled by human hands, and there wasn't a rabid bat in sight.

By the time she'd gotten back to her car, Letty was exhausted and more or less at peace with going home in the morning. Especially as she hadn't heard from Caroline since she'd left Athens.

Rude.

Had she done something to piss her friend off? Maybe Caroline didn't appreciate her last minute fly-by after she'd gone so long without reaching out. But that didn't make sense. Caroline hadn't called her either. And co-dependence had never been their thing. They were more the pick up where you left off, catch-up-over-drinks type of friends.

Letty sat one of her wine glasses on a wide-planked hardwood floor and let herself into the room. The decor inside had the same ruffled burgundy Laura Ashley feel as the rest of the inn. But the bed was soft, and, if she looked past the parking lot, she had a view of the Appalachians. She slid her dinner next to her laptop on a small oak desk by the window.

Letty had missed sunset while she was debating between white, orange, or speckled cheese cubes, but the fading orange pink warmth that spread skyward to purple then blue was still pretty. She popped a speckled cheese cube into her mouth, happy to confirm it was spicy — not old — and opened the laptop.

After her little chat outside the hospital, Letty wanted to confirm what exactly was being done to address the rabies cases and by whom. She clicked through to the Tennessee health department website and read everything they had on the outbreak. Then did the same on the local Hamilton County website. The details were sparse, but it was on their radar, and that's what mattered. As an afterthought, she typed "Chattanooga rabies outbreak" into her search engine.

An article in the Chattanooga Times Free Press showed up as the top result. "Local Authorities Say Risk of Rabies Infection Overblown."

What?

She sat up in her chair and clicked through to the article, skimming past statistics and details of the state's wildlife vaccination program — where, every year, thousands of fishmeal-coated vaccine packets were dropped by low-flying helicopters and airplanes across the forests of Tennessee. Letty skipped down to the end. "Local health officials confirm these two isolated cases should not be of concern to the public. Mayor Jeffries agrees. 'Our hearts and prayers go out to the families of Ms. Canning and Pastor Bullard. And, as always, public safety is our top priority. But our city's response to this tragedy should be based in fact, not fear. There is no reason to believe there's any real threat of further cases. And if we allow irrational panic to drive business away from Chattanooga, the cure may be worse than the disease.'" The article ended with the picture of a young family hiking a trail similar to the one Letty had taken that afternoon, a smiling toddler riding in a carrier on his father's back.

You've gotta be kidding me.

She loaded a cracker with cheese and popped it into her mouth. It wouldn't hurt to stay a few days. See what she could find. Except with Caroline AWOL — which, given the mayor's position, now seemed even more ominous — she'd be doing it with no authority and no way to get access to any of the people or information she might need to trace the disease back to the source animal. She finished the first glass of wine and leaned back in the chair. What would that kind of investigation even look like?

Dr. Hendrick hadn't seemed keen to share notes. But Letty could probably draw some conclusions from what hadn't been on the health departments' websites. If there was any possibility the infection had come from organ donation or travel to a country where rabies was still endemic, they'd have said so. And the second case made both of those possibilities unlikely in any case.

So, they were looking for a good old four-legged reservoir. A mammal. She pulled up a chart of terrestrial rabies variants online and confirmed her memory. In Eastern Tennessee, the source animal was most likely a skunk, a raccoon, or a bat. Her gut still said bat.

She went back to the computer, pulling up everything she could find about the two victims. Emma Canning, the only child of a wealthy Signal Mountain family, had been home from rehab for less than a month when she became ill. By all reports, before that, she'd been on the road to recovery. Even enrolling at UT Chattanooga, where she'd planned to study occupational therapy in the fall. She had been twenty-six when she died.

Randy Bullard left behind a wife, two daughters, six grandchildren, and the congregation of the Chesapeake Hill Baptist Church, where he'd been pastor for more than thirty years. Article after article spoke of his contributions to the community, his dedication to family and God. She scrolled through images — Bullard in a Habitat for Humanity shirt, swinging a hammer. Serving food at a soup kitchen. In side-by-side lawn chairs with his wife at what looked like a church picnic.

What a waste.

Two lives cut short, both leaving behind people who loved them. In a perfect world, she'd go speak to the families. See if she could find out where the victims might've encountered the same animal or animals. But she didn't have any authority to do that and wouldn't feel right approaching the families anyway. They'd been through enough.

So, where did that leave her? There were no obvious connections between the two victims. She took a sip of the white wine and cringed. It was sweet, oaky, and warm.

Blech.

She put the glass down and flipped back through the websites still open on her laptop, stopping at the church's homepage. In a column running down the far-right side of the screen, a map directed visitors where to park. An arrow pointed to one side of an intersection in the middle of the same Signal Mountain neighborhood as Emma Canning's parents' house.

Well how 'bout that.

It could mean nothing. Or it could be there was a reservoir animal living somewhere near Signal Mountain. She tapped a fingernail against the side of the wine glass. If she couldn't talk to the victims or their families to narrow the search area, maybe the next best option was to talk to the people most likely to have encountered an infected animal — veterinarians, doggie-daycares, animal shelters, or clinics.

That might be do-able. And Caroline was bound to surface eventually. Letty could gather information, then once Caroline reappeared, give it to her to push into the right channels. Better to have an answer and owe a mea culpa than to do nothing, right? She topped another cracker with cheese and took a bite. She knew what Jessa would say.

Let's do it.

Letty pulled up the online yellow pages, grabbed a notepad, and started a list. There were two veterinarians in the Signal Mountain area, a half dozen in the surrounding neighborhoods, and an animal shelter just on the other side of Highway 127.

As soon as they opened tomorrow, she would start making calls. It probably wouldn't lead anywhere, but that was the nature of science. For every successful experiment, there were a hundred that'd failed. Perseverance was half the battle.

She stared back out the window. With the sun gone, the distant mountains were now only a series of black mounds against the dusky night sky.

She leaned over, straining to spot her car in the lot. The Inn had seemed like it was in a safe neighborhood when she parked. And, maybe more importantly, she'd been too lazy to carry all the gear she'd packed upstairs. But now that it was dark, the risk of a random smash and grab didn't seem as remote. Plus, at least half the gear in the back of the car wasn't hers to begin with.

Pushing back the heavy curtain, she searched the lot for where she'd parked. Movement in a silver BMW near the street caught her eye. A man sat in the driver's seat, his face lit by a nearby lamp post. Pale, middle-aged, and unremarkable.

Except that he was looking right at her.

CHAPTER 8

May 4, 2018

Pete Hendrick leaned back against the Formica counter in Exam Room Two. "I appreciate your worry, Ms. Edwina, but we vaccinated Ginger right on schedule. She's not at any risk of contracting rabies."

"Well, I knew we'd stayed up to date with everything, even though it cost us an arm and a leg." The old woman eyed him over her glasses, as if he'd personally set the price and pocketed the excess. "But she just don't act like herself." Ginger yapped from under Edwina Brown's seat, growling and biting at a chair leg.

As far as he could tell, the Jack Russell was business as usual. High strung and bad tempered, just like her owner. Pete crouched, his voice soft. "Hey, girl." He reached a hand toward the dog, keeping his movement slow and even.

Ginger inched forward, but her tail stayed low.

"Haven't seen you in church in a bit." Edwina would've sounded concerned to anyone who didn't know her. But he'd spent enough Sundays stuck in a pew with her to know better. She layered on the saccharine. "Everything alright with you and Sue Ellen?"

"Yes, ma'am." He kept his gaze on the dog. Edwina undoubtedly knew it wasn't. Everyone at church did. What she wanted was a nugget of gossip to take back to the other church vultures, and he wasn't going to give it.

Edwina gave an exaggerated sniff that sounded like disapproval.

Pete ignored it, still shifting closer to Ginger. The dog had distrust in her eyes, but her tail gave a slow wag.

Progress.

His phone dinged in his pocket, and Ginger scrambled back under the chair. Nails scratching the floor, a low grumble in her throat.

He ignored the phone. He knew who it was. And he wasn't interested in talking to Sue Ellen, even if he hadn't been with a patient. Pete tried again. "It's okay, Ginger."

Another ding and another spree of barking. Ginger redoubled her assault on the chair leg.

Pete got back to his feet. "I don't see anything of concern, Ms. Edwina. But you let me know if something changes. And, if you're still worried, keep Ginger inside as much as possible. That'll reduce the chances of her coming into contact with animals that might be infected." He washed his hands and pulled a paper towel from the under-cabinet dispenser. "I'll tell you what I've been telling everyone else who came in after they saw the rabies story on the news. The chance of a domesticated dog catching rabies is exceptionally low. Vaccination is mandated by law in Tennessee, and there hasn't been a single case of canine rabies in the state this year. Only one last year, and that was over in Maury County." Pete opened the exam room door. "Of course, you can always give us a call if you have questions or see anything else that worries you."

Edwina huffed past him into the hall. "Might as well have stayed home." She stopped mid-way to the lobby door, bending down to clip on Ginger's leash.

Her rear end all but blocked Pete's path.

He stared down at Ginger's chart, feigning absorption in his notes until Edwina righted herself and the door closed behind her.

Good riddance.

His receptionist's cheerful voice came from the lobby. "Haven't seen you in awhile, Ms. Edwina. That bursitis of yours acting up again?" Nobody managed Edwina better than Trish.

Another ding came from Pete's pocket, and he cringed. He needed to answer it, even if it was the last thing he wanted to do. Sue Ellen wasn't going to stop until he did.

He pulled out the phone. As expected, all three messages were from his soon-to-be former wife.

"Did you get my voicemail?!?"

"CALL ME BACK."

"You're pathetic."

The last one sounded just like his mother. He closed his eyes. Even from a distance, Sue Ellen managed to be a constant source of misery. He'd thought her filing for divorce would make it better. But it hadn't. Demands, insults, manipulation. Like it gave her joy to wear him down every day. He took a deep breath. It couldn't go on forever.

"Dr. Hendrick?"

Pete flinched.

Trish stood in the doorway, her head cocked to one side. "You alright?" She pronounced alright with the hard "i" of a native Tennessean. It was still harsh to his ear, even after living there for years. Nothing like the soft drawl of home.

Should've stayed in Charleston.

He forced a smile onto his face. "Of course, just lost in thought."

"Julie's taking the last of the boarders out for a walk now and Edwina's gone." She smiled. "Thought you'd want to know."

"What would I do without you?" He held Ginger's file out so Trish could re-shelve it.

"Don't thank me yet." She exchanged the file for a new one. "I put Jimmy Coker in Room Three while you were in with Edwina. He says Duke's not acting right."

Crap. Third one today.

He nodded. "Anybody else on the schedule?"

"That Georgia doctor's fixin' to come by in a bit, but otherwise I think you're done after Duke." Trish pulled open the lobby door, talking over her shoulder. "Long as we don't have any more walk-ins."

"Trish?"

She turned back, eyebrows raised.

He held out his phone. "Would you take this, too? Put it in the front desk for me?"

She nodded, a knowing in her face he wished wasn't there.

■ ■ ■

After half a dozen wrong turns, Letty pulled into the parking lot for the Mountain View Animal Clinic. A towering pine forest surrounded her fourth stop of the day and blocked out any view it might once have had, mountain or otherwise. The small brick building had been painted a soft green a few shades lighter than the trees. A shallow covered porch embraced the front and was bordered by a continuous mass of fuchsia azalea bushes, broken only by a ramp leading down to the parking area.

Who was she meeting at this one?

She grabbed her list from the passenger seat and went down the page until she got to Mountain View. This clinic was run by another Dr. Hendrick — hopefully nicer than the last one.

Not that any of her efforts today had amounted to much, even when folks had been open to talk. So far, she'd learned three things. No one would answer her questions by phone. No one had seen anything that might indicate a rabies case in the last year. And most veterinarians' waiting areas didn't smell all that great.

Might as well get to it.

Letty checked the rearview mirror to make sure her hair hadn't gone full frizz in the humidity and grabbed her purse from the passenger-side floorboard.

A loud "thunk" came from the hood.

She jerked up, heart pounding.

Flat black eyes stared at her from the other side of the windshield.

The crow cawed and cocked its head.

She swallowed a nervous laugh. "Hi, bird."

It took flight into the trees, and she leaned forward to watch it go.

Crazy thing.

The bird landed on a branch next to another crow that could have been its twin. Its mate, probably. At least two dozen more filled the branches around it. Another round of caws came from her visitor, and the murder erupted in answer.

Why would so many be gathered this early in the year? They didn't usually collect in large groups until the winter mating season. She scanned the ground around the tree but didn't see anything to explain it. Like humans, they'd congregate around their dead. Whether to mourn or learn from the dead bird's mistake, no one seemed to know.

Letty shook her head.

That went dark fast.

She needed to get a grip. The birds were just being birds. And she was just rattled. Had been ever since she'd seen the weird guy in the parking lot the night before. Which was silly really. He'd probably been staring off into space. If she hadn't been so quick to yank the curtains closed, she'd probably have seen his wife come out after she'd paid their bill. The idea that he'd been watching her was stupid. Why would he be? And besides, no one except Bill even knew she was staying there.

Letty stepped out of the car and into the warm late afternoon sun. She straightened her shift dress, allowed herself one more glance at the crows, and turned toward the clinic.

A shiny black Doberman stood in her path. His sleek, muscled body rigid and still.

Letty froze.

What the hell?

"Oh, sorry." A young woman wearing a low ponytail, scrubs, full sleeve tattoos, and studded combat boots rounded the side of the building. "I hope he didn't scare you. Roscoe's always getting away from me." She offered an apologetic grin and attached a leash to the dog's collar. The Doberman licked the woman's hand, butt wagging back and forth where a tail should have been.

"No problem." Letty returned the smile, the tension easing out of her shoulders.

The dog propelled the young woman off toward a dirt path leading into the woods.

Letty watched them go, then climbed the clinic's ramp and pushed open the door.

A brass bell jangled overhead, and a receptionist with teal eyeliner and a phone pressed to one ear looked up from behind a partial wall. Colorful files lined floor to ceiling shelves behind her. The woman raised her pointer finger in a "just one minute" gesture and smiled.

Letty took a seat between a big window looking out on the forest and a fish tank filled with neon tetras. Other than the fish, this waiting room was no different than all the others she'd been in that day. Plastic chairs, coffee tables with pamphlets, walls covered in ASPCA posters and animal-themed art. And the faint smell of wet dog.

Letty waited while the receptionist carried on a long, hushed conversation. She had read all the pamphlets, named the tetras, and nearly exhausted the internet when a phone finally clattered into its cradle on the opposite side of the desk.

The receptionist cleared her throat. "Can I help you?"

"Yes, hi." Letty got to her feet. "We spoke earlier. I'm Letty Duquesne from—"

A series of thuds and yips came from behind a closed door to the left of the reception desk, and a jowly man in a bright orange Tennessee cap pushed it open. "Which is why I reminded that somna bitch that the first rule of football is you can't ignore special teams." The man spoke over his shoulder as a Boxer puppy danced into the room at his feet. It pulled toward Letty at the end of a leash, front legs windmilling.

"Pardon my language, ma'am." The man handed a credit card to the receptionist. Then turned to Letty and tipped the bill of his hat. "Ma'am."

A second man came through the door. Shaggy brown hair, dark eyes, and, under an open lab coat, the complete preppy uniform — light blue checkered button-down, tailored khakis, and a pair of soft leather loafers with no socks. He leaned on the receptionist's counter. "Almost makes you want to stop watching football altogether, doesn't it?" He laughed, and a double-crescent of smile lines creased his cheeks. "Almost."

Not bad.

The jowly man took his credit card back from the receptionist. "Go Vols." He led the dog out toward the parking lot. "Y'all have a blessed day."

The receptionist looked back to the doctor and tilted her head toward Letty. "Dr. Hendrick, this is Dr. Duquesne."

He stepped forward, holding out a hand. "You can call me Pete."

She shook it. "Letty."

"Nice to meet you. You're the professor from UGA." He looked up, as if searching his memory. "Disease ecology, right?"

Technically, she wasn't a professor until her contract started in August.

Close enough.

She smiled. "That's right. But try not to let what the Dawgs did to you guys in Knoxville last year color your view."

He laughed again, the smile lines re-appearing. "I'm not gonna say forty-one to nothin' didn't sting." He gestured for her to sit in one of the chairs lining the walls of the waiting room. "But no hard feelings."

"Thanks for agreeing to speak with me." She moved toward the closest chair.

A frenzy of barking came from outside. Not the normal bark she'd expect at any vet's office. This sounded like alarm.

They both stopped, turning toward the noise.

Letty searched the forest beyond the window, expecting to see the Doberman she'd met on the way in. But there was no sign of it. Just blue skies, tree trunks, and branches swaying in the breeze.

She looked to the receptionist. The woman had stopped in place, a file half-pushed onto a shelf. She gave a short shrug, and Letty looked back out the window. Still nothing. Then a blur and a flash of blue. The same shade as the tattooed woman's scrubs.

Pete must have seen the same thing, because he went for the door.

The clang of the bell above it snapped Letty to attention. She followed Pete out onto the porch and down the ramp with no idea what she was walking into.

The barking stopped, and the tattooed woman cleared the tree line. Dirt darkened the knees of her scrubs, and her hair had come loose from the ponytail. The dog wasn't with her.

"Julie?" Pete called out to the woman. "Are you okay?"

She shook her head and stumbled down the last of the path. They caught up to her as she reached the grassy patch near the clinic and dropped to her knees. "There's a body in the woods." Her voice came out in a breathless heave. She pressed her hands to a face streaked with mascara and tears, her nails dirt-caked crescents against her skin.

What?

Letty went cold. She stared off into the forest. Maybe the woman had stumbled onto the bones of a big animal. A deer or even a coyote. It wouldn't be the first time animal remains gave someone a fright.

Pete knelt, his voice soft. "It's okay. You're okay. Can you tell me what happened?"

The woman shook her head but didn't speak, hands still pressed to her face.

He tried again. "Julie?"

She spoke from behind her hands, voice muffled. "I took Roscoe up to the top loop of the trail. We haven't been that way in ages, and he seemed like maybe he needed some extra exercise. He got away from me, like he always does." She hiccupped and pulled her hands away, looking to Letty, as if for confirmation. "I chased him down, but when I got over there..." She swallowed hard, head shaking, as if she couldn't make the words come out. She wiped at her eyes with the backs of her hands. "After I found the body, I knew I needed to get help, but Roscoe wouldn't come. He wouldn't move. He just kept staring down at the man, and I didn't know what to do. And I couldn't be there anymore... so I tied his leash to a tree and came to get help." She hiccupped again. "I'm sorry I left him, Dr. Hendrick." She lost whatever control she'd found, and the hiccups devolved into another round of tears.

Pete rested a hand on the top of her back. "It's okay, Julie, really. We'll go get him. Could you show me where?"

She shook her head, tears leaking from her eyes. "The body's in the gulley, and Roscoe's tied up tight right there. But I can't go back." She looked from Pete to Letty, head still shaking. "I can't."

Letty reached into the pocket of her dress, feeling for her phone. Should she call 911? If she did, the police would ask why she was there. And then what would she say? That would be a circus for sure. One she didn't need to endure if the remains turned out to be from a deer.

Even if the "body" was just a few scattered bones, Letty would be able to tell the difference between human and animal pretty quickly. She crouched on Julie's other side. "What if we all go? You'd just have to get close enough to point the way. Would that be okay?"

After a long moment, Julie nodded. She drew in several deep ragged breaths, as if forcing her body calm. Then got to her feet and led them up the path.

They climbed the hard-packed dirt trail in a tense silence broken only by Julie's sniffles and the rhythmic thud of their feet against the dirt. No buzz of insects. No rustle of small creatures escaping through the underbrush. No birdcalls warning of their approach.

Where is everything?

The trail veered right, but Julie kept going straight.

They followed. First Pete, then Letty. Up a narrow path, steep and overgrown with scraggly plants that scraped against her legs. A deep rut scarred the middle of the walkway, probably from rainwater run off.

Letty stumbled over a root and caught herself against the rough bark of a tree. The gladiator sandals she'd worn were comfortable, but they weren't built for hiking.

Pete turned back, his brown eyes kind in a worried face. "You okay?"

"Fine, I'm fine."

A sharp yip came from ahead and to their left.

The Doberman sat thirty yards from the path, his lead tied to a tree in an area covered by ivy. He stood as they approached, gave another short bark, then whined, looking off the edge of a ridge behind him.

Julie spoke in barely more than a whisper. "This is it."

"Okay, hang tight. I'll be right back." Pete tromped through the brush, over logs and fallen limbs. He rested a hand on the dog's head, then peered over the edge of the hill. His body went stiff.

That's not good.

Letty didn't want to follow. Everything in her said to stop, go back. But she went anyway. The undergrowth swished thick around her feet, vines catching in the space between her toes and her sandals and grabbing at her ankles. As if even the forest knew she shouldn't go.

She grew closer, and the smell was unmistakable. Like rancid meat or spoiled milk.

It could still be an animal.

Animal remains can smell like that.

She came even with Pete.

The road she'd driven to get to the Mountain View clinic wound through the woods on the other side of a long, shallow gulley. She inched closer to the edge. A few yards below the ridge where she stood, the remains of a man lay on the ground. His feet pointed out toward the road. Only the bottom half of his body visible from where she stood.

Letty held her breath and took another step forward. Pins and needles spread up her fingers to her arms, prickling across the back of her neck.

What was left of his face came into view.

One eye socket stared up at her. The side of his face she could see was mostly bone, stained brown in places. The stringy, weathered skin that remained had a similar color. Like some sort of disgusting jerky extending from his ear down the side of the face to his mouth. It gaped open, as if in shock.

Letty went numb, even as her mind raced with inane questions.

Was it even a man? Couldn't it just as easily be a woman? Whoever it was had no identifying features left. The body wasn't that big. Their frame was thin, like a teenager's, and what remained of the person's hair — wisps sticking up from a leathery strip of scalp — was only a few inches long. Not that short hair meant anything. The clothes didn't tell her much either. Long-sleeved black t-shirt, dark sneakers, a navy bandana around the neck, and faded black jeans.

A faint circle stood out on one of the front jean pockets. The kind you got from carrying a can of dipping tobacco day after day. She'd lived in the South long enough to recognize it.

Definitely a man.

One of his sleeves looked odd. Too flat.

He's missing an arm.

Letty spotted it in the brush slightly nearer the road, nothing left but sinew and bone. Probably the work of a scavenger. A coyote or a vulture, maybe a possum.

"We need to call the police." Pete spoke from beside her, and Letty jumped. She'd forgotten he was there. Forgotten everything except the dead man lying in dappled sunlight.

She pulled her cell from her pocket. Then stopped.

Something near the body moved.

What the fuck?

She stared down at the darkened leaves and soil around the remains. Volatile fatty acids had leaked out as the body broke down, staining the surrounding ground and killing any nearby vegetation. In that way, it was no different than the animal remains she was accustomed to. But only in that way.

The darkened dirt shifted, and Letty crouched down.

"What? What is it?" Pete asked from behind her.

Letty didn't answer.

It happened again. A slight movement in the soil. Then the flash of an exoskeleton in the sun. The movement wasn't the dirt itself. It was beetles. Busy eating what was left of the man from the inside out.

Letty shot back to her feet. Disgust overrode the rational part of her brain that knew there would be insect activity, especially with a body left exposed on the forest floor.

Julie spoke from the trail behind her. "I chased Roscoe up to the ridge, and then I saw these legs sticking out. I thought maybe a hiker had fallen, so I climbed down. But then the smell… and I saw his face." Her voice grew thick. "And I panicked. I tried to climb up, but I couldn't. The ground kept crumbling. I couldn't get out. And the smell of him. I— " Her words choked off into tears.

"It's okay, Julie." Pete un-looped the dog's lead from the tree. The swish and crunch of brush echoed loud in the woods behind her as they made their way back to the trail.

Letty didn't move. Hearing the anguish in Julie's voice, the fear. It made sense. But the only thing Letty felt was numb. Separate. As if she was there but not really a part of anything happening around her. She stared back down at the body. The disembodied arm in the bushes. The flash of another beetle's sclerite in the sun. The world silent except for Julie's grief and the whisper of wind in the trees.

It wasn't like the raw brutality of nature was any surprise. She'd seen it often enough at work. It wasn't even the first time she'd seen the progression of blowflies, maggots, and beetles that fed on animal remains. But she'd never seen what they did to a human animal. Never seen a dead person before at all.

Jessa's body is still at the bottom of the ocean.

The breeze picked up, a cold breath on her skin. Dry leaves tumbled across the forest floor, and an oak leaf blew up the man's torso. It came to rest on his face. One scalloped edge in the hole that had been the dead man's eye.

She winced away, tears wet on her face. A hungry grief tightened her chest that had nothing to do with the man lying dead at her feet.

CHAPTER 9

Letty thwacked a tiny bottle of shampoo against her palm until it hurt. Nothing came out. She'd already scrubbed her body raw and washed her hair three times with the hotel's rosemary mint shampoo. But the reek of death wouldn't go away. It had seeped into her skin. And her nose, and her mouth. She retched into the drain by her feet, what little remained in her stomach mixing with bathwater and soap suds.

She stayed under the shower spray until the water turned cold.

Fuck.

She cranked off the tap and ripped open the shower curtain to another blast of cold from an overhead air-conditioning vent. Goosebumps prickled skin that had already been cold for hours. The entire time they'd waited at the scene for paramedics to arrive, when she'd given her statement, when she'd watched them haul the body bag away. It was in the low-eighties outside, and Letty wasn't sure she would ever be warm again.

She pulled a towel from the rack over the toilet and, for once, the faint smell of bleach that came with it was welcome.

Her phone rang from the bedroom.

Please let it be Priya.

Or Caroline.

Even her mother would do. She needed a friendly voice. Someone to tell her it was all okay. That it had been a dream. No, a nightmare. Letty turbaned the towel around her hair and padded naked to the bedroom, leaving wet footprints on the carpet.

The phone rang again, but she couldn't tell from where.

She had stripped off her clothes as soon as she was in the room, and they littered the floor, along with her purse, her laptop case, and all the gear she'd finally unloaded from the car that morning before she left.

Another ring.

She rooted through the mess, dumping the contents of both her purse and laptop case on the floor, before finally finding the phone still in her dress pocket.

One missed call.

Double-fuck.

She didn't recognize the number.

Letty tossed the phone onto the bedside table and went back to the bathroom.

She finished drying off, slipped on a t-shirt and sweats, and grabbed the liner from the trashcan. One way or another, she was getting rid of that smell.

The ding of a voicemail came from the side table, and she ignored it. Whoever it was could wait. She shoved the clothes she'd worn to the vet's office inside the garbage bag. She tied it shut, then reopened the knot and added her shoes. No amount of washing would ever make her want to put any of it on again. She left the bag in the hallway outside her room, locked the door, and put on the safety chain.

Having the smell gone helped. A little.

She straightened the room, which helped a bit more.

Letty pulled a throw blanket from the foot of the bed and wrapped it around her shoulders. Then grabbed the phone and carried it to the desk, hoping to find warmth in the orange square of early evening light coming in through her window. She had two messages. One from Bill, earlier in the day. They'd had a burst pipe at the beach house and were heading back to Athens early. Did she want to have dinner with him and Marcia that week?

She closed her eyes. The comfort of home, of friends, of normal life, was exactly what she wanted. Just to go back to Athens and pretend the whole trip hadn't happened. Nothing was keeping her there.

She checked the second message.

"Hi, this is Pete Hendrick." He cleared his throat. "I got your number from Trish. I just wanted to see if you were alright and to apologize for what happened. I… I'm not sure what to say. Anyway, I'm here, if you still want to talk. Or if there's anything else I can do. I'm just really sorry…" His voice faded off, and he stumbled through his phone number and an awkward goodbye.

Letty ended the call. Did she still want to talk to Pete Hendrick? To any of the other vets left on her list? Her rogue search for a source animal seemed silly now.

The phone rang in her hand, and Letty yelped. Her nerves strung tight. She answered, even though it was another number she didn't recognize.

"Is this Colette Du…" The woman stopped, then tried again. "Collette Dew-case-knee?"

It wasn't the worst pronunciation Letty had heard. "Just Letty's fine."

"I'm sorry?"

Letty sighed. "Yes, this is her."

"Evening, ma'am. This is Officer Pearson with the Chattanooga Police Department. I understand you were present earlier today when a body was discovered behind the Mountain View Animal Clinic?"

Another layer of ice formed on Letty's skin. "That's right. Or, at least, I was there not long after. I called 911 to report the…" Letty struggled with her words. "To report what was found." She pulled the blanket tighter around her shoulders and stared out into the parking lot.

"We were hoping you might be able to come into the station tomorrow to give us an official statement? Say, ten a.m.?"

"I'm not sure what more I can tell you, but I'm glad— "

The silver BMW was back, this time parked at the opposite end of the lot, a man's silhouette behind the wheel.

Holy shit.

"Ma'am? Will ten work for you?"

Letty swallowed hard. "I'll be there."

CHAPTER 10

May 5, 2018

Andrew opened and closed his hands, stretching his fingers. Every one of his cases had to be written up and transferred to another detective before he went on leave. And he'd been at it for hours. Head down, trying to ignore the unusual hush in the squad room. He pulled the arson file to the center of his desk. Last one on the list.

He chicken-pecked his notes into the computer. It was a pain in the ass, but necessary. Not even Mary would be able to decipher his scrawl. He got to the line on the notepad where he'd written "dogs" with a giant question mark and stopped. Other than following up with the facility where Richardson claimed the Beagles had been sent, was there anything else that needed doing? Another interview with Richardson for sure. His gut told him there was something there. The guy was too calm, too helpful. But why?

He typed the need for another follow-up with Richardson into his notes and went on to the rest of the list. He'd come back to the dog issue later.

"Any news on Mary?" Phil Williams leaned back in his chair, just enough so Andrew could see him past the file cabinets separating their desks. The old man laced his hands behind his head, biceps straining the sleeves of his dress shirt. Even pushing retirement, Phil still kept himself in better shape than Andrew had been in the day he came out of the academy.

Andrew entered his last note. "Doc cleared her to come back on Monday."

"Thank God for that." Phil popped a stick of Juicy Fruit in his mouth and waved the pack in Andrew's direction.

Andrew shook his head at the gum. "No thanks." It smelled like too-sweet artificial bananas. Although it wouldn't have mattered if Phil had offered him a T-bone. Andrew's appetite had been off since the shooting.

"How 'bout you? Any idea when you'll be able to start picking up your slack again?"

Andrew shrugged. "Shit. Your guess is good as mine."

"Shit's right. Bunch of horse shit." Phil popped his gum. "What were you supposed to do? Wait 'til he cracked her head open like an egg?"

Andrew flinched, his mind replaying the moment Mary's head struck the pavement, and he felt the attention of the other cops nearby turn his way — a subtle stillness in their movements, heads leaning his direction. Andrew logged out of the computer. "Not supposed to talk about it."

Which was an understatement. He had been expressly forbidden by the brass from talking to anyone other than the DA and the shrink he'd been ordered to go see. And, at least for the moment, he was glad for the reprieve. There was nothing he wanted to talk about less. He scooped the last of his things off the desk, nodded to Phil, and tried to ignore the stares of the other cops in the room as he made for the door.

Phil popped his gum again and yelled after him. "Enjoy that paid vacay, buddy."

Andrew shot him the bird without turning, but he did it with a grin. Phil giving him shit was standard issue. It was what cops did. The old man's way of telling Andrew things would be normal again. If not today, someday.

Andrew walked under an American flag tacked up above the squad room door, through the dingy reception area, and outside into a muggy overcast day.

There was nothing remotely resembling a vacation in his future. God knew how long he'd be stuck inside the four walls of his apartment, waiting to hear what DA Nguyen was going to make of him. His face on the news and that damn video playing on loop all over the internet.

He knew he shouldn't keep watching it, but something compelled him back, again and again. The need to know if he might've done something differently. If Randy Bullard could have been saved. Most of all, what stuck with him was the look on Bullard's face in the video's final frame. It had been taken right after Mary had first approached, and the pastor looked almost normal.

It was enough to make Andrew question every choice he'd made before or after. Even though he knew Bullard's moment of sanity had been fleeting, if it'd been there at all. And anyway, now wasn't the time. Andrew crossed the parking lot to his car, popped the trunk, and dropped his crap inside.

Son of a bitch.

He'd forgotten to go back and finish his notes about the dogs. He slammed the trunk. The last thing he wanted was to endure all those "there but for the grace of God" stares on the back of his neck again. Andrew turned his keys over in his hand. He could call Mary and get her to do it. But that seemed like kind of a dick move with her just out of the hospital.

His stomach growled.

That's a good sign.

He hadn't eaten since the cereal he'd had for breakfast the day before. And there was fuck-all in his refrigerator at home. Better eat while he had the chance. He waited for a break in traffic and trotted across the street to Rosie's. If anything could give him an appetite, that would do it.

The meat-and-three joint was a local favorite, especially with cops and the after-church crowd. Rosie's shared a block with the precinct and two churches, not counting the Assembly of God two streets over. But her fried chicken was the real draw. Rosie served it spicy and hot.

Andrew pulled open the door. It looked the same inside as it had since she'd opened in 1978. Low ceilings, a buffet along one side, and a counter dotted with pies under covered glass dishes on the other. Booths and tables crammed the center.

He stepped inside, and the conversation and laughter in the room wheezed to a stop. The whir of the ceiling fans overhead grew loud. One of the fans' pull cords tap, tap, tapping against the glass of its center light. At least half the customers in the crowded room turned to stare. Some had anger in their eyes, but most looked at him with something more like compassion.

He wasn't sure which made him more uncomfortable.

Andrew kept his gaze down and walked straight for the buffet.

If Rosie recognized the sudden quiet, she didn't show it. "Look what the cat dragged in. 'Bout time we saw you back in here." She grinned at him from behind the counter, gold flashing in the back of her mouth. "Want the usual?"

"Yes, ma'am." He smiled at the bald spot on top of her head as she bustled down the line of steamer trays, filling his plate. Fried chicken, mashed potatoes with gravy, collard greens, buttered corn, and a sheet-pan biscuit. Kindness and fried food. What else could a man ask for?

Rosie passed him an overloaded plate. "You want sweet tea with that, sugar?"

Even better.

Andrew took his week's-worth of calories and turned to find a table. He normally grabbed a spot at one of the barstools lining the counter if he came without Mary, but that would mean striking up a conversation with whatever cop or local happened to be in the next seat over. And today, he couldn't imagine what that might sound like.

He scanned the room for an empty two-top and spotted a familiar heart-shaped face. The ecologist lady he'd spoken to outside the hospital sat two booths in from the bathrooms in back, blowing steam from a cup of coffee. Letty Duquesne looked as tired as he felt.

But she had an empty seat at her table and might be just the person he needed to talk to. Assuming she was willing to, after the way he'd behaved outside the hospital. With everything that had gone on that morning, it hadn't been his finest moment.

Still. It's worth a shot.

He carried his lunch to her table. "Ma'am."

She looked up at him with black-flecked caramel-colored eyes. Like a cat's — observant, smart, and judgy. "Detective."

He gestured to the empty bench seat across from her. "May I?"

After a beat, she nodded.

He sat, taking in her plate. Most of her food was still there, silverware on top, like she was done. "Didn't like your pot roast?"

She shrugged. "Not much of an appetite today."

"Same." But the smells coming from his plate were doing their damndest to fix that problem. He broke open the biscuit and spread honey butter on one side. "How'd you wind up here?"

She cocked her head. "Sorry?"

"Rosie's isn't exactly a tourist destination."

She pushed her plate away. "I was across the street this morning, giving a statement."

He stopped spreading butter. "What about?"

She shrugged, and he bit off a hunk of biscuit, waiting for a better answer.

She looked out the window behind him. "I found a body. Or, sort of found it."

"How do you 'sort of' find a body?" He talked past the food in his mouth.

Letty cringed. "I was there right after someone else did. I called 911." She shrugged again. "I guess they just wanted to confirm the details, see if there was anything new I thought of last night."

He recognized the look on her face. He'd bet his looked the same. Some things you didn't need time to remember. Some things you would never forget, no matter how much you wanted to. "I'm sorry you had to see that."

She met his gaze. "I'm sorry for what happened to you, too."

His face warmed. Of course she knew. Everybody must by now.

"Thanks." He took a sip of his tea, waiting for enough time to pass so that he could change the subject. "I was hoping I might be able to ask you a question."

"Me? Why?"

"I looked you up after we spoke outside the hospital."

She raised her eyebrows.

"Curiosity is an occupational requirement." He loaded his fork with collard greens and dipped them into the puddle of gravy on his potatoes.

She picked up the knife on her plate, then put it back down. "And what did you find?"

"For starters, you've got alphabet soup after your name." He'd missed where she went for undergrad, but Letty had a Masters in Public Health from Emory, a Masters in zoology, and a PhD in epidemiology from UGA. She might be where she didn't belong, but she was more than qualified to be there.

And, more importantly, she should be able to give him a feel for whether the heartburn he had over Richardson's missing dogs made any sense.

"Okay." Letty said the word with an implied "and" on the end.

"How familiar are you with animal research facilities?"

She leaned back, brows furrowed. "I don't have any personal experience, but I understand how they work."

"That's a start." He chewed another bite of the biscuit. "I have an arson case at a local research facility where certain animals were released at the time of the fire, which was about a month ago. Rats, mice, rabbits. It also appears dogs were, at some point, used as research subjects. But the facility manager claims there weren't any there when the fire occurred." Andrew took a long drink of tea. "Certain things about the manager's story, about the whole thing really, just don't make sense. And with the recent rabies cases…"

She shook her head, apparently seeing where he was headed. "I'd find a connection between the two highly unlikely."

Good.

If she was right, he didn't need to bother Mary or go back into the precinct.

"Why?" He picked up a chicken thigh and bit in, the crunchy spice of the crust everything he remembered. Andrew set to work on the rest of his plate while she talked.

"Well, first of all, rabies research is a highly specialized, dangerous thing. It's only done at certain designated facilities. One in Colorado, one in Texas, I think." She took a sip of her coffee. "But let's say they were doing rabies research at this facility. There would be comprehensive records."

He had piles of records back at the station. None of them reflected anything related to rabies. "Couldn't they do it on the sly? Just not report it?"

She tapped a short, neat fingernail against the coffee cup. "Is it a licensed facility?"

He nodded.

"Then I don't see how. Animal research is heavily regulated by the USDA. And, by law, every U.S. facility has to have an animal care and use committee. That's an independent group who oversees the facility's operations, including a monthly inspection. If they were doing rabies research, there'd be a trail a mile wide." She put down the cup. "It'd be pretty hard to hide something like that from so many people. Let alone keep all the facility's own employees from—" She stared at something outside, the color draining from her face.

He twisted around to look. Nothing but traffic. "What? What is it?"

"I thought I saw someone."

"Doesn't look like you're too happy about it." He nodded to Rosie, as she approached with their checks. She raised one eyebrow toward Letty in a silent question — one check or two? Andrew shook his head, slowly. It was not that kind of lunch date. He waited until Rosie'd left the checks and moved on to the next table, then spoke again. "Ex-boyfriend? In-laws? Parole officer?"

"I haven't met him." Letty finally looked back at Andrew.

He chewed the last of the biscuit, his curiosity piqued. "I'm gonna need a little more explanation than that."

"Some guy in a silver BMW's been watching me. I've seen him in the parking lot outside my hotel twice now, staring up at my room." She turned the coffee cup in her hand. "Then just now, the same car drove by. Real slow."

He turned again to take in the street outside, but there was nothing noteworthy. An old Nissan puttered past, a minivan with a handicapped tag went the other way, a patrol car pulled into the lot next to the precinct. Just normal mid-day traffic, no BMW. "Did you tell the police? This morning, when you gave your statement?"

She stopped fidgeting with the cup and shook her head. "You think it's related to the dead guy?"

"Probably not. You saw the guy before you found the body?"

She nodded. "And after."

"Still, it's an odd coincidence." He finished his tea, and the ice at the bottom broke loose, crashing onto his face. He wiped his mouth on a sleeve. "What's he look like?"

"White, middle-aged, brown hair…" She shrugged. "Normal."

Except for the stalking.

"That's not much to go on." He leaned back in the booth. "But you should still call the officer you met with and make them aware of it. Even if it isn't related, it's good they know. You remember the officer's name?"

She shook her head. "No, but I got her card. I'll call and let her know." She stared back out the window. "I'm leaving town soon, though."

Andrew pulled several napkins from the dispenser on the table and wiped chicken grease from his fingers. "You see the BMW guy again, you call 911. Or you can call me." He pulled out another napkin, dug a pen from his shirt pocket, and scrawled his name and number. "Here's my cell."

"Thank you." She took the napkin. "Can I ask a favor?"

He nodded. "Shoot."

"Would you let me know who the man we found was? Once he's identified? I think I'll feel better if I know his name."

"You got it." He tilted his head toward the napkin in her hand. "Text me your number."

She'd answered his question and, maybe more importantly, managed to put him at ease. With Mary in the hospital and everybody else acting like he had a stick of dynamite strapped to his gonads, it meant the world to have someone just sit down and talk to him. Like things were normal. Like he was normal.

Andrew dropped enough money on the table for both their tips. "I owe you one."

CHAPTER 11

Letty loaded the last of the gear into her Subaru, the orange-red glow of sunset reflecting off the back glass of the hatchback as she eased it shut. She had the car packed, the hotel bill paid, and a giant Diet Coke in the cupholder. Which meant there was nothing left to do but drive.

Except she couldn't quite make herself get in the car and go.

Why not?

Her trip to Chattanooga had accomplished nothing. Worse than nothing. In three days, she'd found herself a stalker, a dead body, and no sign of a source animal. Any one of which would have been enough to keep her up at night.

Except that hadn't been it at all. She'd stayed up for hours, tossing and turning, kicking off the covers, then pulling them back on. Her mind turning the same question over and over again — what the hell was going on with Caroline? Nothing she could think of explained her friend's silence except that Letty must have done something offensive. What, she had no idea. But that didn't mean it hadn't happened. Like in college, when she'd wake up sure she'd done something idiotic the night before but too hungover to know what.

She'd left a voicemail on Caroline's cell and a message with her assistant at work — who'd told Letty her friend was "in an all-day meeting."

Was that even a thing?

On a Saturday?

But her assistant was there, answering the phone. So something must be going on. Letty sent another text to Caroline. "Heading back to Athens. Sorry I missed you." Whatever was happening, that would have to do for now.

She flew through town in almost no traffic until she reached the intersection leading to I-75. Cars lined the on-ramp, all waiting for their turn to pull onto the interstate. Which would be a challenge, given that those lanes weren't moving either.

Crap.

She had some seriously shit traffic karma — had probably been a tailgater in a former life. No, one of those asshats who didn't give thank-you waves when you let them merge. That would explain a lifetime of gridlock.

Letty's phone dinged in her lap. She glanced down, half-watching to make sure the light didn't change.

Caroline, risen from the ether. "Sorry I missed you! Can I make it up to you next time I'm your way?" Three kissy-face emojis followed the message.

Irritation quickly eclipsed Letty's relief. Three days of nothing, and now that she was leaving, Caroline responded in minutes? What the hell was that about?

The light turned green, but there was nowhere for her to go. The cars on the other side of the intersection hadn't moved. Letty leaned back against the headrest, trying to conjure patience.

The pickup truck behind her blared its horn. The driver red-faced and yelling something she was glad she couldn't hear.

She scowled into the rearview, but her phone rang before she could respond with the appropriate hand gesture for that traffic situation. No doubt Caroline calling to explain why she hadn't reached out sooner. Letty glanced down only long enough to note the Chattanooga area code and tap the speaker button, then looked back up, in case traffic started to move.

It hadn't.

Letty let the irritation come through in her voice. "Where have you been?"

"Sorry?" The man sounded confused and nothing like Caroline.

She looked down at the phone. The caller's number was a few digits off from the one for Caroline's office.

Her face got hot. "No, I'm sorry. I thought you were someone else."

"I got that feeling." He laughed, a soft easy sound. "This is Pete Hendrick. I saw you at the police station this morning and thought I might catch up with you. But by the time I finished giving my statement, you were gone."

She'd been so focused on getting in and out — getting the whole thing over with — she hadn't even noticed him. Which, given how he looked, was just short of miraculous. "Sorry I missed you."

He cleared his throat. "I really just wanted to make sure you were okay. And to thank you for what you did for Julie. She says it helped that you stayed with her while the EMTs checked her out."

"Of course." Letty couldn't remember much about the wait or if she'd even spoken to Julie while they sat together. The whole thing was a blur. "How is she now? Okay?"

His voice got quiet. "She will be. But I doubt she comes back to work."

Letty didn't blame her. The light cycled red again, and she checked her rearview. Pickup truck guy was still staring holes into the back of her car. But at least he wasn't honking. "How are you holding up?"

"Still kind of shaken... It's hard to believe something like that could happen so close and us not know it. It's unsettling." He laughed again, but this time, it sounded sad. "Sorry, I didn't call to dump that on you. I've been terrible company since it happened."

"No, you're fine." It was one thing to find a body. It was something totally different to find it in your backyard. If she could have reached through the phone to give him a hug, she would have. "And anyway, I think I'm the same."

He paused. "What are you doing now?"

Inching my way toward Athens.

Questioning my life choices.

"Nothing." She stared out at a seemingly endless row of taillights.

"Would you want to meet me for dinner? I can answer the questions you came to see me about, and we can be terrible company together."

Was she even looking for those answers anymore?

Either way, the choice between dinner with Pete and gridlock was no contest.

Letty turned on her blinker.

∎ ∎ ∎

Pete scanned the crowd. Waitresses in sombreros buzzed between the bar and their patrons and mariachi music blared from speakers overhead. He spotted Letty at the bar. She sat under a garland of tiny piñatas, and she made a black t-shirt and jeans look good.

Pete cut through the chaos, past massive sliding doors open to a dock lined with tables looking out on the Tennessee River. Almost every seat in the place was full.

He spoke up to be heard over the noise. "I completely forgot it was Cinco de Mayo."

Letty startled, then smiled. "Hi."

"Sorry about that." He chuckled as she moved her purse from the seat beside hers. He slid onto the stool. "Would you rather go somewhere else?"

She shifted her barstool closer. "This is fine. But maybe we should get a table?" She tilted her head toward the guy on her other side, who was shouting into his phone about a no-show blind date while he squeezed lime into a beer. Three empties sat on the bar in front of him.

The corners of Letty's mouth turned up, and Pete matched her smile. "I'll go— "

A woman wearing heavy floral perfume poked her head between them, forcing Pete to lean back to make room. She waved a credit card in the air. "Can I start a tab?"

The bartender flipped on a blender of strawberry daiquiris, either not hearing or not wanting to. And Letty met Pete's gaze above the woman's head, her smile widening. If they had any prayer of an actual conversation, they'd need a different place to sit.

He jerked a thumb toward the entrance. Then mouthed "be right back."

Pete wove through the crowd to the hostess, who wore all black, giant hoop earrings, and her blonde hair up in a twist. She looked up from a reservations book as he approached. "Dr. Hendrick!"

It took Pete a minute to place her, even with the benefit of her name tag. "Well, hi, Savannah. How's Milo?"

"All better thanks to you!" She shook her head, eyes toward heaven. "Although that stinker still tries to run outside every time I open the front door." A habit which had earned the obese Burmese a broken leg and an emergency trip to Pete's office the Thanksgiving before. Which he hadn't minded, except that Sue Ellen had not been pleased when he'd left mid-turkey.

"Are you on the list?" Savannah ran a manicured finger down a long list of names, a crease forming between her brows. She looked up at him.

He shot an apologetic look at the woman standing cross-armed at the front of the line, then shook his head.

Savannah smiled at the woman and turned back to Pete, her voice lowered. "I'm sure I can manage something. How many are you?"

"Two."

Savannah leaned left then right, looking behind him. She stopped short of asking who he was with, but the question was plain on her face.

Pete pretended not to notice. "Thanks so much for your help." Savannah would know he was out with another woman as soon as they were seated. And she'd draw her own conclusions, no matter how innocent his dinner with Letty might be.

"Of course!" She smiled and walked him toward the bar. "Tell the bartender I said to make y'all some on-the-house margaritas while you wait."

Pete hadn't had time to take a sip of his drink before Savannah came back. She led them out to the dock, settled them at a table near the water, and hurried back into the crowded dining room.

"How did you manage this?" Letty looked at the mob clustered inside, then out at the river, glittering in the fading sun behind a short wooden rail. A light breeze played with the edge of the tablecloth and tossed a lock of hair across her face. She tucked it behind an ear.

"Perks of the job, I guess." He told her the story of the cat's run-in with an elderly neighbor's Cadillac.

"It must feel good to help people." Letty used a napkin to wipe the salt from the rim of her glass.

"It does." With everything that'd happened in the past year, his work at the clinic was the one thing that kept him sane. "God knows you don't become a vet for the money."

"I get it. Disease ecology isn't exactly a road to riches either."

He sipped the drink, which was tangy, sweet, and heavy on the tequila. "I shouldn't admit this, but I don't think I know exactly what disease ecology is. Somewhere between epidemiology and environmentalism?"

"You're not too far off. It's more like an intersection between epidemiology, immunology, and ecology. We look at how the environment affects interactions between hosts and pathogens, especially as it relates to infectious disease." She took a drink and hummed her approval. "Most of my lab's work this past year has involved tracking one sort of animal or another. So, when I saw the news about the rabies cases..." She shrugged. "I was hoping I could help."

Pete rubbed a hand across his forehead. When Trish had told him a professor from UGA was coming to see him, he'd expected it to be about some study she wanted the clinic to be part of. Not this.

He took in a deep breath. "What can I do?"

"Answer a few questions?"

He nodded, and Letty dug through her handbag.

She pulled out a phone. "Mind if I record you?"

Yes.

Pete shifted in his chair, its hard wooden slats suddenly uncomfortable. No way he could refuse and have things not be awkward. "Of course not, go ahead."

She started the recorder, recited his name and the date, then looked back at him. Her eyes bright with purpose. "Have you seen anything consistent with a possible rabies case in the past year? In a domesticated animal or otherwise?"

He shook his head. "No, nothing."

"Do you recall any animals presenting with lethargy, fever, loss of appetite or other altered behavior that, for whatever reason, weren't placed in containment?"

Pete shook his head again. "If we have an animal come in with something like that — something clearly viral — we admit them to the clinic for monitoring and treatment. And no, we haven't had anything of that sort. At least nothing that wasn't explained by some other pathogen."

She leaned closer. "Any reports of pets or their owners having contact with bats?"

"None."

"Any reports of contact with a wild animal exhibiting unusual behavior?"

He shifted in his chair. "Nope."

"What about animal bites in the past year?"

"Nothing unprovoked. Our only bite cases were of the usual varieties. A child who took away the family dog's bowl while it was eating. The other was a ferret protecting its young." He shrugged. "I reported both cases to the health department, and in each instance, the animal was placed in containment but never became ill." He stared out over the water. "Although the parents of the child who was bitten chose to have the dog put down anyway." He frowned at the memory, then shook his head and looked back to her. "Sorry I can't be more helpful. But I haven't seen anything that would've made me think rabies."

She closed her eyes a moment before she spoke. "That's okay, thanks." Letty clicked off the recorder and sighed. "You're not alone."

"Who else have you talked to?"

"Several clinics in the Signal Mountain area and that doggy daycare not far from you. No one's seen anything out of the ordinary."

Pete lifted his chin, brow furrowed. "Why Signal Mountain?"

"I thought I'd narrowed down where the source animal might be to that neighborhood. Both of the people infected lived there. But so far..." She shook her head and took a long drink of the margarita.

"What does that mean for your investigation?"

"I think I'm packing it in, heading back home to UGA." She shook the glass, ice cubes rattling. "Although I really do appreciate you answering my questions."

"Of course." Pete finished his drink. With any luck that would be the end of it. He had a beautiful woman out to dinner and couldn't think of many things he less wanted to talk about than rabies.

Savannah appeared with two more margaritas, a basket of chips, and a bowl of guacamole. "On the house." She gave him a smile of approval he hoped Letty didn't notice. Then took their orders and excused herself. "Good to see you out, Dr. Hendrick."

He watched her disappear into the crowd. Would she tell anyone she'd seen him? Did it matter anymore if she did?

Letty snagged a chip and pointed out at the water. "Look."

The river had darkened as night fell, its surface a smooth black except for the reflection of the restaurant's lights. A half a dozen yards from the dock's edge, something broke the surface, a ripple moving gracefully across the river.

Pete leaned out over the water. "He's a big boy."

The snake was at least three feet long. It crossed the river diagonally toward where they sat, the restaurant's lights revealing its skin as an uneven gray-brown, marked with darker bands. The serpent swam with its head lifted while its body undulated through the water, propelling it closer.

"I'm surprised he's not headed for the other shore. You'd think all the noise and lights would scare him away." Letty joined Pete in leaning out over the rail, as the snake disappeared under the dock a few yards from their feet. "I'd swear that's a water moccasin, but I don't think they come this far east, do they?"

"Probably just a Watersnake." Pete settled back in his seat.

Letty did the same. "I met another Dr. Hendrick when I first got here." She pulled a lime from her glass, wiping the salt from the rim again. "Sue Ellen?"

Pete forced his face to stay neutral. Chattanooga was small. But good grief. Letty'd only been there a few days.

She took a sip of the margarita. "Any relation?"

Not a good one.

He cleared his throat. "In a way."

Letty dug a chip into the guacamole, eyebrows raised in question.

Pete tugged at the collar of his shirt. "Sue Ellen's my ex-wife. Or soon to be. We're getting a divorce."

"Oh." Letty sat the half-eaten chip on her plate. "Sorry, I didn't know."

"It's okay." He took another deep drink. "It's a good thing. We met young and married young, long before we'd figured out who we really were." Which was a nice way of saying they'd gotten married before he'd figured out Sue Ellen wasn't what she seemed. When he'd been too in love to notice all the red flags.

"But Sue Ellen's what brought me here to Chattanooga. For her residency. And I wouldn't have started my veterinary practice here if she hadn't." He drank again, more to shut himself up than because he needed the tequila. "I couldn't imagine my life without the work I do at the clinic."

Maybe sensing his discomfort, Letty launched into the story of how she'd followed her sister from California to Georgia, her winding path through academia, accumulating degrees and mounds of student debt. And her upcoming, and dreaded, transition to a teaching role at the university.

As he listened, Pete let himself relax. Let himself enjoy being there with her. He settled back in the chair, forgetting everything except the woman in front of him.

They finished the second round of margaritas as their food arrived. This time, thankfully, delivered by a waitress he didn't know. She slid their plates to the table. "Careful, those are hot. Can I get you another round?"

"I shouldn't." Letty smiled up at her, then spoke to Pete. "I've got to drive back tonight."

"Let me know if y'all change your minds." The waitress collected their empty glasses and hurried back toward the kitchen.

Pete cut into his enchilada, cheese oozing out onto his plate. "When you said you were leaving, I didn't realize you meant now."

"It was a last-minute decision." She shrugged. "After what happened, I just… I wanted to be somewhere else."

"I get that. If I could leave the clinic, I'd be tempted to get away somewhere, too." He looked out at the now black sky. "It's getting kind of late to get started back now, though. Could you go in the morning?"

She emptied a ramekin of jalapeños onto her tacos and reached for the hot sauce. "Maybe. I guess I could check to see if the place I've been staying still has my room free."

He didn't want her to go.

But that was irrational. He barely knew her. He was probably just lonely and looking for distraction from the whole mess with Sue Ellen. And Letty was definitely distracting.

They ate slowly, talking about everything from politics to SEC football. The latter discussion being far more heated. Then searched the water for their snake friend and, having no luck, traded animal war stories, starting with snakes and ending with bears. Him, on a hike in Audubon Acres when he'd happened upon a two-hundred-pound black bear — one of many that seemed to be working their way into suburban Chattanooga. Her, when she'd crossed paths with one in Tahoe.

Letty's eyes danced with the joy of a memory. "—and my dad's at the bottom of the hill waving at me like crazy. I didn't know I'd skied past a bear until I got to the bottom. Me and my homemade skis on a run we had no business taking to begin with. I don't think I've seen Dad's face quite that shade of green since." She laughed until tears came out of her eyes, and, even more than before, she was beautiful.

Pete spoke without thinking. "You're welcome to stay at my place if you don't want to drive back tonight." As soon as the words tumbled out of his mouth, his face grew hot.

I can't believe I said that.

Her eyes grew wide. "That's… really sweet of you."

"Sorry, I didn't mean…" The heat spread from his face to his ears. He hadn't even had that much to drink. Was it just her that made him flustered? He scrambled to explain what he'd meant. "I've got a furnished apartment above the garage. I usually rent it out, but I don't have a tenant now. You're welcome to use it."

The waitress reappeared at the edge of the table. "Anything else I can get y'all tonight?"

Letty gave him a look he couldn't decipher and turned to the waitress. "We'll take another round."

CHAPTER 12

May 6, 2018

"Where's your mama?" Andrew lifted one edge of the tin foil covering a long glass dish on the counter between Mary's kitchen and the den. Few things made him wish he had a wife. Homemade banana pudding made the list.

"She's still on the phone with Daddy." Marcus aimed his XBOX controller at the TV, thumbs flying over the buttons. A cartoon zombie on screen lurched toward a well-armed ear of corn. "She said if you got here before she was done to tell you to make a plate, and she'd be out in a minute."

Don't mind if I do.

Andrew pulled a dish from the cupboard and loaded it with pulled pork, coleslaw, and cornbread. "You already eat?"

"Yes, sir." Marcus flopped back on the couch with a groan. "I lost again."

"That's because you stink at that game." Kaylie appeared in the hallway that led from the back bedrooms and grinned at Andrew over Marcus's head.

A pillow flew in her direction from the couch.

She batted it down. "Your aim sucks in real life, too!"

"Mikayla Patrice Washington." Mary appeared behind Kaylie, her eyes red. "Language."

"Sorry, Mama." Kaylie picked up the pillow, launched it back at her brother, then flew past Andrew and out the back door.

Marcus followed. "You're gonna pay for that." The door slammed closed behind them, followed by the screech of a spigot and a squeal of delight.

Mary seemed not to hear. She pulled cling wrap over the coleslaw and stuck it in the fridge. Then shut the door with a bang. A letter magnet fell free and rolled between his feet.

Andrew stooped down to get it. "Wanna talk about it?"

She swept a pile of silverware into a sink of sudsy water but didn't answer.

"Mary?"

She spoke without turning. "They extended Troy's deployment again."

"That's a tough break." Andrew slid an orange letter 'O' onto the counter next to his plate. "It's just another month, right? Like last time?"

She didn't answer.

"Mary?"

"I couldn't bring myself to tell Troy what happened. With Bullard." Her voice grew thick, hands gripping the edge of the counter. She stared out into the backyard. "And how'm I supposed to tell the kids he's still not coming back? He's gonna miss Marcus's birthday."

Another squeal came from outside, and a soaked Kaylie ran past the kitchen window with her hand out to block the spray of the garden hose.

Andrew waited until Mary turned toward him. "Troy's gonna be pissed you didn't tell him what happened with Bullard." He tilted his head to the backyard. "But the kids'll understand about the deployment, and they're going to be fine. They've got the best damn mama a couple of kids could ask for."

"Hush." She turned away again, scrubbing furiously at the dishes in the sink while he got back to work on the barbecue.

She sounded more like herself when she spoke again. "You want some banana pudding when you're done with that? Marcus helped me make the custard."

"Damn right I do."

She scooped some into a bowl and slid it across the counter. "I can't believe you haven't asked me about the arson case."

He talked past his food. "Off the job, remember?"

"Right." She stared at him.

"And that's why I'll remember none of whatever it is you don't tell me today." He traded his plate for the bowl and licked whipped cream from the back of the spoon she'd left on top.

"Richardson's in the wind. Doesn't answer his door or his phone. And the facility's corporate office says he's 'on leave.'"

"Join the crowd. What're you gonna do about it?"

She rolled her eyes. "We're gonna find his dumb ass."

Andrew had no doubt she would. He ate his way through the rest of the bowl. "Any word on the surveillance video or the missing animals?"

"Nada on the tapes. And, other than some soccer mom on the neighborhood's web forum claiming she saw an army of rats run across Highway 127, nothing on the animals either." Mary shrugged.

"You know anything about that body they found out in the woods on Signal Mountain?" He carried his empty dishes to the sink and rinsed them under the tap.

Mary took a minute to respond. "Why? You think it's related?"

"No reason to." He loaded his dishes into the dishwasher, the hinges squealing as he raised the door and clicked it closed. "I met one of the women who found the body, and I just wondered if they'd ID'd it yet."

"Lemme guess, the witness is young, blonde, and likes a man with a badge?"

He dried his hands on a dishrag and leaned back against the counter. "She's a brunette." He grinned. "And I turned my badge in. On leave, remember?"

"Right." Mary shook her head. "Don't expect an ID on that one any time soon. Pearson told me the body'd been outside so long there were no fingertips left to print. If they don't get a hit from missing persons, they won't know shit 'til the DNA comes back. And that'll take a month. If there's even a match in the system."

They stood in the quiet together, watching the kids play outside the window. Her voice was soft when she spoke again. "Any word from the DA?"

He wasn't sure he wanted there to be. Andrew looked down at his feet. One of his shoelaces had come untied. "That could take weeks." He rubbed at the spot on his arm where he'd gotten his second dose of the rabies vaccine that morning.

Mary touched his elbow. "Drew."

He looked up into warm brown eyes, two shades lighter than the chestnut tone of her skin.

She nodded once. "Thank you."

There in the comfort of Mary's kitchen, listening to her kids laugh in the distance, knowing she'd have done the same for him, a tiny broken part inside him knit back together. The doubt he'd had about what he had done, the buzzing sense of something shameful in the back of his mind. All of it settled into place. Compartmentalized or processed or whatever the hell the shrink had called it. He'd fired his weapon to keep Mary in this world, and he didn't regret that for a minute. Was he proud of what he'd done? No. But Mary was still here, and that's what mattered.

■ ■ ■

Andrew pulled into a parking spot outside his apartment. Six dingy buildings formed a 'U' around the lot. Even the sprigs of grass fighting their way up through the cracks in the pavement were a dead gray-brown. Like a prison yard, minus the fence.

Of all the units he could see, only his windows were dark. Andrew put his hand on the key but didn't turn off the ignition. He could go back out, maybe find company at the bar? Worst-case scenario, that would mean watching the last of the Braves game with a cold beer and the bartender to talk to.

He closed his eyes. Except that wasn't the worst-case scenario. What if he ran into someone who recognized him from the newspaper, or TV, or YouTube? What if he wound up on a bar stool next to one of Randy Bullard's congregation? He rubbed again at his arm where he'd gotten the shot.

Shit.

Andrew put the car in park.

His phone rang, and a picture of Mary with Troy and the kids showed up on the screen. He connected the call. "Miss me already?"

"Did you tell Marcus you'd get him Call of Duty for his birthday?" Mary's tone sounded like he'd suggested she add sugar to her cornbread.

"I feel like you want the answer to that question to be no?" Andrew climbed out of the car and waved a hello to his downstairs neighbors. The two twenty-somethings sat kicked back in lawn chairs outside their unit. One returned the wave, his hand cupped around what probably wasn't a cigarette.

Andrew circled the back of the car and popped the trunk. A long silence stretched out before Mary spoke again. "He's turning eight."

"In that case, no?" Andrew collected his things from the trunk and headed toward the apartment.

She heaved a sigh. "You're hopeless."

"But you love me."

"It's hit or miss. Listen, I talked to Pearson after you left. Still no time of death nailed down from the M.E., but they got lucky with Missing Persons on the Signal Mountain dead guy. Name's Moses

Wilbur, thirty-six, Caucasian, reported missing to the Marietta PD by his girlfriend."

"Reported when?" A pungent breeze told Andrew he'd been right about the neighbor. Definitely not a cigarette.

"She didn't— " Mary stopped with another sigh. "You want me to find out, don't you?"

"Great minds."

Mary hung up.

Andrew carried his crap inside and dumped it on the dining table. The apartment smelled like garbage left a little too long in the can. He grabbed a long-neck Budweiser from the refrigerator and clicked on the TV. Then flipped through channels until he found the Braves game.

Just in time to watch San Francisco get the sweep, four to three. *You gotta be kidding me.*

Andrew surfed through all the other sports stations, past news anchors, and some dude making shrimp scampi. Nothing held his attention. Not just because there was nothing worth watching. His mind was elsewhere, busy pulling threads he'd be better off leaving alone.

He dug out his phone and found the number he'd gotten from Letty Duquesne.

"Hello?" She answered in a raised voice, the back and forth of a vacuum whirring loud in the background.

"Hey, Letty. Andrew Marsh. We got that name you wanted."

The vacuum got louder. "Okay." Even with the noise, the tension came through in her voice.

"Guy's from Marietta, Georgia. Name was Moses Wilbur. Mean anything to you?"

"No." The whirring almost drowned out her answer.

"Didn't figure it would." He waited for the noise to recede. "What's all the racket?"

"Sorry, hang on." Rustling, then the thunk of a door. When she spoke again, her voice had a slight echo, like she'd stepped into a bathroom. "I'm trying to check back into my room at the hotel, and they don't have it ready yet. For now, I'm waiting in the lobby."

"Thought you were headed back to Athens."

She delayed answering just long enough to raise his antenna. "I was, but then, I thought I'd take one more crack at doing some interviews, and… It's a long story."

"Something happen with the BMW guy?"

"No, nothing like that. Just decided to stick around a few more days."

He could tell by the tone of her voice there was more to it than that but, for once in his life, didn't push. "Letty?"

"Yeah?"

"Call me if you see the BMW again."

Andrew hung up, retrieved his beer, and leaned back into the couch cushions. He should have taken the risk and gone to the bar. A little company would go a long way toward making banishment tolerable. He killed half the beer, then scrolled through the numbers in his phone, trying to conjure faces to go with the names. He stopped at one he was pretty sure was a curvy blonde with a dolphin tattoo above her ass. Renee.

She'd smelled like gin and self-tanner, but…

She was fun.

The phone dinged in his hand. An incoming text from Mary. "The girlfriend reported Wilbur missing April 8." Another text followed. "You're welcome."

Son of a…

Andrew set the beer on a side table and went back to where he'd left his files in the dining room. He sifted through piles of paper and old pizza boxes until he found what he was after. A ratty yellow legal pad with a dried splatter of soy sauce on the front. According to his notes, he'd been called to the fire on April 7th.

Less than a mile from where Wilbur's body was found.

And one day before he was reported missing.

CHAPTER 13

May 7, 2018

Like a lot of Chattanooga's mountain roads, the one to Pete's clinic was narrow, winding, and — due to the inexplicable lack of a shoulder — offered no room for error. Letty white-knuckled the steering wheel the whole way.

Last time, the flat stretch of blacktop beside the gulley had been a relief. A chance to change the radio or at least breathe freely.

Not today.

A loose end of crime scene tape waved at her from the other side of the wide depression in the earth where they'd found the man's body, bright yellow and unmistakable. She did her best not to look.

Priya's voice echoed from the Subaru's center console, the cupholder where the phone rested making her voice somehow louder in the car. "Sorry it took me so long to call you back. I got your messages. It's just been super busy. So much to do. And I feel like I've been hungover since I got here, but without the fun part." She groaned. "If my body doesn't figure out time zones soon, I might die."

Letty did the math in her head. It wouldn't even be four a.m. in Cambodia. "Give it a few days, you'll adjust. How's the trip otherwise? Do you love it there?"

"I so do. The food, the people. It's weird working without our team, but the project's off to a great start." Priya ran through the high points of her summer research gig on the outskirts of Phnom

Penh, where she was gathering ecohealth data for Bill with one of the junior professors in their department. "But that's not what I called to talk about. Your last text said you had a date with the hot vet. I'm gonna need all the gory details."

Letty took her foot off the gas, watching for the turnoff to Pete's clinic. "There's nothing to tell." She passed a cluster of realtor signs and one that read "Jesus Saves." That she remembered. The unmarked left turn to Pete's would be coming up any second.

"You break a six-month dry spell, and nothing about it is worth repeating?" Priya whistled. "Poor guy must be hung like a mouse."

Letty groaned as she turned off the main road. "I stayed in a guest suite nicer than my apartment. By myself. He gave me a stack of clean sheets and kissed me goodnight. That was it."

She could almost hear Priya's cogs turning through the phone.

"Does he slobber? Or do that stabby thing with his tongue?" Priya made a gagging noise. "I hate that. It's like making out with a lizard."

"It was good." Letty grinned. And there'd been nothing cold-blooded about it. "I'm meeting him for coffee."

"I really hope that's a euphemism."

Letty laughed, but it died in her throat as she pulled into the clinic's parking lot. The path into the woods came into view, and the sense of normalcy that had come with hearing Priya's voice evaporated. "I gotta run."

"Hey, before you go… I need to fess up."

"Finally gonna spill the beans about Chris?" Letty regretted the words as soon as they came out of her mouth. She knew better than to tease Priya about Chris. Priya didn't just like Chris. She was crazy about him. Which, with Priya's family — who expected to her to marry a nice Indian boy as soon as she graduated — was not going to fly. The last thing she needed was Letty giving her shit, too.

"I don't know what you're talking about," Priya choked out.

Letty pulled into a parking spot. "Sorry, Pri, I—"

"I may have accidentally told Bill you were still in Chattanooga when I called to give him an update on the lab here."

Letty dropped the car in park and closed her eyes. "For real?"

"I didn't know he didn't know what all you were doing."

Shiiiiiiit.

Letty didn't blame Bill for worrying. No question she was way outside her authority. But the last thing she needed was a lecture. Letty smacked the back of her head against the seat. "How mad was he?"

"Not too bad." Priya didn't sound convincing.

"Like how bad is not too bad? Scale of one to ten."

"Ahhh…" Priya hedged. "Hard to put a number on it. Like less mad than when he got passed over for department head. But more than when Chris backed the RV into a hydrant. Maybe a six?"

Letty dropped her keys into her purse. "Dude. You suck."

"But I'm cute."

"True." Letty blew out a deep breath and climbed out of the car. It wasn't like she'd be able to keep it from Bill forever anyway. "Be safe over there and make sure you send me lots of pictures." She hung up and eyed the path into the woods, walking as quickly as she could up the clinic's front ramp.

The bell above the door jangled as she stepped inside. "Hi, Trish."

"Dr. Duquesne, so good to see you again." The receptionist nudged a file cabinet closed with her knee. She looked exactly as she had the first time Letty had been there. Blue scrubs, teal eyeliner, hair styled the same as it probably had been for prom.

"Dr. Hendrick's just finishing up in back now." Trish turned, as if to head through the doorway behind her. "Do you want coffee? I was just fixin' to put on another pot."

"No, thanks. Dr. Hendrick and I are going to run out and grab one together."

"Mmm-hm." Trish's smile widened.

Letty shifted on her feet. Trish would no doubt have noticed when they left for the coffee shop together, but still. Pete might not want her talking to his staff about his personal life. Letty dropped her bag on one of the waiting room chairs and searched for a way to steer the conversation in a different direction. "Any word on Julie? How's she doing?"

"I'm not one to gossip." Trish leaned forward. "But her mama told my sister-in-law she still hasn't slept. Not for more than an hour at a time anyway. Keeps dreaming she's in a grave, being buried alive, and can't crawl out." Trish shook her head. "Terrible. Just terrible."

"Poor thing." An image of Julie crying behind her hands, nails caked with dirt, flashed in Letty's mind. She turned to look out the window into the woods, half-expecting to see the blue of Julie's scrubs through the trees. But there was nothing out of place, everything peaceful and still.

Except the anxiety fluttering in her chest.

Stop it.

She forced the feeling away and looked back to Trish. "I hope she's okay."

"God never gives you more than you can handle." Trish fingered the gold cross she wore on a chain around her neck.

Letty wasn't sure that was true. Had she "handled" Jessa's death? Or what happened after?

If she had, she hadn't done it well.

Trish shook her head, as if getting back to business. "I'm just glad you were here to help. Even though I'm sorry it meant you had to see what you did." She collected a handful of loose documents from her desk and slid them into a Manila folder. "Was Dr. Hendrick at least able to help you?"

Letty furrowed her brow. "Sorry?"

"You came into the clinic because you needed help with something?"

"Right, that's right." Letty flushed, her mind elsewhere. "I've been talking to a bunch of local vets. Trying to see if I might be able to come up with something to help track down a source animal for those rabies cases." She leaned on the counter separating the lobby from Trish's desk. "Haven't had much luck, though."

"All sorts of folks been coming in here worried about it, but we haven't had any animals brought in with rabies. None anywhere in the area I know of." Trish pulled open a drawer to the right of her desk and slid the file folder inside. "Only thing even close was that raccoon a month or so ago."

Letty strangled on her own spit and coughed into the crook of her elbow. "Raccoon?"

"About a month ago, Belinda Peterson came in. She said Davey — that's her husband — was off hunting, a raccoon had wandered into their garage, and it wouldn't come out. She was right beside herself. I mean, she is a good, Christian woman." Trish leaned forward again. "But when she came in, she told me the 'GD' — and she used the real words, now — but she said the GD thing was a devil sent straight from hell." Trish closed her eyes, her body shaking in a silent laugh. "You should have seen me try to keep a straight face."

Letty's mouth went dry, and her pulse quickened. She'd read there'd been raccoon-variant rabies found in other parts of Southeastern Tennessee last year. But not close by.

Of course, that didn't mean it hadn't made its way to Chattanooga undetected. She chewed her bottom lip.

Holy crap.

She waited until Trish's laughter subsided. "What happened?"

"What?" Trish pulled a tissue from a box beside her computer monitor and dabbed it against the corners of her eyes. "Oh, with the raccoon? Dr. Hendrick went over and took care of it. Chased it off, I guess. He should've called animal control, let them deal with it. Raccoons can be proper nasty when you corner 'em. But that's not his way." Another dab. "I will never forget the look on that woman's face."

Letty smiled and nodded, but her thoughts were somewhere else. Her excitement fading as she weighed the possibility of the raccoon as a source animal. The first problem with that theory was the biggest — if there was anything to it, Pete would have mentioned it. And she wasn't even sure it made sense for a raccoon to be the source. They were reservoir animals, yes. But the incidence in that population had peaked a decade ago. She nodded along with whatever story Trish was telling, not hearing any of the details of Belinda Peterson's first marriage or the fight she'd had over custody of Poopsie, who was apparently a standard poodle.

Still, she should ask Pete about the raccoon. Not just because it could be a lead, but because it might give her a reason to stay. Her mind went to Pete's kiss the night before last — the brush of his lips on hers, the urgency that had built between them, the heat still burning under her skin.

Maybe more like another reason.

■   ■   ■

Pete settled next to Letty on a dark green loveseat. The coffee shop's fireplace wasn't lit, but the mineral smell of ash and char lingered. He passed Letty the larger of two cups he'd picked up from the barista.

"Thank you." She took it and leaned in, inhaling the steam coming off the dark roast. "For the coffee, and for letting me crash at your place the other night."

"You're welcome anytime." He'd hated watching her walk away, up into the guest apartment. Wanted so badly to invite her to come into the main house with him instead. But he hadn't had the nerve to ask. Not so soon after they'd met, not with his divorce still pending. And not with someone he liked as much as he did her. "How'd it go this morning?"

"I got through the rest of the places on my list, but none of them had anything new to tell me. Still figuring out what to do next." She blew on the coffee. "Trish mentioned something interesting just now."

"Oh yeah?"

"She said there was a sick raccoon you went out to deal with a month or two ago. For the Petersons. Do you remember anything about it?"

He furrowed his brow. "Belinda came into the office real upset about a raccoon that'd gotten in their garage. She couldn't get it out, and it was none too happy when she tried to shoo it to the door with a broom." Pete shook his head. "I went over to their place to see if I could help. They don't live too far from the clinic, and Belinda was beside herself." He shifted in his seat. "By the time I got there, the poor thing was already dead."

Letty leaned forward. "Did you have it tested?"

"No, it was clear what'd killed it. It still had half a chunk of undissolved rat poison in its mouth and another bait brick under its tail. There's a real problem with rodents out here in the country, and sometimes other critters'll eat the poison."

Letty's shoulders slumped. "Right, I know that can happen."

He rested a hand on top of hers on the couch between them. "I almost wish the raccoon had been rabid, if that meant you'd stay a little longer."

She squeezed his fingers. "I guess you're in luck then."

"Am I?" His gaze drifted to her mouth. Her lips looked as soft as they'd felt against his under the garage apartment's porch light. His hand behind her neck, her body brushing his, the kiss a not-yet-realized promise of something that made his breath shallow and his slacks tight.

"There's no reason for me to rush back." She smiled.

He wanted her to stay. Even as he knew, given his situation, it couldn't help but complicate things.

Letty glanced over his shoulder. "Aren't you supposed to be back soon? You said your next appointment's at three, right?"

He followed her gaze to a clock shaped like a black cartoon cat, the tail swaying back and forth as it kept time. He had twenty minutes before his next patient. "We should go."

He stood and pulled Letty to her feet, the momentum bringing their bodies together again. He pressed a soft kiss to her mouth, trying and failing to keep the heat between them at bay. Her lips curved into a smile against his.

The shop was nearly empty, but he was sure the gesture hadn't gone unnoticed. Not in a town this size and not with his divorce already on everyone's tongues. Pete followed Letty back out to the car, his insides a tangle of worry and desire.

Should he be getting involved with anyone? Now, of all times? What would happen if Sue Ellen heard about it? She'd seek Letty out for sure.

And God knows what she'd tell her.

CHAPTER 14

By the time Letty pulled into the parking lot for South Cumberland State Park, hiking alone in the woods was the last thing she wanted to do. It had seemed like a good idea at first — just rip off the band-aid and go. After all, she was an ecologist. She couldn't be afraid to go into the forest. And the spot Pete suggested had sounded amazing.

But when she closed her eyes, she saw the man's body rotting in the leaves. And the nagging feeling that something dangerous lurked just beyond her view wouldn't go away.

Letty took a deep breath. It was nonsense, and she knew it. She'd been raised outdoors. She'd spent as much of her adult life there as possible. She couldn't let what happened behind Pete's clinic change that.

She wouldn't.

Letty cut the engine, and the car grew too warm in an instant, the late afternoon sun beating down through the windshield. She fanned her shirt against her chest and stared out into the dense forest beyond the parking area. An unusually wet Spring had done wonders for the foliage. It grew thick and heavy, like a wall of green that started where the pavement ended.

Waiting's only going to make it harder.

She forced herself to get out, then followed the muted voices of other hikers to the trailhead and into a hardwood forest.

The temperature cooled as she stepped beneath the trees' canopy. She followed the trail past sandstone cliffs to a short waterfall pouring over striated rock. Children's socks and shoes lined the craggy shore of the upper falls. And a group of them splashed in the shallow pool below, laughing and kicking water at each other. A woman who was probably their mother sat on a boulder. Eyes closed, head turned up to the sun. The way you did when you were at peace.

Letty had been right to come. This wasn't a frightening place. It was a healing one. She hiked to the lower falls, where water cascaded fifty feet into a deep, aquamarine pool. Letty sat on a flat outcropping of rock, letting the mist cool her skin. The water struck the lagoon below with a loud, constant "shhhhhh." As if to quiet the unease she'd been holding inside. She knew first-hand there were scary things in nature, even terrifying things. And sometimes people died.

People like Jessa.

Letty closed her eyes. People who just happened to be in the wrong place at the wrong time. It was a tragedy. One she knew would repeat itself more and more as humankind blindly encroached on the natural world. But there was nothing evil about it.

And Jessa would kick her ass if she let fear keep her from living her life to the fullest. Letty drew a deep breath and let it out slowly. What she wouldn't give to talk to Jessa now. To apologize. To tell her about the past year, about getting forced into a teaching position, about Pete.

The thought of him brought an unexpected warmth to her chest.

Jessa would've liked him.

Letty lingered just outside the waterfall's spray until the sky turned from blue to gray, the clouds gave way to thunder, and lightning rippled in the distance. She almost hated to leave. Letty got slowly to her feet, brushing the dust from the back of her shorts.

A buzz came from her pocket.

She checked her phone. Bill.

Letty cringed. Knowing she'd maybe overstepped the line between offering help and putting herself where she didn't belong was one thing, hearing Bill say it was another.

Might as well face the music.

She took a deep breath and answered. "Hey, I know I owe you an explanation. I— "

"Don't worry about that for now. Listen, I'm calling because Priya's in the ICU. They think she— "

Three loud beeps, and the phone went silent.

Letty jerked it away from her ear.

"Call Lost."

She redialed Bill's number, but the call wouldn't connect. Whatever flicker of service she'd had was gone.

Letty lifted the phone above her head, turning in a slow circle.

Come on, come on.

Still no bars.

Letty hiked back to the car at a sprint. She slid into the driver's seat and checked the phone again. Nothing.

She hit Bill's number anyway and prayed.

Pick up, pick up.

The phone didn't even ring.

"Call Failed."

She tried Priya, then Chris, but couldn't get through. Letty yelled her frustration into the empty car, pelting the phone on to the passenger seat.

A young couple crossing the parking lot from the trail turned to stare.

Letty ignored them and pulled out of the parking lot in a cloud of dust, speeding back toward Chattanooga and cell service. It didn't make any sense. Her friend in some Cambodian hospital. On the other side of the world. Scared and alone.

A whine from the engine interrupted her thoughts.

She glanced down at the dash. The speedometer's needle drifted past ninety.

Letty took her foot off the gas. It wasn't going to help Priya for her to cause an accident and end up in a hospital, too. She needed to relax. Until she knew what was happening, it wouldn't do any good to freak out about it. She clicked on the stereo and scanned through stations until she hit public radio.

The slow, soulful notes of one of Chopin's Nocturnes poured a quiet calm into the car. Which helped, a little.

I'm sure she's fine. And she's getting help, whether I'm there or not.

She checked the phone again. Still no service.

And she wouldn't be alone. The rest of the team on her project is there.

A few fat drops of rain plopped on the windshield, and the lilting voice of a BBC news anchor cut in as the song ended. "Earlier today, the South African government announced closure of their inquiry into the death of a believed poacher killed by a pack of lions near Kruger National Park. The case drew international attention after authorities revealed that the attacking lions left only the man's head and rifle behind."

More raindrops, faster and harder.

What the hell?

Lions didn't behave that way. Leaving the poacher's head on display, almost like a warning. It wasn't normal.

Nothing about anything was normal. Priya in God-knows-what hospital. Dead bodies left to rot in the forest. Rabies outbreaks in suburban Tennessee.

Box jellyfish swarming off the coast of Kauai.

Letty winced as a bright flash lit the sky and thunder boomed. The two so close together there'd been no time to count in between. She glanced behind her. The gray of the early evening sky had gone black with storm clouds. Looming heavy and coming closer.

•   •   •

"Malaria?" Letty paced her room at the inn, phone pressed to her ear. "But she took the meds before she went. And I just talked to her this morning — well, our time this morning. She was a little under the weather but nowhere near needing a hospital."

"Apparently, she's been feverish for a few days. Professor Grayson told her to take some time off. But you know Priya." Bill cleared his throat. "She collapsed in the lab."

"Oh my God." Letty sank to the bed. "Why the ICU?"

"Right now, the main concern is that it may be cerebral malaria, but the fainting could just as easily be the result of anemia or any number of other things. Grayson took her to Royal Phnom Penh Hospital. They're running tests now."

Rain pelted the window, loud in the room as she tried to make sense of what Bill was saying. Her brain spitting out clinical features of cerebral malaria she wished she didn't know. It would be less common to find in an adult, and far more prevalent in Africa. But, if Priya had cerebral malaria, it might mean a coma, permanent brain damage… even death.

Letty straightened. "But she took the meds. It couldn't be malaria unless…" She stopped, shrinking into herself, not wanting to voice the possibility out loud. The Greater Mekong had the worst possible strain of the parasite that caused malaria. She'd been reading in medical journals about it for years. Every time doctors developed a treatment, the parasite adapted to become resistant.

Bill spoke before she could finish the thought. "There's no reason to think she has a super bug, Letty. In all likelihood, this is normal run-of-the-mill malaria that, for whatever reason, wasn't prevented by the prophylactic treatment. They'll probably just start her on an artemisinin-based therapy, if they haven't already."

He was right. He had to be right. "Is she awake? Do you know what number I can use to call her? Her cell goes straight to voicemail."

"They aren't letting any of our people back to see her or even giving us updates. They only do that for family." He sighed into the phone. "I know what I do because I just spoke to her parents. They're boarding a flight to Cambodia now. So, it'll be awhile before we know more. You've taken that trip. They'll be traveling at least a day and..." A pause, then Bill came back. "Letty, I need to jump off. Chris is calling on the other line."

Pain squeezed Letty's heart. She didn't envy Bill that conversation. "Of course, go ahead. Will you call me when there's news?"

"I will. As soon as we know anything."

Letty went through the motions of changing clothes and brushing her teeth, but her mind never left Priya. Round and round, the same worries circled — How could this happen? Was Priya okay? Was she alone? Afraid? She didn't speak Khmer. Would the hospital have an interpreter?

Letty didn't have any answers. Or any way to help her friend. And, even knowing that, the need to do something — anything — burned in her gut. She sent up a quiet prayer for Priya, which felt like a start. But the hours of waiting for news still yawned out in front of her. She climbed into bed, picking up the remote control and putting it back down. There was no way TV would be enough of a distraction.

The only thing sure to hold her attention was work. And even though it seemed weird to worry about that under these circumstances, something about the idea also felt right. She might not be able to help Priya, but if she kept digging into the rabies investigation, there was a chance she'd be able to help someone else.

Letty pulled her computer into her lap and brought up a search engine. She considered getting a Google MD in malaria. Then typed in the name "Moses Wilbur" but didn't hit the search button. Knowing his name was one thing, knowing who he'd been when he was alive was something totally different.

She needed to focus on something that might actually be productive.

Maybe the reason her canvas of Signal Mountain veterinarians hadn't produced results was because she'd drawn her search area too narrow. The obvious next step would be to expand it. She went to the online yellow pages and scanned the list of Chattanooga animal clinics. There were dozens, not counting shelters, doggie daycares, or other possible points of information. Going to all of them didn't seem realistic and choosing among them was too random.

So, what then?

She drummed her fingers on a knee. There had to be other angles she could use. Letty went back to the search engine and typed in the victims' names. A few new articles had been posted since her last search. An obituary for Randy Bullard sung the man's praises. An article with a remarkably unflattering picture of Andrew Marsh confirmed the DA's intention to vigorously investigate Bullard's death. And a short piece in the UT Chattanooga paper had photos from a campus service held for Emma Canning. Students standing around a Magnolia tree planted in her memory.

Sad, but not useful.

Letty pulled up the websites she'd visited before and started from the beginning, re-reading everything she could find about both victims.

Nothing there either.

She went to the online image gallery and clicked through photos.

Letty stopped.

It couldn't be.

She zoomed in on the picture of Randy Bullard and his wife in side-by-side lawn chairs. The same picnic photo she'd seen last time. With each tap on her touchpad, the image got bigger and less clear. But, in the shade of an oak tree, behind the Bullards, a long table sat filled with covered dishes. And behind that, stood Emma Canning.

Holy shit.

The two were connected. Had Canning been a member of Bullard's church? Could the local authorities have missed that? Or maybe they hadn't. Maybe they knew, and it'd been a dead end. But would they have found the photo? Probably not. She'd barely been able to make Emma Canning out in the background. And even now, she only saw the resemblance if she squinted.

She looked again.

It was definitely her.

Letty scanned the small print under the photograph. "Randy and Brenda Bullard enjoying God's bounty and fellowship at the annual Chesapeake Hill Baptist Church picnic, held this year at Signal Mountain Community Park." It didn't give a date, but it did tell her that their two victims had, at some point, been there together. Which meant that place — or, more accurately, whatever animals lived there — could be the answer.

CHAPTER 15

Pete put the Suburban in park and rested his forehead against the steering wheel.

His mother's voice purred through the car speakers. "I was hoping you would make it home for our Derby party at least. We had them put all the tents up on the lower terrace lawn this year, and it was just beautiful. That Gullah caterer I told you about really outdid herself." Darcy Hendrick sounded like she usually did after a party, self-satisfied and tired. "And you know it's your father's favorite holiday."

"The Kentucky Derby isn't a holiday. And Father only likes it because he can drink bourbon in the morning." Pete cut the engine and pressed a button on his rear-view mirror. The garage door rumbled closed behind him, dulling the loud hiss of rain against the driveway.

"Peter." She tsk-ed her disapproval. "What has you in such a mood?"

"Sorry, Mother."

The phone beeped, and he glanced over to the passenger seat, where he'd tossed his cell. Letty, calling on the other line. He let it go to voicemail.

"Everything okay at work?" A coffee pot clattered back into the maker. His mother drank coffee all day, every day. Usually in lieu of food.

He leaned back in his seat. At least she'd asked. She knew how much it meant to him. "Yes, ma'am. Everything's fine. The clinic's doing—"

"Did I tell you Charles made partner at his firm? And at only thirty. You know your father didn't become a shareholder until he was thirty-three, but don't tell him I told you so."

Peter lowered his forehead to the steering wheel again. "You told me."

"Oh, did I?" The tone of her voice told him she knew she had. "And did you call to congratulate him?"

"Not yet, Mother. I will."

"I do wish you boys were closer with one another." She sighed. The same sigh she'd made when he followed Sue Ellen to UT instead of going to Vanderbilt. And when he'd chosen veterinary school over medicine.

"I'll call. I promise."

"Well, alright. See that you do." Her voice grew muffled. "No, Serena. Not there. Put the garden roses in the morning room please." She came back on the line. "Sorry about that. We have so many lovely flowers leftover from the party, and I hate for them to go to waste. I already took two arrangements over to the church for them to enjoy. Beautiful things deserve to be appreciated..." She trailed off, probably arranging a bouquet. "Sorry, dear. Where were we?"

You were lecturing me. Again.

Another beep from the phone. This time, a text from Letty. "Ring me when you get a minute. It's important."

His mother piped back up, answering her own question. "Oh that's right. I was about to ask after Sue Ellen. I don't suppose there's any news you'd like to share?"

His gut sunk to his shoes. "News?"

"Don't be daft, Peter. You know what I mean. Charles and Bridget are on their third baby already, and they married two years after you did. When am I gonna have some grandbabies from y'all?"

He flushed with relief, then guilt. The need to tell his mother the truth about the divorce at war with the fear of disappointing her again. "We're not ready for babies yet. It's not the right time. Not with both of us so busy at work."

"It's never the right time for children. They ruin your figure, turn your world upside down, and then move away and forget to call." She laughed her debutante laugh, still girlish at sixty-five. "But they're the only thing you're gonna leave behind when you die. You need a legacy, Peter."

A legacy, really?

She kept talking before he could respond. "Would it help for me to call and speak to Sue Ellen directly? Some things are easier to talk about when it's just us chickens, you know. And we haven't had the chance to catch up in ages."

God, no.

He sat up in his seat, his throat tightening. "No, ma'am."

"You know I don't care a whit about money. But she wasn't raised like you. Her family is as nouveau riche as it gets, and they just don't see the world the same way we do."

Pete cringed. "Mother—"

"Let me finish, Peter."

"Yes, ma'am."

"Sue Ellen may not realize the doors that are open here for y'all and, someday — soon, I hope — for your children. Just think of how much easier life would be if you were to move back to Charleston." She picked up tempo, the way she always did when she delivered what she thought was a winning argument. "Sue Ellen can even work, if she wants to. Your father has connections at the hospital. And then, when you have babies, you'd have family nearby to help. They can be raised in the same church you were. And those children will be given every possible advantage." She finally paused for a breath. "Will you at least think about it?"

Pete smacked his head on the steering wheel again. This time, hard enough to hurt. "Yes, ma'am."

Andrew stabbed a butter knife into two inches of ice, chiseling at the edges of what he hoped was either lasagna or chicken fried rice. One final jab broke the frozen dinner free.

Salisbury steak.

No wonder it'd been in there long enough to become a part of the freezer.

He paced in front of the microwave while his dinner spun inside. Andrew'd only been home a few days, and he was already losing it. Walls closing in, inactivity wearing at him like a persistent itch just out of reach.

He could call Renee. The microwave beeped, and he pulled out the carton. "Shit, that's hot." He tossed it on the counter.

But that wouldn't work. Even he knew sleepovers two nights in a row would send the wrong message. He used a dish towel to carry his food to the table, pushing aside takeout menus, empty pizza boxes, and old files until there was enough room for him to eat.

He could call Mary to see what they were up to. He glanced at the clock. 8:36 p.m.

Crap.

She'd be putting the kids to bed. Andrew sawed at the meat patty with the side of his fork. He was on his own and needed to get used to it.

He chewed a bite and thumbed through the copy of the arson file he'd made before he left the station. So many pieces of evidence, none of them quite fitting into place. The fire set while animals were still on the scene, the unlocked door, the missing surveillance video, Richardson going AWOL, the timing of Moses Wilbur's disappearance and death. Andrew gave up on the fork and ate the last of the meat with his fingers.

His boss's admonition that he not work on any of his cases while on leave had not been equivocal. And Andrew understood why. His presence in the squad room would be disruptive, and allowing him back on the job before the investigation was over would send the wrong message to the public. But Captain Levinson hadn't said anything about Andrew thinking about a case.

And what was the harm in that? He'd pass anything he found onto Mary, and she could take the credit.

Win, win.

Andrew licked sauce from his index finger, shoved the junk on the table further aside, and pulled everything out of the arson file. One by one, he taped statements, photos, and reports onto the dining room wall. Then pulled them free and rearranged them — playing with the evidence, trying to find links or connections.

He chewed his lip and shifted the papers again. Still nothing.

Andrew went back to the kitchen and searched through the junk drawer until he found half a dozen push pins and an old, folded map of the city. He taped the map up on his evidence wall and sunk a pin where they'd found Moses Wilbur's body. He put another on top of the animal research facility. Less than a mile separated the two.

What did that mean? The gulley was close enough for a dump site. And if you were heading away from the facility toward town, the forest where they'd found Wilbur would have seemed an ideal place to pull over and dispose of a body. The area was empty of everything but trees as far as the eye could see, and because of the terrain, it would have been one of the only opportunities to pull off the road between the facility and the edge of town.

But even if that did support the theory that Wilbur's death was connected to the arson case, it didn't get him any closer to answering the more important questions — Who started the fire? Who killed Wilbur? And why?

Andrew dropped into a dining room chair. No matter how he rearranged the paper, all he really had were questions. Questions he wasn't allowed to go answer.

Fuck.

His cell phone rang from somewhere under all the documents on the table. He dug through until he found it, hiding beneath a stack of leftover takeout napkins.

Letty Duquesne.

She started talking as soon as he answered. "Detective Marsh? I'm sorry to bother you, but I wasn't sure who else to call. I think I found a link between the two rabies victims. Both of them attended a picnic at Signal Mountain Community Park. It might be nothing, but it could mean that's where they encountered our source animal. And someone needs to look into it ASAP. Every minute we wait'll make it harder for us to find and isolate that animal." She finally stopped for a breath.

"Well, hello to you too, Letty." He pushed the ball of his foot against the floor, leaning the chair back on its rear legs. "Don't take this the wrong way, but I'm not sure I'm the right person to call. Wouldn't you be better off reaching out to the health department, or maybe animal control?"

She puffed out a breath. "This wouldn't be in animal control's wheelhouse. And the health department doesn't seem interested. I reported it to them and left a message with my contact in the mayor's office. But I doubt either will do anything about it. They don't seem to care."

He couldn't imagine that was true. Andrew leaned the chair back another inch. "What exactly are you suggesting?"

"The park's about sixteen acres, and I could really use another set of eyes. If you aren't busy…"

He was busy alright. Busy doing nothing.

Letty continued. "I know it's a big ask. But I thought maybe we could meet at the park tomorrow morning. I can show you what to look for, and we can work our way through it like a grid."

"I don't know how much help I'd be." Andrew looked around the cluttered apartment, then at the map. The park sat just to the west of his two pins. "I'm not exactly an outdoorsman. I'm more a 'football and beer' kind of guy than hunting or camping or whatever."

He had no business getting involved... but, at the same time, the rabies cases weren't a police matter. Which meant he wasn't forbidden from helping with them. And if he did a quick drive by at the fire scene on the way, who would know the difference?

"I understand. Really. Thanks, anyway." Letty sounded disappointed but not deterred. "I'm still waiting to hear back from a friend who might be able to come help and, if not, I'm sure I can handle it on my own. It'll just take a little longer."

He leaned back a fraction of an inch further. The fire scene was barely even a detour from the park. He wasn't doing anyone any good on house arrest. She wasn't exactly hard on the eyes, and she'd done him a favor when they'd met at Rosie's.

Plus, it'd be almost irresponsible to send a woman with a stalker out into the woods alone, even if she hadn't mentioned the BMW on this call. When he looked at it that way, it was almost like he had a duty to help.

Andrew let the front legs of his chair fall back to the floor. "I'm in."

CHAPTER 16

May 8, 2018

Andrew spotted the sign for Signal Mountain Community Park at the last minute and braked hard. "I appreciate you calling to check in, Captain. But like I told Phil, everything's fine."

"You been staying close to home?" Captain Levinson spoke in a deep baritone, his words slow and rounded. Like he was talking past a marble in his mouth.

"Yes, sir." Andrew eyed the entrance to the park.

Mostly.

Levinson hummed his approval. "You go see Dr. Cisneros?"

"Sure did." Not that he'd had a choice. An image of the department's shrink, with his too-soft voice and long, purposeful pauses sprang unwelcome to mind. Andrew couldn't imagine anything the man said would help, but if it meant he would get his badge back, he'd suffer through.

"Good, good." A door thunked closed in the background, and Levinson's voice dropped another octave. "Listen, if anyone asks, we didn't have this conversation."

"Yes, sir." Andrew's shoulders bunched. His career, his livelihood, his ability to do the job he loved — all of it hung on whatever Levinson couldn't say with his office door open.

"I got the initial report from Internal Affairs." Levinson paused long enough for Andrew's heart to stop. "They haven't found any breach of procedure."

Andrew straightened in his seat. "That's good news."

"Sure is, son. I thought you deserved to know as soon as I did." Levinson paused again. "You had a hard choice, and you made it. If I'd ever found myself in that situation, I'd have made the same call."

"Thank you, sir. That means a lot."

Levinson cleared his throat. "I do feel like I need to say, even though I'm sure you know already. This is just a preliminary report. IA has a lot of work left to do." The springs of Levinson's desk chair twanged, as if he'd leaned back in it. "From what I hear, they can't make progress on a final report until they follow up with the girl who shot that video. Her parents are insisting she have counsel present. And it seems the family lawyer's on St. Kitts." If there was a verbal equivalent of an eye roll, Levinson's tone nailed it. "Then, of course, there's the DA."

Andrew swallowed hard, and Levinson continued. "In a case this public, DA Nguyen isn't likely to feel she has much choice but to send it to a grand jury. And you know as well as I do…"

"They'd indict a ham sandwich." Much less one who shot a mentally ill, local preacher in the back of the head. And once Andrew was indicted, anyone who didn't already think he was a murderer, would. A long break in oncoming traffic gave Andrew plenty of time to turn into the park, but he didn't go.

He forced himself to take a deep breath. Levinson had called with good news about the IA investigation. Andrew needed to focus on that. He glanced in the rearview — and put his foot back on the brake.

What looked like a silver sedan pulled to a stop behind a paneled van at the last light.

Was that a BMW?

Levinson's voice came through the car speakers. "Andrew? Did I lose you?"

He snapped back to attention. "No, sir. I'm here." Andrew searched the intersection but couldn't find the silver car anywhere.

Probably just a glare.

Andrew pulled through the park gates.

"Hang in there, son." Levinson hung up.

He would. But only because he didn't have any other choice.

Andrew left his car in a small lot next to a Subaru with Georgia plates he assumed was Letty's, then wandered into the park. The sun hot on his shoulders, the air sharp with the smell of cut grass. Under other circumstances, it might have been peaceful. But not today. Not with the prospect of an indictment. Or a civil suit by Bullard's family. That could mean enough attorneys' fees to put him in the poor house and keep him there. He scrubbed a hand across the back of his head.

Focus on what you can control.

Wasn't that what Cisneros had said? While Andrew had been edging toward the door, waiting for the clock to strike an hour so he could leave.

Maybe the shrink hadn't been completely useless. Even though Andrew going on a rabid goose chase — and poking around a crime scene where he wasn't supposed to be — probably hadn't been what Cisneros meant.

Beggars can't be choosers.

Andrew scanned the park. A huge play structure built to look like a pirate ship dominated the end closest to where he'd left his car, but the rest of the park was green space. It alternated between rolling lawn and thick patches of trees with picnic tables underneath. Everything quiet and still, not even a breeze moving through the leaves. And no sign of Letty.

He pulled out his phone and dialed her number.

She answered on the first ring. "Oh, hey. It's you."

Not exactly the welcome he'd hoped for. "Expecting someone else?"

"No... Yes, sort of. Sorry." She laughed, a short mirthless sound. "My friend's sick. I'm waiting for an update on how she's doing. But so far..." Her voice went rough, then she spoke again. "Are you here? I don't see you."

She rattled off directions to where he'd find her.

Andrew did his best to follow them and, after doubling back twice, found Letty behind a thick clump of trees. She stood on top of a picnic table with her hands on her hips, staring up into the branches of a broad oak tree.

"See anything interesting?" He leaned on the table, peering into the dense mass of bright green leaves above her head.

"There you are." She crouched and jumped down. "Not yet." Letty gestured to a grassy spot a few yards away. "But I think that's where the Bullards were, in the photo. The food table was about where you're standing. And Emma Canning was just over there." She shifted to point behind Andrew, toward a series of well-used charcoal grills bolted to a concrete base.

He looked back up into the tree, but there was still nothing to see. "What were you hoping to find up there?"

"Scat." Letty collected a backpack from where it lay against the tree trunk.

He watched her dig around inside the bag. "You're looking for shit?"

"Tracking animals largely comes down to finding and identifying sign, which can be prints, chews, rubs, hair…" Letty pulled out a map and smiled up at him. "Or shit. With bats, it's mainly shit." She unfolded the map. "Usually small piles of black pellets which are flecked with shiny bits from the undigested pieces of insects' wings."

He kept his face neutral until she looked back down at the map. Watching ESPN alone on his couch was starting to sound a whole lot better than this.

Letty spread the document out on the table and pointed to a light green section on the far right side. "We're here." She swept her hand to the left. "And this is the developed area of the park you can see from where we're standing." She gestured to the darker green area above it. "The rest is natural forestland, wild except for the marked trails and the other entrance here on the Eastern end."

She pointed to another, much smaller swath of light green. "The forest'll be harder to cover, but it's only about twelve acres. So, nothing the two of us can't handle." She put up a hand to shield her eyes from the sun and stared out toward the trees lining the back edge of the mowed area. "Although I may change my mind once it's dark."

He made an exaggerated show of checking his watch.

It wasn't even ten in the morning yet.

Letty raised an eyebrow but seemed to catch his meaning. "We'll only need a few hours to cover the ground we need to cover. But the animals we're looking for are mainly nocturnal — bats, skunks, foxes, raccoons, bobcats, coyotes — they all come out at night." She pulled on the backpack. "So we'll do a canvas in the daylight to get an idea of what we're looking for and where they might be. Then come back tonight, preferably at dusk."

She didn't wait for him to respond. Letty started back the way he'd come, talking over her shoulder. "It's always easier to make out tracks when the sun is low in the sky. That's when the bats'll be leaving their roosts. And if we're going to capture anything, that's when we're likely to do it."

Andrew followed a few paces behind.

What have I gotten myself into?

Letty continued. "We'll start out together, working our way from that end. Then back again. I'll show you what to look for. And then, when you're comfortable, we can split up to cover more ground." She stopped in the shade of another oak tree, waiting for him to catch up. "Sound good?"

Good wasn't quite the word he would use.

Something buzzed in Letty's backpack before he could say so. She flipped the bag to the ground, knelt in the leaves, and pawed through it, yanking out her phone. Letty grimaced at what he guessed was a text message.

If she'd gotten news on her friend, it must not be good. Not with that look on her face.

He put out a hand to help her back to her feet, smothering any complaints he had about a search for literal shit. "Let's do it."

She took his hand with a nod. "You sound like my sister."

They kept moving through the woods, but Letty went silent. No more easy chatter about where to look for tracks or how to distinguish a dog's print from a fox's. She had the same worried look he'd seen on his own face in the bathroom mirror that morning.

Andrew searched his mind for anything that might be a distraction. "What about armadillos?"

She turned to him. "What?"

"Don't I need to know about armadillo poop?"

"They're too cold-blooded to carry rabies. But they can carry leprosy." The tension in her face gave way to a smirk. "So, if you see one, don't hug it."

He picked up a long stick and swished it through a patch of brush, looking for prints in the soft soil underneath. "Is that why I see so many dead ones? Because of leprosy?"

"Nah, it's just that armadillos tend to die in public. They jump when they're startled, which works great if you're trying to escape a bobcat." She disappeared around an overgrown cluster of saplings and brush. "Less so if it's a Chevy, if you know what I— "

Andrew waited for her to finish the thought, but she didn't. "Letty?"

No answer.

He rounded the bushes.

Letty stood frozen in place, a finger pressed to her lips. Half a dozen yards behind her, sat a small cinderblock building spray-painted with graffiti, a door standing open on each end. Probably bathrooms. She pointed to a dark spot in the undergrowth below the building's eaves.

Something lay in the dirt. A lump of gray-brown fur, with a sharply angled wing tucked at each side.

A bat.

"Is it dead?" He came closer.

"No, but it's sick." Letty held up a hand, as if warning him away. "I'll go get what we need to trap it. I wasn't sure what we'd be catching, so didn't know what to bring. You stay here and watch. If it tries to fly off, pay attention to where it goes. Follow at a safe distance, if you can. But do not—" She paused, as if for emphasis. "—do not get near it."

He nodded. He'd already been bitten once that week.

That was more than enough.

Letty backed away slowly, her footfalls soft in the leaves. When she made it a few dozen yards, she broke into a jog toward the parking area.

He watched until she was out of sight, then looked back at the bat. The animal shivered, opening and closing its mouth, as if gasping for air. Exposing a row of tiny, sharp teeth.

Yuck.

Andrew took a step back, and a twig snapped under his foot.

He looked to the bat, but it hadn't moved except for the slow gaping of its mouth. Open, close. Open, close.

He waited, watching.

What would happen if he was bitten again? Would the first two shots he'd gotten of the series Sue Ellen prescribed be enough? Would a second bite affect how the other shots worked? If they would work? Had there ever even been a case of someone bitten twice? He stepped further away.

A rustle of leaves, this time behind him.

Andrew jerked around.

"Got it." Letty carried a ten-gallon bucket and a small piece of cardboard into the clearing.

Andrew did his best to look like she hadn't scared him half to death. "What're you gonna do with that?"

She sat the bucket on the ground and drew out a pair of thick leather work gloves and a roll of tape. "You'll see." Letty dropped the tape to the ground, pulled on the gloves, and edged toward the animal, carrying the bucket in one hand and the cardboard in the other.

The bat twitched, and Letty stopped in place. "Don't worry, friend. I'm not here to hurt you."

She moved forward again, and the bat responded, dragging its body along the ground in a slow circle. As if it sensed Letty approaching but was too far gone to decide between fight or flight.

Letty took another step.

The animal pushed the webbed membrane of its wing against the dirt and lurched in her direction.

She moved closer.

Two yards, two feet.

One.

Letty lowered the bucket over the bat in a single, fluid movement. Then lifted the edge a fraction of an inch and slid the cardboard underneath.

She grinned up at him. "Got it."

CHAPTER 17

Letty paced the patchy strip of grass in front of Andrew's car. "No one picked up at animal control. And the woman who answered at the health department was even less helpful than the last time I called." Which was saying something. "I doubt they call back."

"Why wouldn't they?" Andrew tilted his head toward the bucket where it' sat in the shade of a pine tree. "The health department's the ones who're looking for that thing, right?"

"Supposedly. But I called them when I found the link between Bullard and Canning, and they didn't seem interested." She shrugged. "I passed that off as maybe they'd already made the connection. Maybe it wasn't news for them. But, just now, I couldn't even get past the receptionist. I have a possible source animal in hand, and she dropped me in the voicemail for public relations." Letty threw up her hands. "Public. Relations."

"What does that mean?" Andrew leaned against his sedan's hood, the metal protesting under his weight.

"PR is where they send people who need to be managed." Letty paced faster. "I think they're ignoring me because they've decided I'm nuts."

"Oh." Andrew crossed his arms. "So, what do we do with the bat if the health department won't take it?"

"We need to get it to a testing facility. And, to do that, we need to find a 'permissible submitter,' because they won't take a specimen from just anyone. It has to come from the health department, or animal control, neither of which seems interested…"

Or a veterinarian.

Which would be a fine solution if Pete was calling her back. But she'd already left three messages and texted. She checked her phone again.

Still nothing.

It was enough to give a girl a complex.

Letty pulled the tape free on one side of the bucket and peeked inside. "Our friend here doesn't look so good. Whatever we do, we need to do it fast."

Which meant stalking Pete might be her only choice.

"I thought you said they'd have to euthanize it anyway?" Andrew eyed the bucket as if he thought the poor half-dead animal might stage a prison break.

"They will. The test's done on brain tissue. But the longer it lives, the better. The sample will start to degrade as soon as the animal dies." She replaced the cardboard and rubbed her hand across the tape to re-seal it. "Refrigeration will help. But it'll only buy us so much time, forty-eight hours from death max. And that includes however long the specimen spends in transit."

Letty tapped her phone against her leg. She had one more option before she dialed Pete again, and it was a long shot. She hadn't spoken to Caroline since Letty'd texted she was leaving town, and there was no reason to think reaching her would've gotten easier.

Worth a shot.

Caroline answered on the second ring. "Hey, girl. I'm so sorry I didn't catch you while you were in town. Did you manage to have fun without me?" The steady thump, thump, thump of footfalls and the whir of a treadmill came over the line. Even at a full run, Caroline didn't sound winded.

"I found something."

The footfalls slowed. "What do you mean?"

"Randy Bullard and Emma Canning were together at a picnic at Signal Mountain Community Park earlier this year. I went down to check it out, and I—"

"Letty, you know I love you." A beep sounded, and the footfalls stopped. "But I can't get involved."

Letty blinked. "Wait. What?"

"The rabies outbreak was an isolated incident. It's over. You need to let it go."

"Over?" Things clicked into place. Caroline not calling her back, then responding only when she thought Letty had left town. The health department's refusal to give her the time of day. All the suspicions she'd been carrying, not wanting to admit them, even to herself. It made sense now, and in the worst possible way. "I think you mean Mayor Rafferty wants it to be over."

Caroline barked out a short, harsh laugh. "Is there a difference?"

"I'm sure the next person who comes down with rabies will think so." She tried to keep the snark out of her voice. If there was any chance Caroline could be persuaded to get her boss on board, Letty needed to make it happen.

"Look, I know you're just trying to help. But the authorities have assured Mayor Rafferty they've done everything possible to make sure this is all behind us. He's not inclined to disregard what they're telling him, just because you say so. Maybe if you hadn't shown up uninvited, it'd be different. But, as it stands now, it's almost like you're saying our folks can't be trusted to handle the situation without outside help. You have to see why that won't go over well." Something rattled metal against metal, probably her gym locker. "And please take this with all the love it's intended, but I think you're being overly dramatic."

"Am I?" Letty glared out at the park, her patience wearing thin. "Two people are dead. I may have found the source animal. And, as crazy as it sounds, it seems like I'm the only one who's interested."

"Okay, Nancy Drew." Caroline's tone was carefully casual. Everything about it said "we're just friends having a chat." Even though Letty had no doubt they both knew that wasn't true. Caroline continued. "If the health department thought there was a risk anyone else would get sick, they'd be all over it. It's handled, Letty."

"The sick bat I just captured in the middle of a public park says otherwise."

A long pause stretched out before Caroline spoke again. "You don't know that bat has rabies. It could be anything."

Letty blinked. "Is that really a chance you want to take? That the mayor wants to take? I can't imagine letting constituents die would be good for re-election." An angry heat rose under her skin. "If anyone else gets sick, you can bet the public will know why. I'll make sure of it."

"I'm going to pretend I didn't hear that. You need to be reasonable. Go through normal channels. Call the health department. Hell, go there and leave the bat with them. If they think it's worth checking into, they will. But I can't do anything for you." Caroline lowered her voice. "Rafferty ran for office on a platform of public safety and economic growth. You have to see why we can't get involved. Not in this political climate and especially not with festival season on the horizon. Riverbend alone brings in millions of dollars to the— "

"Right. I'll let you get back to your work-out." Letty hung up. "Bitch."

Andrew raised his eyebrows. "That sounded like it went well."

She scowled at him. "It's bullshit. Pure political bullshit." Caroline had always put her career first, her sights set on making it to the next rung of whatever political ladder she was climbing. But this was insane.

"So, what now?" He shifted his weight off the car.

"We get proof they can't ignore."

CHAPTER 18

"Thanks for all your help." Letty took the insulated container from Pete and slid it onto her passenger seat, trying to decide whether it'd stay put when she hit the brakes. The bat was well-wrapped in layers of plastic, ice packs, and newspaper. Not to mention already dead.

But still. She only had one specimen.

Letty moved the container to the floorboard, closed the door, and turned back to Pete. "Sorry again for coming by unannounced."

"I'm glad you came. Just sorry I couldn't get back to you earlier. Things have been so hectic here with Julie gone."

"Don't worry about it. I understand, really."

"I'm glad someone was able to come help you at least." He followed her around to the driver's side.

"I know, me too. I wish you'd gotten the chance to meet him." She opened the door and leaned against the frame. "You've probably seen him on TV. Poor guy's been all over the news."

Pete's eyebrows went up. "Really?"

"Yeah. Andrew's the detective who shot Randy Bullard. I met him at the hospital right after it happened. He'd just gotten the first of his rabies shots. And I was there to…" talk to your wife. She cleared her throat, wishing she could think of any other plausible way to end that sentence.

Pete's face had gone unreadable. He checked his watch. "I guess you need to get going if you're going to make it to Knoxville before the testing site closes. It's almost three now."

"Really? Crap." The drive would take two hours, and that's if she didn't hit traffic. Still, Letty lingered. "Thanks again."

Pete leaned in for a hug, but it was quick, perfunctory. And from the side. "You're more than welcome." He gave her a wave and turned back toward the clinic. "Good luck."

She watched him climb the front porch steps before she put the car in reverse. He hadn't done anything wrong. He was kind, polite, the perfect gentleman. But something had felt off. Even before she'd stuck her foot in her mouth.

It wasn't just the side-hug, it was the way he'd looked when she'd gotten there. Just for an instant, when he noticed her in the doorway. His expression had almost been... what? Petulant? Then he'd smiled, with that same boyish charm he always had. And everything had been fine.

Letty pulled out of the clinic's parking lot.

Maybe he was just conflicted? His divorce wasn't final yet. That could make anyone uncomfortable starting something new. Especially growing up the way he had, in a place where divorce was something you didn't do. She'd probably just caught him at a bad moment. And besides, she had other things to think about. Like getting the specimen up to Knoxville. And then celebrating their discovery of the bat with a well-deserved bottle of wine.

Letty sped up.

And spotted a police cruiser, mostly hidden behind a thick grove of trees.

Shiiiiit.

She took her foot off the gas and watched the cop car in her mirror.

No way she would make it to Knoxville in time if she got pulled over.

The cruiser didn't move.

Thank God.

She checked one more time just to make sure its lights were still off.

Something silver flashed two cars behind her. Sunlight glinting off the hood of a silver BMW sedan. The bulky silhouette of a large man behind the wheel.

He's back.

Her throat tightened, and she shifted in her seat.

What now? She could call Andrew. But he was at the hospital getting the next of his rabies shots. He probably wouldn't even answer. Maybe call 911?

But what would she say? That she'd seen the same car a few times? It wasn't like the guy had threatened her or even done anything wrong. They'd think she was ridiculous.

Letty flipped on her turn signal and made a quick right onto a side street.

She watched the BMW in her mirror.

Keep going, keep going.

The car didn't follow.

Thank God.

Letty made another right, and another. Circling around to the main road. She checked the mirror again.

Mother fucker.

The BMW pulled out into traffic, coming up quickly behind her. As the sedan grew closer, the man's face came into focus. Dark sunglasses, brown hair, his mouth a thin, flat line.

She went faster.

Two blocks until the on-ramp for the interstate.

She could drive to the police station. Chances were good the BMW wouldn't follow her there. And if it did, all the better.

But the precinct was on the other side of town.

She glanced at the Styrofoam container.

There wasn't time. Every minute that passed, the specimen degraded. The chance of getting an accurate result fading with it.

And she was almost to the overpass. She needed to make a choice now — go find help and risk her one chance to track down the source of the rabies outbreak. Or see if she could lose the BMW and do what needed to be done.

I can always report him after.

The light at the intersection ahead turned yellow, and Letty slowed.

Then floored it.

She checked the rearview. The BMW jerked to a stop at the light. The man behind the wheel yelling something she couldn't make out.

Letty let out a whoop. "Fuck you, ass— "

Tires shrieking against pavement cut her short.

A wrenching crunch of metal. And her car lurched to the right. Spinning off its axis, drifting in a way it shouldn't have been able to. The force of the impact threw her sideways into the center console. Even as the seatbelt held tight against her chest.

The world outside blurred. Her car flying through the intersection, out of control.

Letty stomped the brake. Shock finally giving way to self-preservation. Her tires bit at the road, trying for traction. Found purchase.

And lost it.

She slid toward the parking lot of a cheap hamburger joint. The kind that sold small, steamed burgers that smelled of onions and armpits. Letty put all her weight on the brake, stomping down until every muscle in her leg ached. Still, the car didn't stop. It drifted as if drawn toward the metal support for the restaurant's oversized sign, which glowed overhead orange and white. Like some kind of beacon.

Letty gripped the wheel, closed her eyes, and waited for impact.

CHAPTER 19

The change from chaos to stillness came in an instant. Everything suddenly silent except for the ragged heave of Letty's breath and the creaking protest of the Subaru as it came to rest. She took quick stock of herself.

Nothing hurt. But that might not mean anything. Not if she was in shock.

Letty eased open her eyes, bracing herself for what she might see. Her car sat half on the curb, half jutting out into the intersection. Traffic around her had come to a stop. Her hands were still locked, white-knuckled on the steering wheel.

She forced herself to let go.

Holy shit.

Letty took a deep breath and turned off the engine. The car grew even more quiet, and into the silence floated a single terrifying thought.

Did I hurt someone?

She jerked around in her seat. Checking for other cars. For whoever had hit her. A Nissan Altima sat on the diagonally opposite corner, its front-end crumpled. A shaggy-haired man wearing several gold chains and a Lynyrd Skynyrd tank top leaned over the hood with a phone pressed to his ear, probably inspecting the damage. She scanned the inside of his car, squinting into the back, praying not to see a car seat.

The Altima looked empty. The windows unbroken. No sign of damage except for the smashed bumper.

Thank God.

She let herself breathe a little easier as she un-clicked her seatbelt and climbed out. Traffic creeped forward, cars edging around the back end of her Subaru. Every one slowed as they passed, no doubt to make sure they got their turn to gawk. She didn't make eye contact despite the press of their stares on her skin. Letty skimmed the intersection — a big, brown delivery van, a few economy cars, more pickup trucks than she could count — but there was no BMW.

Was that good or bad? Would the police even believe her that he'd been there?

Would it matter?

The other driver glared at her across the intersection. She waited for a lull in traffic, took a step in his direction, and hesitated. What was the etiquette for "so sorry I almost killed you"?

She stepped back onto the curb and looked away, her gaze rising to the fast food sign still towering overhead. Its lights made a dull, constant buzz that reminded her of the bug zappers outside cheap convenience stores. She walked around the front of her car for a better look.

She'd missed the metal support by less than an inch. If she hadn't, if the impact had caused the sign to fall on her...

Letty closed her eyes and said a quick prayer of thanks.

A siren wailed faint in the distance, and she cringed. Things could still get worse. And maybe she deserved it if they did. This was her fault. She knew the light was turning red, and she went anyway. She caused an accident that might have gotten her killed. Could have gotten other people killed. And the fact that no one had gotten hurt didn't mean there wouldn't be consequences.

She sucked in a breath.

The specimen.

Letty hurried around the car, peering in the front passenger window. The insulated container sat where she'd left it. Safe and undisturbed in the footwell.

Except there was no way she'd get it to Knoxville now.

Letty slumped into herself. How had she messed things up this badly?

A police car pulled up behind the Altima, lights flashing.

She looked from the police car to the specimen, pulled out her phone, and did what she should have done to begin with.

Pick up, pick up…

The call connected. "I need your help."

■ ■ ■

Letty inched her way up the Inn's staircase, purse in one hand, grocery bag full of supplies in the other. Her body ached. The adrenaline that had kept her in motion since the accident all but gone.

A muted ringing came from down the hall, and she stopped. Was it coming from her room? It could be Andrew. Or Bill. He'd promised an update on Priya. If she'd missed a call on her cell, he might ring her room.

If it was an emergency.

Letty hurried up the rest of the stairs, ignoring her body's protests.

The phone rang again as she dug the key from her purse, fumbling to get it into the lock.

Or it could be the police, summoning her down to the station.

The policeman had taken her statement after the accident, listening without reaction as she'd explained what happened. But he hadn't said what would happen next, and she'd been afraid to ask. Letty stopped, key in the lock.

A strange smell hung in the air.

Cigarette smoke.

Another ring from inside her room.

If it was Bill, she needed to answer. Needed to know Priya was okay. The lock clicked open, and she stepped inside.

She still smelled cigarettes. Letty wrinkled her nose and grabbed the cordless receiver. "Hello."

"Ms. Duquesne, this is Charlene from the front desk."

"Yes, hi."

"My manager came in right after you went upstairs. He says he hadn't seen any BMWs parked outside either. But we're gonna keep a look-out for ya. Okay?"

"Thanks for checking." The smell persisted. Not an old, dingy-ashtray smell. More like she'd walked in right after the smoker had been there.

Letty edged over to the closet door and jerked it open.

A handful of metal hangers swung in the draft. A small safe and an ironing board sat underneath, but it was otherwise empty.

The front desk lady continued. "You are certainly welcome, I— "

"Do you know if anyone's been in my room?" Letty stepped into the bathroom, and a silence fell over the line.

The shower curtain sat closed and opaque.

Letty shoulders tensed, and she fought the urge to run.

She swept it open.

Nothing waited but a dripping faucet and a new set of tiny toiletries.

"I'm sorry?" The hotel receptionist finally responded.

"Is it possible maintenance has been in recently? Or maybe housekeeping?" Letty pulled the shower curtain back into place.

"No, ma'am. Housekeeping finished up hours ago, and we don't really have a maintenance crew. It's just me and Bobby down here. Did you need something? I can bring up more towels, or…"

"No, thank you. I just… thought I smelled something." Letty went back to the hotel room door, engaged the deadbolt, and put on the chain.

"Oh, okay." The woman spoke with a clear "bless your heart" intonation. "You have a good night now."

Letty hung up. There didn't seem much of a chance of that.

She went to the window and checked the lot for the BMW again, but there was still no sign of him. Which should've made her feel better, but it didn't. Not knowing where he was, where he might be, was making it impossible for her to relax. She yanked one of the drapes, trying to close it — desperate for whatever separation she could get between her and what waited outside. But the heavy, lined fabric resisted, and pain flashed across her chest. She let go.

Fuck.

Letty peered down the neck of her shirt. A bright red stripe marked the spot where her seatbelt had held her in place. The welt ran from her left shoulder, between her breasts, to her right hip.

No wonder it hurt.

Letty retrieved the grocery bag she'd dropped by the door and dumped its contents on the bed. Ibuprofen, a Snickers bar, a six pack of Sierra Nevada — probably all foam now, thanks to the rough trip upstairs — and two ice packs. She conquered the Ibuprofen's childproof lid on the third try, shook several into her palm and cracked open a beer to wash them down. Then took another peek down her shirt.

Could've been worse.

That's what the officer at the scene had said — after he'd finished bitching at her for not moving her car out of the way of traffic. If she'd seen the impact coming, if she'd tensed before the other car hit her, she'd probably be in a neck brace. Or worse.

Letty bent one of the ice packs in half until it cracked and grew cold in her hand. She settled back on the bed and lay the pad across the sore spot on her chest. Not that it helped.

Priya's parents should be at the hospital by now. Why hadn't Bill called with an update?

Her phone dinged the arrival of a text message, as if she'd summoned it.

Finally.

She tossed the ice pack to the bed and ignored the pain as she dug the cell from her purse.

A text from Andrew. "Dropped off the bat."

Thank God.

At least there was one thing she hadn't screwed up. She'd expected Andrew to balk when she'd asked for his help — it was a big ask to come on notice and make the two hour drive to Knoxville. But he'd come as soon as she called, picked up the specimen, and after he made sure she was okay — and that her car would still run well enough for her to get home — he'd raced off without blinking an eye.

She might have a psycho following her around, might get charged with reckless driving, might go insane waiting for news about Priya. But, thanks to him, she might also still have a chance to do some good.

CHAPTER 20

May 9, 2018

Letty tapped the glass of the pastry case. "That one." She pointed at the fattest of the Pain au Chocolat. Layer upon layer of flaky, buttery goodness filled with chocolate and the comfort of carbohydrates.

God knew she needed it. She'd been up half the night, jerking awake at every creak of a hallway floorboard or distant slam of a door. Heart pounding, straining to see into the dark, half-expecting one of the room's shadows to shift into human form. She'd spent the last hour before dawn staring at the door, in case something tried to creep through it.

Now, in the light of day, it all seemed silly, but... she hadn't imagined the BMW following her.

The tidy man behind the bakery counter placed her pastry into a white paper bag. "Anything else, mademoiselle?"

She eyed the other offerings — beautiful tartes tatin, mini-french baguette sandwiches, and quiche with small sprigs of thyme or dill on top. If ever there was a day to order one of everything, this might be it. "Just a large coffee please. Black."

The baker gave a quick nod and creased the bag closed.

With any luck, caffeine would clear the cobwebs from her mind.

The man hurried off to a bank of gleaming coffee tureens, his bright yellow Crocs squeaking on the Linoleum as he went.

She needed the clarity, needed something that would help her make sense of what was going on.

If that's even possible.

The baker returned with a steaming cup. "Have a seat wherever you'd like."

She carried her breakfast to a small table against the back wall of the café. The spot gave her a view of the door and the parking lot outside. At least she'd know if someone was watching.

I sound like a crazy person.

She wrapped her hands around the cup, letting the comfort of its warmth seep into her fingers. The shop's front window had been hand-painted with a garden scene done in cheerful spring colors. The word "Patisserie" arced through the middle, written in a floral cursive. But, outside, the morning loomed gray and lifeless, brightened only by a single blue jay perched on the windowsill.

The bird cocked its head, as if it was thinking.

It jumped to one side, then back again, on repeat. The movements sudden, almost aggressive.

Is it nesting season?

She searched her mind but couldn't remember. Blue jays were territorial, especially if they felt threatened. The bird stopped moving, beady eyes peering inside the shop.

Looking right at her.

Letty's phone rang, and she jerked, splashing hot coffee onto her hand. "Crap." Her nerves were shot.

She wiped the wet on her sweatshirt and scrambled to dig out her cell.

Bill.

Finally.

She connected the call. "How's Priya? Your text didn't sound good."

"She's okay, she's stable." He paused, and Letty could tell something was wrong before he spoke again. "She's just not responding to the treatment the way we hoped. They may need to try another variation."

And if that doesn't work, what then?

Letty didn't bother asking. If the therapies didn't work, if Priya did have a super bug, there was nothing anyone would be able to do to help her. She remembered that much from the malaria case studies she'd read in grad school. Letty's hands clenched into fists.

"Letty?"

"I'm here."

"Her parents are at the hospital now. They've promised to tell us more as soon as they can. Although I don't know when that might be." Bill let out a deep sigh. "Almost makes me wish I had a big stack of papers to grade. Or really anything to keep my mind busy."

"I get that." Even though she'd had more distraction than she could handle.

He cleared his throat. "How are things with you?"

"Good." She touched the red mark on her chest, the skin tender beneath her shirt.

Part of her wanted to tell him everything. But the bigger part, the less selfish one, knew better. Telling him about the man in the BMW, the car accident, the body in the woods — it would only give him more to worry about. Which was the last thing he needed. She struggled for what to say.

Bill filled the silence. "Any progress on your work there?"

She straightened in her chair, grateful for a safe topic. "You could say that." Letty caught him up on the connection between Bullard and Canning, the link she'd found to the park, her spat with the mayor's office, and, finally, the discovery of the bat. "My friend dropped it off at the testing facility in Knoxville yesterday." She allowed herself a smile. "I'm hoping we'll have results by tomorrow."

"Well, I'll be." Bill chuckled. "I suppose, if anyone could've pulled it off, it'd be you. I've never met anyone so attuned to animal life. It's what makes you so amazing at field work."

She flushed at the compliment. "I just caught a lucky break."

Letty's phone dinged the arrival of an email.

"Hang on a sec." She pulled the cell away from her ear. The first few lines of an email appeared on the screen. Pete forwarding a message from the Tennessee Department of Health.

Oh my God.

"Bill, I need to call you back."

■   ■   ■

"I don't get it." Andrew pressed the phone to his ear and peered into his refrigerator, but no food materialized. Unless the brown lump in the crisper drawer could still be called cheese. "Why wouldn't they run a test?"

"Apparently, the health department decided it wasn't worth doing. Listen to this shit." Letty's voice flattened. "'The Tennessee Department of Health has not authorized testing on the submitted specimen. Testing is reserved for those situations where the results will impact public health-related decisions. Submitter has identified no known exposure, and testing has, therefore, been deemed unwarranted.'" She laughed, but there was no mirth in it. "Can you believe that? Basically, they won't test because we didn't actually see the bat bite anyone."

"That's fucked up." He flipped open last night's pizza box, hoping for a stray slice. "What're you gonna do now?"

"Regroup, I guess. I'd bet anything that bat had rabies." Paper crinkled on her end of the line, and Letty went quiet.

He closed the empty pizza box. "Are you eating something?"

"My feelings, mostly."

The jingle of a bell and a man's muted "Bonjour!" sounded in the background, the voice familiar. Andrew's stomach rumbled. "Are you at the bakery on Sixth? Tell Jean Marc to save me a couple beignets."

More crinkling paper. "I feel like I should make a crack about cops and doughnuts."

"They're not doughnuts if they're French. Bring me some, and we can spitball ideas for what to do next. I'll give you cash when you get here."

A second passed before she responded. "You're still game to help?"

"I can probably squeeze you in somewhere on my busy schedule." He rattled off his home address and his breakfast order — the beignets, a ham and Swiss croissant, and a large coffee with cream and three sugars. "Not that fake crap either, real white cane sugar."

"Seriously?" Letty did not sound amused.

Andrew grinned. "Man's gotta eat."

"Consider this payment for last night's courier service." She hung up.

His grin faded as he took in the state of his apartment. The dining room was a lost cause, but he might be able to make the kitchen and living room presentable before she got there. If he hurried.

He swept the beer bottles from the coffee table into a trash can, picked clothes up off the floor, and gave the kitchen a once-over. After a trip down to the dumpster and back, Andrew considered cleaning the bathroom, but that would require finding something to clean it with. Did he even have a scrub brush? He closed the door instead.

A knock sounded through the apartment.

Breakfast.

Letty waited on the other side of the front door with a paper bag and a coffee.

"Oh, thank God. I'm starving. Come on in." He snatched the bag and carried it to the kitchen. Something about company made him feel like he should eat off a plate. He rummaged unsuccessfully through cabinets.

"I put your coffee on the dining table. Good luck finding it." Letty's voice floated into the kitchen from the other room. "What's all this stuff on the wall?"

Andrew stopped, plate half out of the dishwasher.

Crap.

He'd left the arson case file — which he wasn't supposed to have, much less show to anyone — taped up in the dining room. "Just some evidence in a case I was working." He carried his breakfast to the dining room.

Letty stood with her back to him, inspecting the evidence she wasn't supposed to see. "And are you still? Working it, I mean?"

"No, just moving paper around." Which was accurate, given that his efforts had gotten him nowhere. Andrew scouted out his coffee and took a seat. He needed to change the subject. Preferably to something that wouldn't get him fired. "How're you feeling this morning? That kind of thing always seems worse the second day."

She shrugged but didn't turn from eyeing the pins on his map. "I was better before I looked up the penalties for reckless driving in Tennessee. D'you know you can get six months in jail?"

Andrew stuffed half a beignet in his mouth. "Jail time's usually reserved for repeat offenders. Or a wet reckless."

"A what?" She looked back at him. "Like when it's raining?"

"Nah, more like…" He finished chewing and mimed tilting a bottle back against his lips.

"Oh." She kept moving along the wall.

"At worst, you're probably facing a fine and some points on your license, assuming they decide it's your fault." He washed another bite down with a gulp of coffee. "Looked to me like maybe the other guy came off the interstate too fast to stop. You said you thought it was yellow when you went, right?"

Letty stopped in front of one of the pictures he'd tacked up.

He ran his finger through the powdered sugar on his plate. "Earth to Letty."

She didn't answer.

Andrew went to stand beside her. "What do you see?"

"That guy." Her voice sounded strangled. "He's the one who's been following me. In the BMW. The one I was trying to outrun last night."

Her finger shook, but she pointed right at Stuart Richardson's photo.

CHAPTER 21

Andrew stepped outside, holding the phone to his ear with one shoulder. The patio door tended to stick, and he needed both hands to get it closed. One final tug, and it slid into place. "So, what do you think?"

"What do I think?" Mary's voice echoed out of the receiver.

He pulled it away from his ear.

Her voice got louder with every word. "I think you disobeyed a direct order. I think you showed evidence in an active case to someone who just might be involved in it. Evidence you shouldn't have copies of to begin with. And I think Levinson's gonna chew your ass, spit it out, and stomp on what's left."

Andrew checked through the glass door, but Letty hadn't looked away from Richardson's photo. He swept a pile of dead leaves out of a lawn chair he'd repurposed as patio furniture and took a seat. "Not if he doesn't know."

"How're you planning to manage that?"

He grimaced. Mary wasn't gonna like it. "There's nothing about me being on leave that prevents me from spending time with friends. And if those friends happen to talk to each other when we're together... Like say, if you'd come to meet a new girlfriend of mine, and she told you about a strange guy who'd been following her. Maybe you'd have recognized the similarity between that guy and one you're already looking for. It'd be like any other break in the case. A feather in your cap, and Levinson none the wiser."

"That's your plan?" Mary snorted a laugh. "I love you, but not enough to write parking tickets for the rest of my career."

"You know I wouldn't ask if I didn't have to." He tilted his head side to side, trying to work the tension from his neck. "But this is about more than just an ass-chewing. If people think I'm still working when I'm on leave, it'll look like the department isn't taking the Bullard investigation seriously. And if they think that..."

She finished the thought. "It'll give them a reason to question the results. I get it, but still— "

"It's not just that. If IA finds out I kept copies of evidence I shouldn't have, if they think I shared it with someone involved in the case... aren't they gonna see that as confirmation that I don't play by the rules?" He stared out into the sparse woods behind his apartment. All pine trees and unkempt brush. "And if they think I'm willing to ignore the rules now, what would they think I'd do when your life was in danger?"

She went quiet, and he cringed.

"I didn't mean..." He hadn't thought of how that might sound, like he was trying to pull some sort of "you owe me" bullshit. He squeezed his eyes shut.

Shit.

"I know you didn't." All the anger had gone out of her voice. "I'm just not sure this is something I can do. You're asking me to lie to the captain, Andrew. And we aren't the only ones who'd know it was a lie. What if Letty Duquesne tells a different story?"

He looked inside again. Letty had moved to his couch. She sat with her knees pulled tight to her chest, head resting on top. It made her look younger, vulnerable. He had no real reason to trust her, but he did. She was there, trying to do the right thing. Trying to help people, even when it had put her own life in danger. "She won't."

"If we do this, you'd better hope, for both our sakes, that's true."

"So, will you? Do it, I mean?"

Mary didn't answer.

He wouldn't blame her if she didn't help. It was a big ask — maybe too big.

He took a deep breath. Either way, it was out of his hands. Whether Mary covered his ass or not, they had to follow the lead. "You learn anything more about Richardson?"

"Not that I should share any of it with you. But, yeah. I did some digging when I got your message. Some of it we already had in the file, the rest I had to pry out of a half a dozen databases..." Keystrokes clattered in the background. "Here we go. John Stuart Richardson, aged thirty-eight. No priors. Grew up local, son of Leonard and Kay Richardson. Father got popped in '89 on a charge of possession with intent but died in custody before his arraignment. The wife raised a hell of a stink, claimed Leonard was innocent. That his death was some kind of cover-up. She died a year later from a heroin overdose. After that, Stuart — he went by John then — went into the system. Disappeared after that."

Andrew shifted in the chair, the rusty metal creaking under his weight. "Disappeared where?"

"From what I can tell, Tampa. Got his GED and went to community college. Wound up with a degree in Animal Health Science. Worked in a research lab there for a few years. Never married. Came back to Chattanooga two years ago when a position opened up at the research facility."

"I don't know why anybody'd want to do that." He fanned his shirt against his chest. Five minutes outside, and he was already sweating.

Mary spoke to someone else, her voice muted, then came back on the line. "Do what?"

"Torture animals for a living." Movement through the trees caught his eye. A woman stepped into the clearing with a shaggy dog on a leash and a plastic bag dangling from the other hand. Andrew relaxed back into his seat.

"You know that's not actually what those facilities do, right?"

"If you say so." He'd seen the inside of the one where Richardson had worked, and he couldn't imagine the kind of person who'd choose to do what he did for a living. All those animals penned up the way they were, the scientists doing God-knew-what to them. "What's his connection to Letty Duquesne?"

"Beats the hell out of me. Both of them work with animals, but that's about as much of a connection as I can find." Mary paused. "There's something else, though. Not about Richardson exactly, but maybe related."

"Tell me."

Mary continued. "Remember when you asked about the body they found out by the Mountain View clinic, whether it might be connected to the arson case?"

"Right, Moses Wilbur. The timing of his death and the location of the dump site made me think it might be related." Andrew picked up a dead leaf and crunched it in his hand.

"Turns out Wilbur's real name was Matthew Wilkes. Wanted in Florida on charges of assault and disturbing the peace. He's also suspected of sending death threats to a scientist at Emory University's animal research center."

"Holy shit." Andrew sat forward, letting the dry leaf bits fall through his fingers.

"Wait, it gets better." The tap, tap, tap of Mary typing followed. "Wilkes's social media is bananas. I'll print the highlights for you. Real left-wing wacko stuff. Guy self-identified as part of the Animal Rights Militia."

"The what?"

"It's a militant animal rights group. Doesn't see the need to avoid human casualties. Some shit about existential self-defense." She said the words like they tasted bad. "Whatever that means. But the ARM's no joke — car bombs, letter bombs, contaminating food or medicine that's been tested on animals, vandalism, grave desecration... arson."

His eyebrows lifted. Well, that was certainly something. "How come I've never heard of them?"

"They're leaderless, just a bunch of isolated cells. Most active in Europe, and even there, they've been quiet in recent years. But you wouldn't know it from what Wilkes posted online." A printer whirred in the background. "What the hell is your friend involved in?"

"I have no idea." Andrew glanced back in at Letty.

But he was damn sure gonna find out.

CHAPTER 22

Letty checked the parking lot. No BMW. She closed her eyes and gave herself a second to relax. The night air carried the chirp of crickets, the faint scent of rosemary, and a lingering damp from yesterday's rain. Fresh, clean. Exactly what she needed after a day spent cooped up in Andrew's stuffy apartment. She typed out the text she'd promised him. "Made it. Everything's fine here. Heading to bed soon."

He responded before she had her phone back in her pocket. "Okay. Text me if anything feels off. Mary'll pick you up tomorrow morning at 8."

Super.

Andrew's partner had shown up mid-morning, grilled Letty for an hour, and hardly spoke to her the rest of the day. At first, she'd thought Mary and Andrew might be more than work partners, maybe Mary thought Letty was edging in on her turf. Even though the idea of that was ridiculous. But it hadn't taken long for her to realize that theory didn't make sense. For one thing, Mary wore a wedding band. And even if she hadn't, Andrew and his partner couldn't have been a less fitting match. Mary, slim and no-nonsense, her jeans creased down the front of the legs. As if she'd ironed them.

And then there was Andrew.

Letty had only realized later — the second or third time she caught Mary watching her, face tight with skepticism — it was something else. Mary didn't trust her.

At least Letty had convinced them to let her head back to the Inn alone. She needed the break. Letty popped the Subaru's trunk, gathered her things, and stuffed them into her backpack.

Here goes nothing.

She tossed the bag over her shoulder and set out into the woods.

■   ■   ■

Andrew tapped his phone against the couch cushion. Something about Letty's text seemed off, but he couldn't quite put his finger on what.

"That her?" Mary sat on his living room floor, surrounded by neat stacks of paper, discarded binder clips, and a laptop.

"Yeah, she's at the inn."

Mary shrugged, her expression flat. "One of us can take a ride over there, if you're worried."

He was, but God knew how long it would take for them to bring Richardson in. They couldn't spend every waking minute watching over Letty until then. "Nah, I'm sure it's fine." He nodded toward Mary's laptop. "You got more on our guy?"

"Not exactly." She turned the computer around so he could see the screen. It showed the University of Georgia's website, open to the disease ecology department's page.

"You're digging into Letty?" He'd meant it as a statement, but it came out sounding like a question.

She frowned at him. "We can't just assume her version of the facts are the truth."

"Of course not." He would've been thinking the same thing if he hadn't been pretty sure he'd seen the BMW himself. And even with that, it made sense to confirm the rest of what Letty had told them. "What did you find?"

Mary navigated through the website to a page showing five or six small headshots, each with a bio beside it. The second photo was of Letty. Mary looked up at him. "We think of animal research as what happens in a facility, like the one that burned here. But if you really look at the work Letty's doing, it kind of sounds like the same thing." Mary clicked again, this time on one of the links next to Letty's picture. "See this?"

The print was too small for him to see anything except for what looked like a bunch of mathematical tables. If he squinted, he could make out the title, "Methods for Determining Pathogen Virulence in Field Mice."

Whatever that means.

Mary scrolled down. "It's still animal research. They're just doing it outdoors... Which means the same folks who burned down the research facility might take issue with your new friend."

He rubbed a hand across his chin, stubble prickling his fingers. "That all tracks. But, as far as I know, there's never been any local activity by these animal rights militia guys before. Assuming it's them. What're the chances of them conducting two separate operations here, at the same time?"

She shrugged. "Maybe they're not separate."

He gave a short nod. That seemed more likely. "Except Letty isn't a local. How would they have known she'd be here? She said the BMW showed up for the first time at her hotel. Which means Richardson didn't just know she was in Chattanooga. He knew where she was staying."

"Could've followed her there from somewhere else. The bigger question I see is why her? Why not the rest of her department? Why not the professor in charge of it?" She used the cursor to circle the first of the photos on the webpage. An old hippie looking dude with a scraggly ponytail and a lop-sided smile.

He let Mary's questions roll around his brain. "You're saying it might be about her work specifically. Maybe a project she's done independent from the group?"

She nodded. "It's a thought."

"Which is why you're digging into Letty's work."

"Bingo." She snapped the laptop closed and reached for her bag.

Andrew checked his watch. "Doesn't the sitter usually stay 'til nine?"

"I want to make sure I get to see Kaylie before she heads to bed." Mary slipped a pile of paper into the battered messenger bag, then edged her laptop into what little room there was left.

Andrew shifted on the couch. "She okay?"

"Just a little under the weather. At first I thought she was trying to get out of a math quiz." Mary closed the bag and fastened its clip. "But she had a low-grade fever when I left this morning, so it's something."

He hated when the kids got sick. "You sure you're okay to grab Letty tomorrow? I can go if you think Kaylie'll be home from school."

She smiled at him. "Kaylie will be fine. I can always run her over to her grandma's on the way. And it's just a bug. You know kids, they get everything. And besides, I've gotta go get Letty either way." Mary stood, pulling the bag onto her shoulder. "Unless you're gonna take her in to give a statement."

Andrew blinked at his friend. "When you said you'd pick her up, I just assumed you meant you'd bring her here or—"

"Shut up." Mary adjusted the bag, lifting the strap over her head so that she wore it cross-body. "You know I've got your back."

He did, and he'd always have hers, but it wasn't something he took for granted. Especially when taking Letty in to make a statement meant Mary would be officially in the middle of whatever this was. Mary went on before he could say so. "Besides, once Letty makes an official statement about Richardson, this'll go from me tracking down a witness to a full APB on a person of interest in a murder case." She strode out, her words floating in as the door closed behind her. "It'll be over before it starts."

■ ■ ■

Letty stopped near the tree line and swung her backpack to the ground. This was the part she liked best. Outside, on her own, her mind alive with the need to know what things meant or how they worked. It was the same fascination with the natural world she'd had since she was a little girl with a butterfly net.

She felt around in the backpack until she found what she needed — a thick, brick-shaped device with a small nub on one end. She pulled the bat detector free. Letty had borrowed it from the lab, and the detector was a good one. Self-scanning, digital display, capable of recording results in the field. Top-of-the-line. Letty clicked it on, tuned to forty-five kilohertz, and rubbed her fingers together in front of the mic. The friction came through, loud and clear.

We're in business.

Letty lay the device in the leaves and peered back into the bag. What else would she need? The moon had risen full and bright, giving her more than enough light to see, so she could do without the flashlight. Which was good. Her chance of actually finding bats depended on her not scaring them away. And she didn't intend to go so deep into the park that she'd need the map. Just a quick trip over to the area where they'd found the sick animal, see if she got any hits with the detector, and back out again. Easy peasy.

Not that Andrew or Mary were likely to see it that way.

Letty cringed. Under any other circumstances, she wouldn't either. Not with Richardson lurking around. But if the bat they'd found had rabies, there was a decent chance others in its colony did, too. And that meant she didn't have time to go convince Andrew and Mary to let her do a second canvas of the park. God knew how long that conversation would take — or if convincing them was even possible. And, in the end, it didn't matter.

She didn't need their permission. And any amount of time spent trying to get it would be more time than she had. If there were other sick bats, they would die soon. Or be dead already. The samples degrading. Her chance of finding the outbreak's source fading.

Or worse. Those bats could be spreading the disease to other people.

Even knowing that, she almost hadn't come. She'd watched the road behind her the whole way there, checking the mirror at every turn and a dozen times in between. But there'd been no BMW. Nothing out of the ordinary. And the closer she got to Signal Mountain, the better the plan seemed.

Letty zipped the backpack closed. If she didn't find anything, she'd be back in her room at the Inn in a few hours, and Andrew would never have to know.

She continued into the near-darkness under the trees' canopy, sweeping the device left to right. Hoping for the cartoonish ping, ping, ping of a bat's high-frequency call.

The device stayed silent. The world quiet except for her soft footfalls and the night song of the forest. Branches swished in the wind. A frog croaked out for a mate, and a Great-horned owl called out its distinctive "hoo-hoo-hoo."

Letty passed the tree where she'd met up with Andrew, moving through the forest with comfort. One of the few advantages to spending so many years of her childhood in a tent. She panned the detector side to side.

Part of her worried what would happen if she did find something. Andrew would be pissed if he found out what she'd done. And Mary would trust her even less.

If that was possible.

Even though it'd been Mary's idea.

Sort of.

It would never have occurred to Letty to come back to the park to try again. Not with Richardson on the loose. And not when she'd already succeeded once and been shut down by the health department. There was no purpose in catching a bat she couldn't test. She'd known that, and she'd basically come to terms with the fact that any further search of the park would be a dead end.

But then Mary had drilled her with questions about her research with the university — what they studied, what they did in the field, how they did it...

And, just like that, it'd hit her. She didn't need anyone else to do the testing.

She could do it herself.

Letty slowed as she rounded a thick copse of trees, and the cinderblock outbuilding housing the park's restrooms appeared. Squat, dark, and marred with spray paint. Everything just as she remembered it. She scanned the ground where they'd found the sick bat. Nothing but weeds and brush. But, if she was going to find the bat's roost, find the others that might be infected, the forest nearby was the most likely spot.

She panned the detector again. Left, right. Left—

A series of rapid, irregular ping, ping, pings erupted from the bat detector. Like tiny popping bubbles. Too many for her to pick up a pattern, so she couldn't be sure of the species. But, if she had to guess, they were the same type of brown bats as the one she and Andrew had found.

I knew it.

She swept the detector over the area again, pausing when the pings grew more frequent. There must be dozens of bats flying above her. She struggled to spot them, trying to catch a silhouette against the light of the moon. Searching for darker spots in the trees.

She scanned back and forth, looking over the outbuilding.

The outbuilding.

That's why she hadn't spotted the roost. She'd bet anything they were holed up in the building. Probably somewhere in the roof or the rafters. She'd been so caught up with handling the sick bat when they'd found it. She hadn't even thought to check—

A branch cracked behind her.

Letty froze, listening. And another burst of pings came from the detector.

Shit.

Letty clicked it off and slipped it into her backpack, easing the zipper closed.

A rustle in the bushes, coming from the same direction as the first noise. Something big moving through the forest. Letty's throat tightened as she tried to tell how close it was.

What the fuck is that?

She wasn't sticking around to find out. Letty moved as fast as she could without making noise. Watching every footfall to make sure she didn't step on anything that might give away her position.

Another sound, closer this time. The snap of a twig?

The cock of a gun?

Her breathing went shallow and her skin cold.

A light flashed on a few dozen yards away, the beam broken by branches and brush. Then a man's voice. "Stop!"

Like hell I will.

Letty broke into a run, noise be damned. The backpack, heavy with her gear, slamming into her back with every step. She leapt over branches and logs, barreling through the underbrush. Each obstacle becoming visible only an instant before she had to react. She raced full tilt through the forest. Back toward her car.

The man called out again. "Hey!"

She cut left, through a denser section of the woods. Maybe she'd be harder to see. She changed direction again, and a pine branch smacked her in the face. The bristles clawing their way across her cheek. Not enough to slow her down but enough to sting.

Please God let me be going toward the car.

She knew how to find her bearings at night, but she couldn't see the stars through the tree limbs above her. The ground had no incline. And she was moving too fast to get a feel for any landmarks. It all flew by in a blur.

She strained to hear if the man followed, but adrenaline roared in her ears. Any sound of her pursuer drowned out by the thundering crash as she plowed through limbs and brush. What if she was running deeper into the woods instead of back toward the parking lot?

Tears of panic burned behind her eyes. She looked back again.

The beam of his flashlight bounced through the trees. Up, down. Up, down. The rhythm steady. Relentless. He was getting closer, and he wasn't slowing.

Letty stumbled but didn't fall. She forced herself to keep her eyes forward. Her breath came in jagged bursts and her lungs burned with the effort, which didn't make any sense. She hadn't gone that far into the park. Had she doubled-back on herself, running in circles? Back toward him. Another branch grabbed at her, catching in her hair.

She kept going anyway. The limb yanking strands of her hair out by the root.

Letty hardly felt it.

A huge silhouette loomed in the distance.

The pirate ship-shaped play structure that sat just beyond where she'd parked.

Thank God.

A burst of hope powered her sprint to the car. She fumbled with her keys, forced her hands steady, and jammed the key into the lock.

Turn, damnit.

She looked up, checking to see how close he was.

The flashlight beam pointed at her. Blinding her to whoever might be behind it. But the man didn't come closer. He waited at the edge of the woods.

Watching.

CHAPTER 23

May 10, 2018

"I really am sorry." Letty held the police precinct door for Mary, who followed her out onto the ancient building's front steps. "I know it was a stupid thing to do, but I thought I was being careful. I must have checked a hundred times, and I could've sworn there was no one following me."

Mary stopped half-way down the stairs. "Stupid doesn't quite cover it." She looked at Letty a long minute before she went on. "But I get it. You did what you thought you had to. However idiotic it might have been." She started back toward the street, talking over her shoulder. "Just so you know, you did good in there. You'd be amazed how many witnesses can't remember anything. Or if they do, it's a jumbled mess of what they might have seen or thought they did." Mary shrugged. "Now that the wheels are in motion, it won't be long before we've got Richardson in custody." She stopped in the shade of a giant candy-pink crepe myrtle.

Letty joined her under the tree. At half-past ten, the temperature was already over eighty. The sun beat down from a cloudless sky, and even the spotty cover the crepe myrtle offered was a welcome relief.

Mary pulled a pair of sunglasses from her bag. "Although next time you decide to play tag in the woods, a call first would be nice."

Letty grimaced. She'd told Mary everything, except what she planned to do next. "About that…"

Mary raised an eyebrow.

"I— " Letty stopped.

Pete's Suburban pulled into a parallel parking spot just past the police station.

What's he doing here?

Pete leaned out of the front window. "Everything okay?" He glanced up at the precinct and back to her. "Did something happen?"

She turned to Mary. "I'll just be a minute."

Mary nodded, slipped on the sunglasses, and stared in the direction of Pete's truck. Probably memorizing the plate.

Pete popped open the door and climbed out. His khakis were creased from where he'd been sitting, but otherwise he looked like he'd stepped out of an issue of Southern Living. Same as always. He'd left the engine running, and the door alarm dinging in the background. "So sorry I didn't get back to you yesterday. Things are still crazy with work and, you know... everything. What's going on?"

Letty wasn't even sure where to start. She gave him the thumbnail sketch — the man following her, the accident, her identification of Richardson. "I just gave my statement to the police, and I've basically got a full time escort." She tilted her head back to Mary. Who, judging by the scowl, could hear what they were saying. "So, I think everything'll be fine now."

"Jesus, Letty." He touched her face, probably inspecting the scrape she'd gotten from going toe-to-toe with a pine branch and pulled her into a hug. This time he didn't leave any distance, and he didn't let go. "I'm so glad you're okay."

Letty breathed in the scent of his skin — Irish Spring soap and a hint of sweat. She let herself relax, wrapping her arms around him, and holding on tight. "It's really good to see you."

When he finally stepped back, a smile pulled at the edges of his mouth. "It's really good to see you, too."

"We should go," Mary called from the sidewalk.

Letty's face got warm. All it had taken was the press of Pete's body against hers to make her forget she had a chaperone.

"I need to run, too. I was just coming back from a consult in Nashville when I spotted you. Should get back to the clinic before Trish kills me." He trailed a hand down her arm as he let go. "Call you later?"

She nodded and followed him the few steps back to his car.

A bouquet sat on the passenger seat. Lilies and daisies and baby's breath. The whole thing wrapped in cellophane. The kind of thing a man might pick up at a grocery store on his way to a first date.

If he noticed that she'd seen the flowers, he didn't let on. "Bye now."

She returned his wave, a knot of uncertainty in her belly, as he pulled away from the curb.

He might have picked up the flowers as a mea culpa to Trish. Or for a sick grandmother. She watched his truck disappear around the corner.

Or Sue Ellen.

■   ■   ■

Andrew walked with Letty around the backside of an enormous RV. The monstrosity was bright red, despite the road dust, with an image of a six-foot tall bulldog in a spiked collar and the University of Georgia logo painted on each side.

Subtle.

Andrew squinted into the sun and rubbed the top of his head, wishing he'd remembered either sunscreen or a hat. "I can't believe you got Mary to agree to this."

Or that he had. He picked at the edge of the band-aid covering the spot where he'd gotten his third shot of the vaccine.

"I don't think she would've if you hadn't been able to come with me." Letty came even with the RV's door, and Andrew scowled at her back. Four years on patrol and countless hours of grunt-work to make detective, only to wind up babysitting while Mary was off doing actual police work.

The RV's door swung open, and two men climbed out — the old hippie Andrew had seen in the picture on Letty's website and a younger man with a sad face and shaggy white-blonde hair. Both stretched, as if they'd sitting for a long ride, then hugged Letty.

Letty kept an arm around the older one, still smiling. "Chris, Bill." She nodded toward the younger and older man, respectively. "This is Andrew. The detective I told you about. Andrew's gonna ride shotgun with us to make sure we don't have any more unwelcome visitors."

Bill came forward, hand extended. "Glad you're here. Nice to meet you, Detective."

"Just Andrew's fine. I'm off-duty." Which was close to true. And off-duty sounded better than on leave. He shook Bill's hand, surprised to find Bill's grip strong and his palm dry. In person, Bill looked more like Jimmy Buffett than the fruity yoga-and-incense type Andrew had expected.

The one she'd called Chris hung back but lifted his head in greeting. "Hey, man."

Letty started toward the park. "You guys ready to see what you're here for?"

They followed her over the grassy area toward the woods. Bill and Chris walked with Letty, and Andrew pulled up the rear. Letty glanced at Chris every now and then, concern on her face. But Andrew couldn't tell why. Letty talked as they went, explaining how they'd found the sick bat and her problems with the health department. Bill asked few questions, steering the conversation back to her run-in with the man in the park the night before.

When she'd said she was safe at the Inn.

Annoyance took root in his gut, even though she'd already apologized, and he'd already more or less forgiven her. Andrew rolled his neck. He wasn't upset with Letty, not really. He was mad at himself. He'd known something felt off and let her go back to the Inn alone anyway. It wasn't a mistake he would make again.

The building that housed the park's restrooms came into view, doors open at either end, graffiti tags across the front.

Letty sped up, pointing to a dirty spot where the building's eave met cinderblock. "See here." She stepped closer. "And here." She pointed higher, to another dingy spot near the roof's peak.

Andrew went for a closer inspection. "Just looks like some smudges on the paint."

She shook her head. "It's the bats' body oils. They rub off when the animals go in and out." She pulled on a glove and shoved her thumb in a crevice between the wall and the roof. "And look, plenty of room for them to fit."

Bill came to stand beside her. "Got some guano here, too." He motioned to a few small, dark spots, just under the peak of the roof.

Letty shook her head. "I really don't know how I missed it the first time around. When we found the sick bat, I was just so focused on getting it in to be tested. Trying to get it there before it died or at least as soon as we could after that." She stared off into the trees.

Bill took a few steps back, as if to get a better perspective, and peered up at the slightly darker spot near the roof's peak. "Any of us would've done the same. If you think you've got a potentially rabid animal, you deal with it right then. Do the rest of your due diligence later." He turned, looking down his nose at her. "Although, preferably not by yourself, without telling anyone. When you know someone's following you."

Andrew joined Bill in giving her the stink eye.

Letty closed her eyes. "I know, I— "

"Ah, shit." Chris piped up from behind them.

They all turned to look, but Chris stared at his phone. "Exclusion season ended a week ago."

"What?" Andrew waited for him to explain.

Letty got there first. "It's a time set by the state. A limit on when you can remove bats from a roost. They restrict it to avoid the months when the bats are forming their maternity colonies during the summer."

Andrew's confusion must've shown on his face, because she kept talking. "You know, when the bats have pups, they cut off exclusions. Usually sometime in May to sometime in August."

"Started May first." Chris looked up from the phone. "We're screwed."

"Shit, I assumed it was the same as in Georgia." Letty frowned. "But either way, we're only a week outside of season. That shouldn't be a deal-breaker."

"Don't shoot the messenger." Chris raised his hands, palms out. "All I'm saying is, if we do it, it wouldn't be a legal exclusion. And you know as well as I do, if we start this, and we get shut down before the full four days pass, we won't know if—"

"Right, right." She interrupted. "But under the circumstances, it—"

Andrew half-listened to the two of them argue. He found a fallen log and sat, arms crossed over his chest. He should be out looking for Richardson. Or doing any sort of actual police work. This had been his year to go up for a position in the major crimes division. And instead, he was here, listening to two dorks debate bat babies.

"But the one we found was male!" Letty threw up her hands. "We wouldn't find a male bat outside a maternity—"

Bill tromped his way back into the clearing with a thick roll of black mesh sheeting under one arm, a small ladder under the other, and a staple gun in his hand. Andrew hadn't even realized he was gone.

Bill carried his supplies to the outbuilding, pulled a tube of caulk from his back pocket, and tossed it to the dirt by his feet. "Chris, come give me a hand."

The younger man hesitated but went to join Bill. "Are you sure?"

"Look, if we wait, we risk the further spread of infection, maybe we miss our chance to track down the source. This is one of those situations where we ask for permission after-the-fact." He held the mesh up to the soffit and spoke to Chris. "Hold this here."

Chris replaced Bill's hand with his, and Bill stapled the mesh to the wooden overhang.

Bill spoke between the loud bam, bam, bam as he fired staples to hold it in place. "Letty, you've got a friend in the mayor's office, right?"

Bam.

Andrew let out a low whistle. Friend wasn't exactly the word he'd have used.

She glanced over at him before she answered. "Yeah, but— "

Bam. Bam.

Bill spoke without turning. "Good. Go get us permission."

CHAPTER 24

May 11, 2018

Letty followed Caroline into a cubicle-sized office in the bowels of City Hall that smelled like old coffee left in the pot too long. Caroline's desk held a silver-framed photo of herself, a fern, somehow lush despite the room's lack of a window, and nothing else. Not even a laptop. The only sign indicating that actual work might take place there hung on the back wall. An oversized cork board bore a few maps and notices mixed with decorative inspirational quotes: "Your only limit is you" and "#Blessed."

Ick.

Caroline slid behind the desk and waved toward one of the two chairs wedged between the far side of the desk and the wall. "Have a seat."

Letty took her time getting settled, still wrapping her head around the coming conversation. Ass-kissing had never been her forte. But then, it wasn't like she had a choice. "Thanks for meeting me."

"Of course." Caroline eyed her from under mascara-thick lashes. She leaned back in the desk chair, playing with a charm on her necklace. A filigreed monogram that glinted a cold silver in the office's florescent lighting. "Although, I have to say, after the way our last conversation ended, I was surprised to hear from you."

"I know hanging up on you wasn't the most mature thing to do." Letty forced what she hoped looked like sincerity onto her face. "I was upset."

Caroline raised a pencil-thin eyebrow. "Obviously."

Letty sighed. Why bother trying to look like a supplicant? With Caroline, blunt was almost always best. "Buy you a round tonight? Make up for it?"

Caroline waved her off. "I'm on a juice cleanse. But I guess you're forgiven." She shook her head, face softening. "So, what's with the cop in the lobby?"

Letty blinked. "What?"

"The guy you're with. It took me a minute, but then I recognized him. From the news." Caroline toyed with the necklace. "He's kinda cute, in a blue-collar sort of way. And it's not like you gotta take 'em all home to mom, am I right?"

Caroline grinned, and Letty suppressed a wave of annoyance. Caroline talking about Andrew rubbed her the wrong way. Big time. "He's just a friend." Who was doing her a favor that would probably get him in trouble with his boss. He hadn't said so, but she couldn't imagine being her bodyguard was what "on leave" was supposed to mean.

"Hmm." Caroline swiveled her desk chair back and forth. "And what about the other one?"

Letty cleared her throat, afraid she knew the answer before she asked the question. "What other one?"

Caroline smiled, like a shark scenting blood in the water. "A little birdie told me you've been going out with Pete Hendrick. I mean, damn girl, you've only been here a few days, and you're getting more action than I have in a month."

Letty suppressed the curse that sprang to her lips, focusing instead on picking non-existent lint from her skirt.

Small towns are the worst.

She crossed her arms over her chest. "It's not what—"

"He's a nice catch. His father's family owns half of Charleston." Caroline's smile widened. "But you know he's still married, right?"

Letty gripped the edge of her seat, her face growing hot. Pete's divorce, whatever was going on between them, was none of

Caroline's business. None of anyone's business. And Letty wasn't going to add fuel to the gossip fire by telling Caroline anything more than she already knew.

How were we ever friends?

Probably because they'd never hung out sober. Not in college and not since. Letty gave herself a second before answering. "It isn't like that."

Caroline shrugged, as if she'd had her fun. "If you say so." She ran a hand over her hair, smoothing icy blonde strands that weren't out of place. "Anyway, I'm sure you didn't come see me to talk about Pete and Sue Ellen. What do you need?"

Letty struggled to get her mind back on track. She'd planned to come in, smooth things over, and ask for help. But now...

She'd just as soon kick Caroline in the shin as ask for a favor.

Except the alternative was going back to Bill with empty hands. Or worse, the city telling them all to pack up and go home. Letty closed her eyes. There was no helping it. "The health department declined to test the sick bat I found in Signal Mountain Park."

"I'm aware of that."

Son of a bitch.

Of course you are.

Letty clenched her jaw, the room suddenly stuffy. Did Caroline know because the health department kept the mayor informed? Or because the mayor's office had something to do with the refusal?

The likelihood that the mayor had influenced the health department's decision was slim. The department was autonomous, a state agency not controlled by the mayor. And refusals weren't uncommon, especially when the animal hadn't bitten anyone.

But still.

Her gut said otherwise. If the mayor wanted the issue closed, he'd know how to do it. Politics in the South had always been that way. Letty leaned forward, elbows on the desk, close enough to Caroline to smell her expensive lavender shampoo.

Letty bit her tongue before she said something she couldn't cure with a round of beer.

Suck it up.

You've got a job to do.

Letty settled back in the chair. "I found what I believe is the sick bat's colony. My team from UGA is here with the department's mobile lab. And we're prepared to test the rest of the bats we find on site. The results will tell us if we've found a possible source of the rabies infections suffered by Mr. Bullard and Ms. Canning. It may be the only lead we're going to find and we need to be able to set up an exclusion so we can—"

Caroline frowned. "Why bring this to me?"

"The blackout period for exclusions began May first." Letty rushed to get the rest out before Caroline could stop her again. If they had any hope of tracing the source of the outbreak, of preventing the further spread, they had to be allowed to test the rest of the bats. "We have no reason to believe the colony is a maternity colony, and we're barely into the—"

Caroline raised a hand, but she didn't look like someone savoring the power of saying no. "You're here because you can't legally do whatever this thing is you want to do."

Letty nodded. Maybe she was wrong about what'd happened with the testing. Maybe this would work. She could do something important. "I was hoping the mayor might be willing to grant us a waiver. I know it's a little outside his usual scope, but if ever it was warranted, this is the time."

Caroline shook her head.

"What does that mean?" Letty's chest grew tight. "You're saying you won't help?" She had expected as much when she'd come there, but the answer still stung.

Except Caroline wasn't gloating. If anything, she looked uncomfortable, and she'd stopped toying with the necklace. Caroline lowered her voice and glanced out the office door. "It's not up to me. I'm happy to ask. I'll even plead your case for you.

But you should know, as far as Rafferty's concerned, this outbreak was over when Randy Bullard died."

■ ■ ■

Andrew adjusted the A/C vent, aiming as much of the refrigerated air toward his face as possible. Rafferty had always struck Andrew as the typical glad-handing type — his every public word about God, guns, or tradition. Even though everyone knew the man had a standing Sunday morning tee time. But what Letty'd told him of her meeting with Caroline made Rafferty sound like he was something worse. Andrew glanced over at her.

She sat in the passenger seat, cardigan wrapped tight around her like she'd gotten caught in an unexpected winter storm.

He turned the air back down as they pulled in next to the RV. "What're you gonna tell Bill?"

She shrugged. "Nothing to tell right now. We asked for permission, and we're waiting to see if we get it. Until we know otherwise, we assume we will and keep working." She un-clicked her seatbelt. "Besides, it's Friday afternoon. What're the chances Caroline connects with the mayor before Monday? By then, we'll be done, and it won't matter if he says no."

"What if the bats don't come out?" He cut the engine.

"They will. They have to eat. We started yesterday, which means we only need the weekend to finish. And it's possible we'll have an answer before that. We had at least a dozen bats captured overnight. Enough to be absolutely certain this was no maternity colony. And any one of them may be our positive."

"What if the mayor calls in an hour and says no?"

"Let's hope we don't have to find out." She climbed out of the car and leaned down, looking back at him. "You coming?"

"I think I'll wait out here. Not a fan of bats." He grimaced. "Even dead ones."

He waited until Letty climbed into the RV, then dialed Mary's number.

She answered on the first ring. "You got my message?"

"Yeah." Although he wished he hadn't. It had given him instant indigestion. "Did Phil say anything else?"

"That was it. Just that he heard Internal Affairs finally had their sit-down with the girl that got the video of the moments leading up to the shooting. And a few hours after, they sent a bunch of materials to the DA."

The back of his throat burned. "And what do you make of that?"

Her answer came a little too slowly. "Could be nothing. IA's probably just following procedure. You know what they're like."

Right.

It might be easier if he didn't know what they were like. Andrew dug through the glove box until he found Renee's cigarettes, a soft-pack with a few slightly mangled smokes and a lighter inside.

Who the hell buys menthols?

He lit one anyway and cracked the window. "Any news on Richardson?"

"No, but it's early yet. Just got the APB in place yesterday. Found a little more on Matthew Wilkes, though. Atlanta PD went through his apartment. The girlfriend seems to have cleared out. No sign of her, none of her clothes in the closet. But they found a laptop. They're supposed to be sending us a copy of the hard drive."

"You gonna try and track the girlfriend down?"

"I'd like to talk to her, sure. But right now, it's not a priority. She's alibied. On the west coast when Wilkes died. No evidence she was involved in anything he might've been doing. And she left Wilkes's computer behind."

"Which doesn't seem like something you'd do if you were covering tracks." He took a deep draw on the cigarette. "Unless she knows there's nothing on it."

"Are you smoking?"

"No."

"Uh-huh. I thought you quit."

"I did... mostly." Knowing the DA was gathering evidence against him might change that. He'd take his comfort where he could find it. "Fifty bucks says the hard drive's nothing but porn."

"Wouldn't be the first time. But I doubt it. We know this guy was active online. Mainstream social media and a bunch of wacko animal rights blogs. If he's got a connection to Richardson or to Letty Duquesne, that's where we're most likely to find it."

"My money's on porn."

He'd been joking, mostly. But Mary's tone wasn't. "I know she's your friend. And you want to give her the benefit of the doubt. But Richardson isn't following her for nothing. She either has something he wants or knows something she isn't saying."

CHAPTER 25

Letty stepped out of the RV, arms stretched high overhead. Her back ached from hours sitting hunched over a worktable and her hair clung damp to her neck. The lab had grown stuffy in the afternoon heat, and she was glad for the break. Especially given Bill's mood.

She crossed the short distance from the RV to the picnic area and found Chris sitting cross-legged on top of a weathered table. Grocery bags scattered around him, spilling out a mess of cookies, hot dog buns, and condiments. On the opposite side of a wooded clearing, Andrew loaded charcoal into a grill.

"I see you've been making yourself useful." She waved a hand toward the groceries and dug two SweetWaters from a cooler sitting in the table's shadow, the beer ice cold and dripping. "Bill kick you out, too?"

Chris nodded, taking his drink. "Probably right before you got here. Apparently, I hover."

She opened her beer and snorted a laugh. "You totally do."

He scowled but lifted the SweetWater, clinking it against hers. "How's it looking in there now?"

"Only got two of the bats we pulled in last night left to go." She tore open a pack of Oreos and snagged a cookie. "Or at least, that's where we were when he kicked me out."

"Hovering?"

"He says I talk too much."

Chris raised his eyebrows and grinned.

"Shut up." She smacked his arm, moved one of the grocery bags out of the way, and sat beside him. Letty washed another cookie down with beer, which was surprisingly not terrible. "Uh oh." She nodded toward the grill, where Andrew squirted half a bottle of lighter fluid onto the charcoal.

They were too far away to be in actual danger, but she and Chris both leaned back as Andrew struck a match.

Fire shot skyward, and Andrew hooted with joy.

Men.

He tended the fire while she and Chris did the same for their drinks. Comfortable in only the way you can be with someone who knows you well. For the first time since he'd arrived, Chris seemed like his old self, laughing and joking, telling her the same stories she'd heard a dozen times before.

He looked down at his watch, lips moving without speaking out loud. No doubt counting cricket chirps so he could do his favorite parlor trick.

Letty rolled her eyes but waited until he'd had time to do the math in his head. "What'd you get?"

"Forty-four chirps in fifteen seconds, add thirty-seven." He smiled. "Crickets say it's eighty-one degrees out."

"You know your phone'll tell you the weather. It's easier and more accurate."

"Way less fun though." He popped the top on another beer.

Letty leaned back on her elbows. He was right, his way was more fun. The smokey sizzle of hot dogs on the grill, the sky going purple as dusk fell, the heat of the day finally subsiding into something that still felt like spring. Being there, safe with friends, doing what needed to be done — it was all so good. She almost didn't want to ask the question she'd been holding since he arrived.

But she had to. "Have you talked to Priya?"

His face tightened. "No." He picked at the edge of the label on his bottle, one small tear after another. "Between the doctors and her parents, it's like there's a brick wall built around her. The only information I can get comes through Bill. And there's no way for me to get there to see her in person. The damn flight costs two grand. Forget whatever I'd need for a hotel. Or a car to get around. And, oh yeah, I don't speak Khmer." He tore at the label again.

Letty put down her beer. She'd been so focused on what was going on in Chattanooga, she hadn't even considered Chris's situation. Not really, not enough to realize there was something she could do about it. Shame colored her cheeks. "I can get you a ticket. I have the money in savings. I'm sorry I didn't think of it before." She leaned forward, putting a hand over his where it rested on the table between them. "I'm such an asshole."

He squeezed her fingers. "You're not an asshole. And I love that you offered to do that for me, but I can't let you."

No way was she going to let his pride stand in the way of getting him there. Or let it stop her from helping Priya find some comfort. "Of course you can. I would've offered earlier if I'd thought—"

He squeezed her hand again and let go. "There's no point in me going to Cambodia."

Letty swallowed hard. That didn't make any sense. Not unless he knew something she didn't. She searched his face, the beer turning sour in her stomach. "Why not?"

Chris's eyes widened. "No, no. Nothing like that. I just meant she wouldn't want me to. Even if I had the money, I can't go with Priya's parents there. The last thing she needs, on top of everything else, is the drama me showing up would cause. You know what they're like."

Letty collapsed into herself. "Oh, thank God." She glanced up. "Sorry, that came out wrong. The part about her parents sucks. But for a second, I thought you were saying Priya really did have a super bug."

"Actually…" He smiled. "Bill says he's pretty sure it isn't one."

She held her breath. "What do you mean?"

"According to the professor she's working with there, Priya day-tripped into an area outside Phnom Penh that wasn't on her schedule. Which means she might have come into contact with a parasite carrying a malaria strain she wouldn't have been vaccinated against. Bill says that's the current theory, anyway. It's just a matter of finding the right therapy. And now that the doctors know where she went, they know what strains to target."

"Oh, thank God."

"I know. I had the same reaction. Well, that and to be pissed off Priya didn't check to make sure she had the meds she'd need before she went." He ripped the rest of the label from his beer. "I mean, this is what we do every day. Other people might not understand how dangerous the natural world can be. That it's getting worse every day. But she knew better." He crumpled the label into a ball in his fist. "And she went anyway, unprepared, not thinking what it could mean…"

What it could mean to him.

That's what he'd meant. She leaned forward until she caught Chris's gaze. "We all do stupid shit sometimes. But what matters is that it sounds like Priya's gonna be okay."

It was by no means certain. But as she said the words, Letty believed them.

He raised his now-naked beer bottle in her direction. "Here's to that."

"You guys want dogs?" Andrew carried over a paper plate mounded with half-singed sausages. A look of pride on his face.

"Definitely." Bill appeared in the growing darkness, coming from the direction of the RV.

"There he is." Chris hopped down from the table. "Any positives?"

Bill shook his head.

Letty helped Chris clear grocery bags off the table. They had plenty of time left to find what they needed. "We'll test the next batch tomorrow." She opened a beer for Bill.

"Sorry I bit your head off earlier." He offered an apologetic smile as he settled in at the table next to Chris.

"It's okay." She dumped a bunch of chips on her plate and passed the bag down the table. "We all know how you get when you don't eat."

"What?" Bill looked to her, then Chris, eyebrows raised.

Chris talked past a mouthful. "Why do you think I kept..." He huffed past a still-too-hot sausage. "Offering you protein bars?"

Bill scowled, but his eyes sparkled with good humor. "I'm old. I'm meant to be crotchety."

They worked their way through the mountain of hot dogs. Andrew with a smear of ketchup on his face and a dedication that would've been admirable if it hadn't been disgusting. He'd only just met the other men, but he didn't seem like an outsider. He laughed and teased and goaded Chris into a third hot dog she was sure he'd regret. But after all the fear and worry and stress of the last few days, this normal, silly moment felt wonderful.

A text dinged its arrival as she pushed her plate away, and Letty dug out her phone.

A message from Pete. "Can I see you tomorrow?"

There were lots of reasons why she shouldn't. She was leaving soon. He was still married. The flowers. The gossip. Richardson. But in that moment, none of it seemed enough of a reason not to see him. She texted a quick response. "I'd love that."

CHAPTER 26

May 12, 2018
Daylight faded, leaving a golden glow above the mountain peaks outside Letty's hotel window. She pulled the curtains into place. Another day gone.

She peeled off the clothes she'd worn in the mobile lab all day, ran a washcloth under the bathroom tap, and scrubbed her armpits. She'd showered before Andrew picked her up that morning, but after a third hot day in the park, she'd left the RV clammy and tired.

With no positive test results.

Again.

Should she have surveyed the rest of the park again? Was she too quick to focus on the colony they'd found in the outbuilding? Or maybe she was looking in the right place but had just gotten there too late.

Shake it off.

It was too early to jump to any conclusions. If there were sick bats in the colony, it made sense they might be the last to leave the roost. And she didn't have time to dwell on work anyway. Not with Pete waiting downstairs.

An alfresco dinner in the Inn's lobby wouldn't have been her first choice. But it'd been the best compromise she could find with Andrew — if she didn't leave the Inn, he wouldn't ride shotgun on her date.

And Pete had volunteered to bring takeout from what he said was the best Italian spot in the city. The least she could do was not look like she'd come straight from wrestling bats.

She rifled through her suitcase.

Shit.

She didn't have a single decent bra. She'd be out of underwear come Monday, and the clean clothes she had left looked more hand-me-down than dinner date.

Double shit.

Letty sniffed the jeans she'd worn the day Bill arrived.

They'd do.

She tossed them on with her only pair of heels and a tank top she didn't remember packing. A pair of gold hoop earrings, a swipe of mascara, and she was as ready as she was going to be. She checked the mirror anyway, combing her fingers through her hair, trying to coax the dark waves into something that looked intentional. It'd been a year since she actually cared what a man thought about how she looked.

Letty flinched. Thinking about the past wouldn't lead anywhere she wanted to go. She checked twice to make sure the door was locked and hurried downstairs.

Pete waited by the mostly empty happy hour table. The hors d'oeuvres were well picked over, as they usually were by half-past eight. Pete held an over-laden bag with 'Vito's' printed on the side. His hair was shower-damp, and he seemed to have dressed up for her — dark jeans, button down shirt, and a blazer.

Who needs dinner?

"Hi." Letty's heels sunk into the thick carpet as she crossed the room. She lifted onto her toes to kiss his cheek. "Sorry I made you wait."

He pressed a hand to the small of her back as he returned the gesture. "It was worth it."

Letty flushed, missing his hand when he pulled it away. "I know this is an odd way to have dinner together, but—"

"It's perfect." He shifted the bag to his other hand.

"Well, it's better now that you're here anyway. That looks heavy. Want to sit?" She led him to a polished mahogany table nestled into one of the Inn's bay windows. As Pete unpacked their dinner from the bag, she updated him on Priya, the lack of any news on Richardson, and finally the day's work at the lab.

Pete lifted the lids off the takeout containers. Stacks of fried eggplant with fresh basil and mozzarella. A shrimp and linguine dish, flecked with parmesan and red pepper. Meatballs bigger than her fist swimming in a rich sauce. Salad, and bread, and…

"It's enough to feed an army." She leaned over to smell the garlicky deliciousness.

He gave a short shrug. "I wasn't sure what you wanted. I didn't want to bother you while you were working to ask. And, anyway, I wanted to do something nice for you. Something to make up for how out of touch I've been."

No question he'd been distant, but it wasn't something she'd expected him to acknowledge, and she didn't see any purpose in making a thing of it. She'd known he was mid-divorce when they met. She couldn't expect him to act as if nothing was wrong. And it wasn't like she didn't have her own share of baggage. "Not at all, you're fine."

Pete looked out the window and back at her. "I know this is something I'm not supposed to talk about on a date, but I want to be honest with you." He swallowed hard. "Sue Ellen's trying to take half the clinic from me. So I either have to buy her out, which I can't do without asking my parents for the money. Or I have to sell the practice." He looked down at his hands. "Everything is a mess. And I have been trying to fix it. But…"

"I'm so sorry. I know what the clinic means to you." It'd been one of the first things he'd told her about himself the night they'd had dinner on the river. And one of the things she'd liked most about him. She could feel that he loved his work as much as she loved hers.

He nodded, but he didn't look up. "I made a mistake, and I have to live with the consequences."

Hearing him blame himself for Sue Ellen's bullshit was too much. Any guilt she'd had over the relationship disappeared. Along with any sympathy for his soon-to-be former wife. Letty might not know their situation, but Sue Ellen had been a thin step above bitchy when they'd met at the hospital. And she'd left poor Pete broken in her wake. That was enough.

She put her napkin on the table and went around to where he sat. She cupped his face in her hands, a hint of stubble scraping her palms as she lifted his chin and pressed a soft kiss to his mouth. "You deserve better."

The light came back to his eyes, his shoulders relaxing. Everything so different in that instant, it was as if she'd changed the channel on a TV.

Pete leaned down, rummaging around in the takeout bag. He pulled out a corkscrew and a bottle of wine so dark it was almost black. "Can I pour you some?"

"Definitely." She blinked at him. Maybe he'd been embarrassed by whatever impulse caused him to share so much so quickly. She turned to go back to her seat.

And locked gazes with the woman from the Inn's front desk. The receptionist was mid-way through clearing the happy hour spread and — judging by her raised eyebrows — had gotten an eyeful of what had passed between Letty and Pete.

Fuck it.

Letty turned back and planted another quick kiss on Pete's lips. The woman had already seen them. There was no reason to hide anything now. Letty gave her a tight mind-your-own-business smile as she grabbed two empty wine glasses from the happy hour table and went back to her seat.

She piled their plates with food. "Want salad?"

"Mm-hmm." He opened the wine and poured a deep purple cabernet.

"Can I ask you about something?" She held her glass by the stem, swirling the wine inside. He'd trusted her enough to open up about the divorce. There didn't seem to be any reason not to ask about the flowers. "So the other day when— "

Andrew strode into the lobby. He wore the same dirty sweatshirt he'd had on in the park all day, and a set of keys dangled from one hand. He gave a quick jerk of his head. "There you are."

Letty stopped swirling the wine. "Andrew?"

Pete turned, and the two men gave each other an awkward nod. A strange look passing over Andrew's face before he refocused on her. Recognition? Something else?

Either way, it didn't make any sense for him to be there.

Not unless...

Letty pushed back from the table. "What's going on?" She glanced out the window, but the BMW wasn't there. Just Pete's Suburban, her battered hatchback, and a handful of other cars. Nothing out of the ordinary.

Pete sat stiff in his chair, leaning toward the wall as if to put space between him and Andrew.

Andrew patted the air in a "calm down" gesture that made her want to smack him. "I was driving by, and—"

"You just happened to be driving by?" she asked, her tone bone dry.

"Not a coincidence I'm here." He crossed his arms over his chest, and his brow furrowed. "I wanted to make sure your car was in the lot. That you were actually where you said you'd be this time."

I deserve that.

Letty relaxed in her chair, but, if anything, Pete looked even less comfortable. Not that she blamed him. "So you've confirmed I'm here, now what?"

Andrew seemed to notice the spread on the table for the first time. "Is that from Vito's? God, their meatballs are good."

Letty sighed, her mind flashing to Lady and the Tramp eating spaghetti. But with a big, sloppy bulldog sitting between them, chomping meatballs. She tried again. "So you were driving by, and…"

Andrew finally tore his gaze from her dinner. "Mary called. You didn't answer your phone, so I thought I'd come tell you in person." He smiled, big enough she saw the caps on his back teeth. "Missouri state police picked Richardson up near Kansas City. We'll have him in the hot seat by morning."

CHAPTER 27

May 14, 2018

Letty waited in the shade of an old oak, its thick green canopy the only thing between her and the blazing afternoon sun. No hint of a breeze moved through the leaves or against her skin. The world so still it seemed as if time had stopped. And maybe it had. She'd expected Bill to emerge from the RV with their final test results an hour ago. She adjusted the phone against her ear. "Has Richardson said anything?"

"Nothing yet." Andrew mumbled, like he spoke past something in his mouth. "But Mary's in with him now. Won't be long." A rasp, and he sucked in a deep breath.

Must be smoking.

Andrew went on. "Still no reason to think he was working with anyone else. But until we confirm that for sure, you need to keep being careful."

"I will." The static of worry and waiting buzzed in Letty's ears. She drew a line in the dirt with the toe of her sneaker, connecting two patches of grass that'd grown high enough to go to seed.

"And I can always come back to the park if anything doesn't feel right." A long exhale. "How're things going there?"

"The same." She drew a circle in the dirt. The buzzing louder in her ears. "Just trying not to think too much about what happens if we don't find our positive." An outcome which loomed more and more likely as the minutes crept by. "I finally heard back from Caroline."

"And?"

"Rafferty says we have until nightfall to pass whatever we've found onto the health department and get out of town." The buzzing changed in pitch, the low hum now a whine. She wasn't imagining it, and it was getting closer. Letty looked around but couldn't find a source. "After that, we're officially persona non grata."

"Shit."

"Basically." She turned, searching the woods behind her. But the trees stood empty, not even a squirrel or a bird hopping branch to branch. An airplane? Letty peered out at the horizon, shielding her eyes from the sun.

The cloudless sky stretched bright blue and empty into the distance.

Except for the noise.

A swarm of bees pulsed out over the oak tree.

Letty ducked.

Even knowing they weren't dangerous, the swirling black mass triggered something instinctual. Her body on high alert, a cold sweat slicking her skin. The frenzied whine pressing down on her.

The swarm pushed further into the parking area, moving toward the RV. Thousands of bees, maybe tens of thousands, shifting together in a coordinated path. Slicing through the air.

A living, buzzing saw blade.

She swallowed hard.

"Letty?" Andrew's voice came loud through the phone.

"One second." She whispered.

"Everything okay?" His voice, still too loud, now edged with worry.

"Shhh."

The swarm pulsed one way, then the other. An angry mob. Deciding.

Andrew again. "What's going on?"

She clapped a hand over the receiver. The bees would be more attracted to the smell of her sweat than any noise. But still.

The hive veered toward the RV. Darted back toward Letty.

And disappeared over the trees.

Gone as suddenly as they'd come.

She drooped in relief, leaning back against the tree trunk, its bark scratching rough between her shoulder blades.

"Letty?"

"I'm here. I'm okay." She wiped a hand over her forehead. "It was nothing. Just some honeybees looking for a new home." She forced her voice calm. What would Jessa have said about her? Hiding from bees under a tree.

Ridiculous.

She needed to calm down.

The RV door smacked open, and Letty jumped.

Bill stood in the doorway. His shirt damp with sweat, a clipboard in one hand, his face unreadable.

"Andrew, let me call you back." She hung up, hope making her throat thick. "So?"

She knew the answer before Bill shook his head.

■ ■ ■

Letty fought the mesh, one knee on the center of the roll to hold in place while she wrangled obstinate loose ends. It'd taken her an hour to dismantle the exclusion. Longer because her borrowed work gloves were a size too big, the stiff leather not yet broken in. Her own were left forgotten somewhere at home. She'd run off to Chattanooga so half-cocked, she'd only brought about a third of the equipment she needed. She leaned back, surveying her work. At least now, the outbuilding looked just as it had when she came.

She'd made no difference at all.

"Need help with that?" Bill trudged into the clearing.

"I got it." She lifted the roll, pushed the last end into place, and tucked it under an arm. "You guys get everything stowed in the RV?"

"All set." He picked up a staple from the dirt. One she must've missed when she gathered all the others she'd removed. He tucked it in his pocket. "Do I still need to call the health department with our results?"

She shook her head. "Took care of it a few hours ago." And it had been every bit as unpleasant as she'd expected. The woman who'd been ducking her calls all week, suddenly available and saccharine sweet.

"Good, good." He folded the step-ladder and lifted it onto his shoulder. "Chris's gonna go fill the RV's tank before we hit the road. I thought maybe you and I could chat while we waited?"

"Yeah, of course." She started toward the parking area.

Bill's footsteps crunched over dead leaves as he followed behind her. "I know you think this project was a failure."

She let out a low sigh and glanced back. "Well, we killed an entire colony of bats for nothing. So I'm not calling it a win."

"It wasn't for nothing." He caught up with her, adjusting the ladder on his shoulder. "You formed a reasonable hypothesis and tested it. There's nothing wrong with that. And it's just as likely you were right as wrong."

"How d'you figure?"

"Who's to say the sick bat you found didn't have rabies? Or that it wasn't the source animal? Maybe the reason you didn't find more is just that the disease hadn't spread within the colony yet. Any of those things are possible."

Possible, maybe. But likely?

No.

She shrugged. "If you say so."

"Either way, even if your theory was wrong, I'm proud of you for trying."

"Really?" She stopped, eyebrows raised. "Because proud wasn't exactly how I read your reaction when I told you I was coming."

"You have to admit coming here was kind of a crazy thing to do." He put down the ladder, letting it lean against his hip. "But then, once you were here and I talked to you about the work, I could see why you'd come. Which is why we're here, too. But more importantly, I saw the difference in you." He held her gaze. "You're more yourself. Engaged in the work because you love it, not because you need the distraction. You're more like you were... before."

Letty winced.

Before Jessa died.

He put a hand on her arm. "I'm sorry. I know thinking about it upsets you. But I'm worried. I've been worried for a year, watching you bury yourself in work to avoid dealing with what happened. And now..." He grimaced and let go. "I just want to make sure you let yourself be happy in whatever you decide to do next."

She lowered the roll of mesh to the ground, careful to hold it tight so it wouldn't unspool. Something about what he'd said sounded off. "What do you mean, whatever I decide to do next?"

He looked away. "I got a call from the chancellor's office. They tried to reach you and couldn't get through."

"My battery died about an hour ago." She waited until he met her gaze again. "What's going on?"

"The university's withdrawn their offer for your teaching position."

"What?" Letty let the mesh go. "Can they do that?"

"Apparently, you didn't return the last of the documentation they asked for. They were missing a signature, so your new position wasn't official yet."

Her mouth went dry. "But why would they..."

"Chancellor Bryant got a call from Rafferty's office claiming you had concocted the story about the bats to try to make a name for yourself. That you pursued it without proper authorization, after the health department determined the investigation was unwarranted. And..." He frowned. "They say you threatened to go to the press. To create a public panic if the city didn't support your version of events."

He shook his head. "I tried to tell them that wasn't what happened, that you wouldn't do that. I told him I supported you one hundred percent. I mean, except for Rafferty's waiver on timing, we had every approval we could need. We wouldn't be here otherwise." He paused. "But Bryant wouldn't listen. Whoever called must've been pretty convincing."

Letty sat on the gnarled root of a tree, the mesh in a messy heap by her feet. Her words to Caroline ringing in her ears.

"If anyone else gets sick, you can bet the public will know why. I'll make sure of it."

She hadn't meant it as a threat, not really, but... "Holy shit." She looked up at Bill. "I mean, I didn't really want to teach anyway. But how am I supposed to hold my head up on campus next semester, knowing what they think of me? That stain on my record is going to follow me for the rest of my career, no matter—"

The lines deepened around Bill's eyes.

Letty swallowed hard. "What? What aren't you telling me?"

"I'm so sorry." He scrubbed a hand through his hair, his words spilling out in a nervous jumble. "I thought you were leaving to take the teaching job, and you know what it's like with the budget. If the department doesn't use the money, we lose it." He looked at his feet. "I already filled your old position in the lab."

CHAPTER 28

Letty found an empty bench mid-way across the Walnut Street pedestrian bridge. She ignored a dried spatter of bird poop and sat, watching the river meander south beyond the rail. A group of kayaks floated out of sight beneath her feet. The air carried the happy chatter of families and joggers as they passed, strollers thunking over the wooden planks of the bridge. The whizz of a bicyclist zipping past the slower foot-traffic. Everyone going somewhere.

Except me.

Not unless going to her apartment to start packing counted. She leaned back until her head rested against the top of the bench, staring up at steel trusses painted a bright robins-egg blue. They crisscrossed overhead, like a cage. Almost invisible against the darker blue of the sky.

She had nowhere to go. No idea what to do next.

Although that wasn't technically true. The hard ball of anger in the pit of her stomach told her exactly what she needed to do. Assuming Caroline had the balls to show up.

Letty checked her phone. Six-thirty. Half an hour past when Caroline said she'd be there. One way or another, that bitch was going to face her. Letty pulled up her text messages, scrolling until she found the thread where they'd made plans to meet. She jabbed a message into the phone. "Where the fuck— "

"Letty?"

Caroline stood at the opposite end of the bench, the collar of her silk shirt damp with sweat. Dark circles not quite covered by concealer under her eyes. She clasped and unclasped her hands. As if Letty made her nervous.

Smart woman.

Letty put down her phone. "I wasn't sure you'd actually come."

"I almost didn't." Caroline took a short step closer but didn't sit. "I knew how angry you'd be. But you have to know I didn't mean—"

"You didn't mean what? Are you trying to say it was an accident you told the head of the university that I'm an attention-seeking lunatic?"

Heads turned in their direction. Strollers veered wider around them.

Caroline kept her voice low. "That's not what—"

"Don't bother denying what you did." Letty didn't care who heard or that she was making a spectacle of herself. "You're the only one I said anything to about the press. And you know I wasn't serious. I don't even like having my photo taken, much less want to be on TV. And now..." The reality of her situation caught in her throat. The truth too big to fit. "And now..." Her voice broke, and she stopped again, not wanting to cry. Especially not in front of Caroline.

Caroline sat beside her. "I know you probably won't believe this. And, after everything that's happened since you came, I don't blame you for that. But I really was trying to help."

That's one seriously fucked up idea of help.

Letty leaned back, crossing her arms over her chest.

"Just listen." Caroline went on. "Rafferty called me Sunday afternoon. I guess he finally checked his messages, and he was pissed when he found out you guys were working in the park. Not just a little pissed. Scary pissed. He says you being here is an insult to his administration. Like saying they can't handle their own business. Our health department says it's contained, and that's good enough for him." She turned in her seat so she faced Letty. "I did my best to convince him that your work here wouldn't turn into anything, that letting you finish would be the end of the matter. But he wouldn't hear it."

Caroline swallowed and pulled at the neck of her blouse. "So I told him what you'd said. That if we didn't let you finish the testing, you'd go to the press." She cringed, not meeting Letty's eyes. "I thought it would help. I— I really did. I thought I was giving you leverage. That he'd leave you to it if you thought you might go public. And it seemed to work. He said he'd give you through today." She stared out over the water. "I never thought he'd go to your dean."

Letty laughed, but it came out as a dry, unhappy sound. "He skipped the dean and went straight to the chancellor. And in a way, what he did was brilliant. If he discredits me, it doesn't matter what I found. No one's going to listen to me anyway. Problem solved." Letty stood, wiping what she hoped wasn't bird poop from her jeans. "And it doesn't matter now anyway." She turned away, talking over her shoulder as she headed back over the bridge. "It's over."

■ · ■ · ■

Andrew scanned the police precinct's top floor, trying to remember which window was the captain's. Was his office the second or third from the left? The orange-red blaze of sunset reflected in every pane of glass. For all he knew, Levinson was looking out at him now. Barking at someone to go drag his ass upstairs for a reckoning.

Andrew slumped down in the driver's seat and pulled his ball cap lower over his face. At least the unmarked sedan wouldn't draw notice. Half the cars parked around the precinct looked the same as his.

The last thing he needed was to get caught lurking exactly where Levinson had told him not to be. Andrew scanned the windows again, but there was still nothing to see.

The station's front doors swung open, and Mary came bounding down the steps.

He rolled open the passenger window. "Over here."

She jogged to the car. "Not that I'm not grateful for the dinner invite, but I'm pretty sure you being here right now isn't the greatest idea."

"Well hurry up and get in then." He pushed open the door for her.

She slid into the passenger seat and dumped her purse on the floor. "Do you do anything but eat?"

"Occasionally." He pulled away from the curb. "But Renee's busy tonight."

Mary groaned past a laugh. "Ew."

He didn't bother asking where she wanted to go. She always picked the same thing on Mondays. "Any progress with Richardson?"

"I thought we had him, but... I don't know what happened." She stared out at passing traffic, her arm resting on the open window frame.

"Might help to talk about it." He made a left on Market Street, and even as they picked up speed, the night air did little to cool the car. It blew in sluggish and humid, like hot breath on the back of his neck.

Mary shrugged. "He's been clammed up tight all day. Then a few hours ago, I brought up what happened in the park with Letty. And he got twitchy. Said he wasn't there, never been there before. So I pretended to believe him, asked him some softballs. And he got comfortable. Talked about the lab, told me about the rats. How they're so smart and they make great pets." She rolled her eyes. "Anyway, I was just bringing him around to what happened the night of the fire when Phil came in. Just to observe, you know. Didn't say a word."

She turned to face him in the seat. "And Richardson freaks out. It was like he'd seen a ghost. He went pale, got sweaty. Then he wouldn't say a damn thing after. Just chain-smoked one cigarette after the next. Until I couldn't breathe anymore and had to leave the room."

"Did Phil come stomping in like he was gonna kick Richardson's ass or something?"

She shrugged. "Not at all. And he didn't get near the guy."

"So what then?"

"You got me."

Andrew waited his turn to pull into a parking lot lined with food trucks and stalls selling tchotchkes. Why Mary liked the place so much was beyond him. A few other customers milled around the weekly market. Mostly young couples. All the families had probably already gone home to put their kids to bed.

A break opened up in the cross-traffic, and Andrew pulled through, the car dipping as his tires rolled off the edge of the pavement and onto the dirt lot. Both of them jostled in their seats. "D'you talk to Phil? See if they know each other."

She scowled, rolling up the window. "Course I did. First thing I considered is maybe Phil picked him up for something before. Could be he let him off with a warning, that's why it's not in the system. Maybe left a less-than-favorable impression."

"Makes sense."

"Except Phil says he never met Richardson. Wouldn't have been able to pick him out of a crowd before today." Mary shook her head. "And if it was anybody else, I might wonder if there was maybe more to it. But, it's Phil. Guy's so by-the-book he probably alphabetizes his underwear drawer." She grabbed her purse from the floor. "And now Richardson's as good as mute again."

"What about Leonard? You said Richardson's old man got popped in '89, right?" Andrew pulled up in front of a taco truck and put the car in park.

She stopped, her hand hovering over the door handle. "What?"

"Phil would've been on the force when they brought Richardson's father in. He'd have been a rookie then, and Richardson would have been a kid, but..."

"But maybe it's something." A smile spread across Mary's face. "I think I might just have to buy you a taco."

■ ■ ■

Vodka hummed warm under Letty's skin. Garth Brooks sang about crashing an ex-girlfriend's fancy party. And the mirror over the bar reflected the busy press of bodies behind her. A mostly after-work crowd by the looks of them — suits, women in pearls, a few people in scrubs. Here and there, a couple with their heads bent together, trying to talk over the noise. And then there were the ones she'd guessed were regulars. Older folks, drooped over a drink. Sitting alone.

Like me.

Letty eyed the lime floating in the bottom of her glass. Smashed and limp, brown around the edges. She downed the rest of the vodka and soda anyway.

The alcohol would cure whatever was wrong with it.

And maybe, if she drank enough, it'd cure her, too.

Cure her of ever thinking she would live a normal, happy life. That she'd ever amount to something. Ever do anything that would've made her sister proud. For the briefest moment, she'd thought maybe this was it. Maybe she could do something useful — track the source of the infection, stop other people from getting sick. Keep them safe the way she couldn't do for Jessa.

More like, make up for what I did to Jessa.

She shrank into herself, as if she could disappear into the bar stool. Except no matter how hard she might try, there was no hiding from herself. She raised a hand, waving at the bartender. She needed a refill.

The bartender gave a quick jerk of his head, hands flying through the mechanics of making half a dozen drinks at once. She understood it as the universal language of barkeeps everywhere — she was in the queue, and he'd get to her when he was able.

But it was already too late.

Whenever the next round came, it wouldn't be soon enough.

The memories were already there.

Jessa inviting her out to San Diego so Letty could help with wedding planning.

Mark kicking her ass at chess.

Jessa texting her a dozen times — was she sure she couldn't make it? Did she really have to work? The wedding planning would suck without her.

Mark in PJ bottoms flipping pancakes for the three of them.

The moment she'd realized she loved her sister's fiancé.

Letty squeezed her eyes shut tight. It hadn't been on purpose. And she'd fought it. God she'd fought it. But it wouldn't go away. His nearness sucked all the air out of the room, her awareness of his body close to hers eclipsing everything else. Had he felt it? Had she imagined it?

It didn't matter.

Either way, once she knew, she couldn't go. Couldn't bear to see the two of them together. Couldn't stand the weight of her guilt.

So Jessa had gone out on that damn boat instead.

She never would've been there if it wasn't for me.

Letty had as much as put her sister in that water.

Her sister, who had been there for Letty when she'd most needed it. Had taken care of her when their parents were off doing God-knows-what. Jessa had been the one thing she could count on.

And she'd died alone.

Letty's face grew warm, tears building behind her eyes.

And then, there was Mark.

He'd nearly died, too. Been stung so many times trying to save Jessa, he had been in the hospital for a week. His body ravaged by the jellyfish venom, fighting to overcome an overload of hormones and proteins that might have killed him.

She'd let him lie there by himself, alone and in pain. Not able to face him. Not able to face her parents. Letty looked down at the scarred bar top, her chest so tight she could hardly breathe.

Her only solace had been her work. And now...

The bartender leaned over the counter, cocktail in his hand. "You driving?"

She scrubbed a hand over her face, trying to look normal. Knowing it was a lost cause. "Not anymore."

He gave a quick nod and slid the vodka across the bar.

She took a deep drink. This one didn't even burn going down.

"I know you."

A flash of movement in the mirror above the bar.

Letty twisted around in her seat. "Sorry?"

A mane of thick red hair framed a perfectly structured face. The kind of curves Letty only dreamed of. Cold green eyes, under heavy lids.

Sue Ellen wore the same scrubs as the group Letty'd seen before. She'd probably been there the whole time, and Letty had just been too wrapped up in her own shit to notice. Had she chosen a bar near the hospital on purpose? Maybe a part of her hoping to run into Pete's ex? To face the consequences of her choices.

The way she hadn't done before.

Whatever I get, I deserve it.

Sue Ellen swayed closer, her skin flushed. Damp tendrils of hair sticking to the sides of her face. "You're the one who came to see me about the rabies case." She swayed again. "Cases. The rabies cases. Letty? Right?"

Holy shit.

Maybe she didn't know about Pete?

She had to.

Letty reached to steady her. "Right, we met at the hospital."

Sue Ellen jerked away, the movement throwing off her balance, or what was left of it. She listed left like a boat unmoored, gripping the back of an empty bar stool. Then righted herself, holding on as if the stool was the only thing keeping her from floating away. She leaned in again, her voice a hiss. "If you know what's good for you, you'll stay away from Pete."

Sue Ellen pushed the bar stool, metal legs shrieking against the floor as it slammed into the bar. Even over the clamor and commotion of the bar, it was enough to turn heads. Sue Ellen stumbled back, bumping into a couple of college kids before she turned away, weaving side to side as she went for the front door. One of the men in scrubs followed, but Sue Ellen never looked back.

What a bitch.

And who the hell did she think she was? There might've been a time when Sue Ellen could tell another woman to back off, but not anymore. She had no right to Pete. And Letty had nothing to lose.

She pulled her phone from her bag and dialed. If she couldn't escape herself at the bottom of a bottle, there were other ways.

CHAPTER 29

May 15, 2018

Pete rolled on his side, careful not to jostle the mattress. He lifted onto an elbow, trying to see the alarm clock past where Letty slept beside him. The digits glowed green in the dim pre-dawn light: 6:26 a.m.

Four minutes until he was supposed to get up. An hour and a half before he should be prepping for an ACL repair on a Rottweiler. And that surgery was just the first of the day. He needed a shower. Needed to be where he was supposed to be. Do what he was supposed to do.

He lay back down instead, watching Letty sleep. One arm thrown over her head, dark hair tumbling across the pillow, her back rising and falling in a steady rhythm. Under the covers, she wore nothing but his undershirt.

Maybe a few more minutes wouldn't hurt.

He leaned over her. Careful, quiet. Reaching to turn off the alarm.

She smelled of his soap, his scent. As if she belonged to him.

The thought kindled a warm satisfaction in his belly.

He closed his eyes, leaning further. He needed to stop thinking that way. She'd be gone back to Athens soon. Whatever this was between them would be over. And — as much as he didn't want to admit it — that was for the best. He hadn't meant to get involved with anyone so soon. And he had too much at risk already.

His fingertips brushed the clock. He stretched another inch. And pushed it out of reach.

Crap.

"Morning." Letty mumbled, sleepy eyes smiling up at him from under a fringe of dark lashes.

He settled back in beside her. "I was trying not to wake you."

"Well, since that didn't go as planned, we might as well make the best of it." She pulled him to her, the kiss an invitation sealed by the press of her body against his. He ran his hands up under her shirt, white cotton stretching over his knuckles as he lifted it over her head.

God, she was beautiful, even with the bruises left from her accident.

Smiling up at him from his pillow. Her naked body tan against the ivory sheets. He pulled the blankets over them both and dropped his head to her breast. Licking the soft velvet of her skin, her nipple hardening under his tongue. Leaving a soft trail of kisses over the mark that crossed her chest. She tasted of cocoa butter and just slightly of salt.

She wove a hand into his hair and gave a tug, her voice a half-sigh. "Come here."

He moved back up her body, reaching out from under the sheets. Feeling for the drawer on the side table where he kept the condoms.

The alarm shrieked to life, and Letty jerked under him. "Ouch." She rubbed her palm against one eye. "I can feel that sound in my brain."

Pete tossed back the covers, reaching across her to silence the alarm. He smacked it twice before it finally turned off. "Sorry about that." He let himself collapse back into bed, his body half-draped over hers. Their heads rested side-by-side on the pillow. He wrapped a lock of her hair around his finger, then let it slip loose. "You okay?"

She shifted her hand to the other eye, rubbing circles against the socket. "Just hungover." A smile played at the corners of her mouth. "But it's nothing a little bed rest won't cure."

He laughed. Nothing restful would come from more time in bed with her, and he was absolutely fine with that. Except he really couldn't be late. Not today. Not with back-to-back surgeries on the books. He glanced to the window, where the morning light had gone from leaden to ash gray. It sliced in through the plantation shutters, alternating bands of shadow and light. "If I don't get in the shower and get going soon, Trish'll have my head."

"I should go, too," she said, but she leaned closer, teasing her lips against his mouth. She slid her leg between his, her thigh brushing against him. Turning want into need.

He ran his hands down her back, cupping her ass, pulling her tighter against him. The kisses grew hungrier, their bodies pressing together in an urgent rhythm of give and take. Every embrace making it harder to remember the reasons he needed to go.

All the reasons he needed to let her go.

Didn't he deserve to be happy? Wasn't it finally his turn to be with someone who wanted the same things he did?

He broke away from a kiss. "Are you sure you have to go home today?"

Letty lay back on the pillow, her face flushed, her breath uneven. "Yeah, I think so." She pulled the covers up around her, a sadness replacing the playful spark in her eyes.

He pulled her closer, tucking her against him.

"The project's over." She gave a soft shrug. "And even if Rafferty can't make me go. After the stunt he pulled with the university, I'm not sure I want to find out what he'll do if I don't."

Pete scrubbed a hand through his hair. She was right to leave. Because there would be consequences for both of them if she stayed.

But he was tired of letting other people make his choices. And for once, he had someone on his side. Someone who'd seen what Sue Ellen had tried to do to him and known he didn't deserve it. He found her hand under the blanket and clasped it in his. "Can I come see you in Athens? Maybe next weekend?"

She rolled on top of him, smiling as she kissed him again.

■ ■ ■

Do drug stores even sell drugs anymore?

Letty dodged displays for sunscreen and lip balm. Her head pounded. Her thoughts shot like arrows into her skull, one after the next. What was she going to do about work? How long would it take to find another job? She'd definitely have to leave Athens. Would anyone even hire her? And what would she live on until then?

She rounded another aisle.

Dog toys.

Son of a bitch.

Letty kept moving, the headache a steady one-two punch to the temple. She had a little cushion thanks to the money her parents had given her, but it wouldn't last forever. And even if she bartended in the meantime, how long would she be able to stay in that holding pattern before the gap on her resume got too big to explain?

At least there was Pete.

A smile snuck onto her face as memories surfaced from the night before — the two of them on the floor, on the couch, in his bed. What must Pete have thought when she called from the bar? Whatever it was, he hadn't seemed to mind what happened after. Her smile widened, and her cheeks warmed. She glanced around, but the pharmacy was mostly empty. No one near enough to see her mooning like a love-struck teenager.

Thank God for that, at least.

She backed up so she could read the signs hanging overhead and crossed two aisles over.

Row upon row of pain relievers.

Finally.

She grabbed a bottle of Advil and hurried to the refrigerated cases at the back of the store, searching until she found the water that came with electrolytes. Once she took something to make her head feel better, she'd go to the Inn and pack. Then get on the road. She ripped the safety seal from the ibuprofen and shook two into her hand. On the way home, she could make a few calls. Reach out to friends at other universities to see if they knew of any openings, follow up with Bill on the feelers he'd said he'd put out for her. And when she got back to her apartment, there were places she'd look online.

She shook out a third pill for good measure and washed them down with half the bottle of water. By the time Pete came to see her next weekend, she'd have a job plan in place. It was time to move on anyway. Time to stop obsessing over things she couldn't change. To stop blaming herself for things that weren't her fault.

Letty carried her purchases to the register, humming along to Phil Collins as he whined over the drug store's intercom. She might not be able to stay in Athens, but she'd be okay. She'd land on her feet.

A heavy-set man in a beanie and a too-tight Grateful Dead t-shirt stood behind the check-out counter, staring at his phone. A silver hoop hung from his top lip, and he breathed through his mouth. Or maybe he just couldn't close it comfortably around his piercing.

Letty slid the water and the Advil onto the counter, waiting for him to look up.

He didn't.

She pulled out her wallet, digging until she found a twenty. "Here you go."

"Sorry." He took the money and tossed the phone beside the register. It landed on a messy stack of newspapers, face up.

The phone showed an image of Sue Ellen, smiling into the camera. A headline ran above the photo, but she couldn't make out what—

The screen went dark.

What the hell?

The clerk tapped keys on the register, each one a shrill bleep. "The world just keeps gettin 'crazier, man."

"The thing you were reading when I came up? What was it? If you don't mind my asking?" Her voice came out gruff, the question sounding more like a demand.

He scratched the top of his nose, really looking at her for the first time. "Another rabies case. This one's the doctor that treated the other two."

Letty stood frozen in place. How could that be possible?

The clerk held out her change. "Like I said. World's going to shit."

*   *   *

"What do you think?" Letty leaned over the vent, waiting as the hotel room's ancient air-conditioner rattled to life. She closed her eyes against a rush of ice-cold air that smelled like mildew. "Bill?" She checked her phone. The call was still connected. "You there?"

"Yeah, just thinking. A third case in a city the size of Chattanooga is bizarre. The national average is what, one or two a year?"

"Right. And all three in less than two weeks." Which, given that the incubation period for rabies could be anything from a week to a decade, meant there almost had to be more cases. It didn't seem statistically possible that all the infected would just happen to become symptomatic in that short of a time period. Letty rubbed her fingers in a tight circle against her temple. "What I meant was, what do you think I should do now?"

"That's an easy one. Get out of there. The CDC's gonna be on the ground any minute, if they're not already. They'll do whatever's needed from an epidemiological perspective. More importantly, for your purposes, Rafferty's gonna be in full damage-control mode, especially when the national press rolls into town. Sue Ellen getting sick might validate what you've been saying 'til now, but there's no way he can acknowledge that and save face. You know how politicians work. The last thing you need to be is in his way."

"I'm sure that's all true." But she couldn't help feeling she was leaving things unfinished. And, even more than that, Sue Ellen becoming ill had changed things. From a contact tracing perspective, nothing made sense. The few small pieces she could see didn't look like they belonged to the same puzzle.

Something clicked on the line, and Bill gave a puzzled grunt. "Hang on." The phone went silent.

Letty moved to the bed so she could see the TV. If online news outlets were covering the outbreak, the local television stations probably would be, too. Maybe they'd have an update on Sue Ellen, perhaps even something that would explain how she'd gotten sick.

Could she have encountered the same infected animal as Bullard and Canning? It was possible but didn't seem likely. And if she hadn't, what did that mean for how the virus had been transmitted? Sue Ellen had treated Emma Canning, which meant she'd had at least face-to-face contact, but human to human transmission was virtually unheard of except in cases of organ donation. None of it made sense.

Letty stared past the television. Sue Ellen contracting the disease raised a possibility she was afraid to think. Much less name.

"Sorry," Bill said as he rejoined the call. "That was Professor Grayson from the lab in Phnom Penh. Nothing new since the last update we got on Priya. She still seems like she's responding to the treatment. But I'm trying to pick up every call, just in case."

"No, it's fine." Letty ran a hand over the bed's ruffled comforter. She'd been afraid to ask. Letting herself believe Priya was getting better felt risky. Like if she did, she would jinx it. And it would no longer be true, and—

"You ready to head this way?"

Letty glanced at her still unpacked suitcase, yawning open on the floor. "Almost."

"Good."

She went into the bathroom and ran a washcloth under the tap. If she got some comfort from Bill on the transmission issue, she'd feel a lot better about leaving. "Did you read the story I sent you from the local paper?"

"I did."

She waited for him to say more, but he didn't. Letty wrung out the washcloth, draped it over the back of her neck, and tried again. "She didn't have any bites or abrasions. Same as the other two."

"I saw."

Letty rolled her eyes.

Like pulling teeth.

She settled back at her post in front of the TV not sure what to—

"Let the CDC handle it." He spoke before she'd decided what to say.

She rolled her eyes, shifting to the edge of the bed. "I will. It's just..." She tried to force herself to finish the sentence. He really was going to think she'd gone insane. "Something's been bothering me. I know it's a little outside the box and, I'm probably way off base, but I can't stop thinking... And God forbid I was right, but it would explain things, and— "

"Just spit it out."

She took a deep breath. "What if it's airborne?"

Bill went silent.

Shit.

The idea that one of the most fatal viruses known to mankind had, after twelve thousand years, suddenly and inexplicably mutated in such a fundamental way was impossible. Except, as much as she'd tried to convince herself otherwise, given the situation in Chattanooga, it wasn't.

Not anymore.

Bill finally spoke. "That's a terrifying thought."

"It is," she said, and they both went quiet again.

Now that she'd finally said it out loud, her mind ran wild with worst-case scenarios. If she was right, there was no telling how far the disease might have spread, especially if asymptomatic carriers were contagious. The entire city might be infected — the virus creeping silent through people's central nervous systems, biding time until it was able to cross into the brain. And once that happened, there'd be nothing anyone could do to help them.

For all she knew, she could be a carrier. Sue Ellen had been six inches from her face the night before. Letty's stomach clenched. Would it be crazy for her to go get the vaccine? Would they give it to her? If the virus had mutated, would the existing vaccine even work?

She forced herself to relax. "I'm praying there's a different explanation for how Sue Ellen got sick. I mean, I know there has to be." Even though she'd already checked all the photos she'd found of the Signal Mountain picnic. None of them included Sue Ellen. And it didn't make sense for her to have been exposed in the hospital's lab. A facility that size would have an entire department dedicated to laboratory tests. She'd have seen Canning as a patient, but there'd be no reason for her to be in the lab. "Shouldn't the city be thinking about mass vaccination? Just in case. At least trying to source enough vaccine in case it's needed on such a large scale."

Bill let out a low whistle. "We don't know they aren't. But what would that even look like? No way to know who's been exposed. No way to test for it either, not before they're symptomatic and it's too late. And I doubt folks are gonna volunteer. Rabies shots aren't the twenty shots in the stomach they were years ago. But still four shots over as many weeks. Which would cost thousands of dollars for each of those seemingly healthy folks." He paused. "That's a hard sell, even if the government picks up the expense."

Which Rafferty isn't going to want to do.

Bill went on. "You know it's far more likely Dr. Hendrick got infected in a lab accident. She could easily have been exposed to infected tissue from one of the other two."

Letty mopped the washcloth against her neck, but it had already gone warm and did little to help cool her. Had she been too quick to disregard that possibility? When a lab-related transmission happened, it was usually the result of a needle stick or an improper procedure which turned infected tissue into aerosol. Either of which would explain Sue Ellen's lack of an injury. Letty looked at the television without actually seeing it. The more she thought about what Bill had said, the more possible that seemed.

At least more so than some spontaneous, catastrophic mutation of the virus.

"I'm not saying the airborne theory shouldn't be investigated. But you have to know the CDC will consider the possibility. Even if it's just one of a hundred they pursue." Bill continued as a game show host spun a giant colorful wheel on television. "My guess is, they're already chasing leads down. And they'll have their answers as soon as they talk to Dr. Hendrick, if they haven't already."

He wasn't wrong. Chances were good Sue Ellen would have some idea how it might've happened, whether it was a slip in the lab or a trip to the same park visited by Bullard and Canning. And it wasn't like Letty could stroll into the ICU and ask her lover's wife for a chat. She needed to let it go. "You're right."

With two squealing contestants looking on, the giant wheel on television finally stopped, its needle pointing to "lose a turn."

Sounds about right.

Bill's voice came back over the line. "Let me know when you make it home, okay?"

"I will." She disconnected the call, wadded up the washcloth, and launched it into the bathroom, where it plopped on the tile.

That's it then.

She should pack and get going.

A "Breaking News" graphic interrupted the game show.

Letty scrambled for the remote, finding the volume button as the camera settled on a familiar face behind an anchor desk. The reporter she'd seen interview Sue Ellen the week before shuffled a stack of papers with a sober smile. "Dr. Sue Ellen Hendrick, the third patient admitted to CHI Memorial Hospital suffering symptoms of rabies, remains in critical care today under the watchful eye of doctors dispatched from the Centers for Disease Control in Atlanta." The woman clasped her hands, resting them on the stack of paper. "The CDC is working closely with Mayor Rafferty's office to prevent any further spread of the disease."

A small image appeared in the top left corner of the screen as the reporter rehashed the details of the first two cases. It showed Rafferty and a group of white-coated men and women sitting around a conference table in what looked like deep discussion.

Oh shit.

What would Rafferty tell the CDC? Or, more accurately, what wouldn't he? Would he pass on what she'd found? Even if it meant admitting he'd been warned there might be additional cases. And ignored it.

Probably not.

And if the CDC didn't know to ask Sue Ellen about the church picnic, or any other time she might've spent in the park, what then? Would they find that connection on their own?

Letty tossed the remote on the bed. It wasn't like she could go tell them. Rafferty would probably have her arrested for trespassing, or disturbing the peace, or God knew what. And, even if he didn't, why would they listen? Her credibility was as good as destroyed. Which meant what? She went home, washed her hands of the whole thing, and hoped for the best? Left Pete there, knowing he had a dozen or more animals in and out of his office every day? Any one of them a possible carrier.

The news anchor tapped her stack of papers against the desk, straightening the edges. "The District Attorney is expected to convene a grand jury in the case against Detective Andrew Marsh for his role in the shooting of local pastor Randy Bullard. Sources close to the investigation report that new evidence has recently come to light which may result in further charges. We'll keep you updated as this part of the story progresses."

Poor Andrew.

What now? A witness? They already had a video of everything but the final moments of the shooting. Maybe something forensic? Andrew had to be losing his shit. Not just from the trauma of the shooting but the whole thing being so public. All while his life was on the line — his career, his reputation, his freedom.

A larger version of the photo showing Rafferty and the people she assumed were with the CDC replaced the news anchor on the screen, this time overlaid with text — the number for a hotline where animals exhibiting any signs of rabies were to be reported, along with a list of symptoms to look out for. Letty scanned the faces sitting around the table. None were familiar except Rafferty's. She stopped.

Behind them, just within the frame, Caroline wilted against the conference room door. Her face pale, dark circles under her eyes, a shine of sweat on her forehead.

Holy shit.

Caroline hadn't looked like herself when they'd met on the bridge. Her hair disheveled, cheeks flushed. But now she looked just like Sue Ellen had in the bar. Could be nothing. Could be a cold. But what if it wasn't? Letty rubbed a hand over her forehead.

The chances of Caroline having had a lab accident were non-existent.

■ ■ ■

Letty rolled to a stop in front of a clapboard house virtually identical to all the others on the block — gabled roof, perfect postage stamp of grass, and a walkway lined with boxwoods. Caroline's shiny black Mercedes sat in the drive.

She parked behind the flashy convertible and dialed Caroline again. It went straight to voicemail. Caroline was probably ignoring her. Which would be understandable given their argument the day before.

But what if that wasn't it? What if Caroline couldn't answer? No matter how bitchy she'd been, no matter what she'd done, Letty wouldn't wish rabies on her. And what if she was just one of a lot of people who were infected and didn't know it?

She followed the walkway to Caroline's front door, where a thick palm fiber doormat printed with "Welcome Friends" squished under her feet. At this point, Caroline probably wouldn't see her as either welcome or a friend.

Letty hit the doorbell and waited.

No answer.

Her phone rang from somewhere deep in her bag, and she scrambled to pull it out.

Mark.

Her thumb hovered over the phone, but she couldn't make her herself accept the call. Why would he be reaching out? Now, after all this time? She hadn't seen him since Jessa's memorial service. And after all that had happened...

Letty squeezed her eyes shut tight. She didn't have time to think about that now. She sent Mark's call to voicemail and put the phone away. Nothing good would come from thinking about him.

She rapped a brass pineapple-shaped knocker against the door. Maybe a little harder than she actually needed to.

Still no answer. Letty stepped back so she could see in the front windows. Floral curtains had been drawn over the one to the left. She peered into the other, but there was no sign of Caroline. Just a couch with too many pillows and a cheerful blue rug striped by the overlapping passes of a vacuum. No noise behind the door, no movement behind the glass.

She tried the doorbell again. After the chimes stopped, the house remained quiet.

Letty walked around the side of the house, the ground sloping down toward a dry creek bed at the far end of the property. Maybe Caroline wasn't home. She could've carpooled to work.

Letty braced herself against the neighbor's fence as she inched down the grade and rounded the back of the house. Unlike the front yard, it had not been landscaped. Dead leaves and pine needles covered the ground. A deck jutted out from the second story, but no stairs led down to the backyard. Which meant there was no way to get up to where she might be able to see inside. She walked under the deck instead, peering into Caroline's basement.

A washer and dryer. An old dog crate. A few boxes of unpacked who-knows-what.

Maybe this whole thing was stupid.

Letty circled around the other side of the house, this time moving up the incline. Caroline probably just had a normal, run-of-the-mill bug. Nothing more than that.

Please let it be a cold.

The alternative was unthinkable. For Caroline and for everyone else.

Letty dug an old receipt and a pen from her purse, holding the paper against the other neighbor's fence so she could write. "Please give me a—"

The fence jerked beneath her hands with a crushing thunk, pushing toward her. Something on the other side slamming into it full-tilt.

A raw snarling fury.

She stumbled back, and another assault landed against the other side of the fence. The barking a pure, undeniable message of territorial rage.

The neighbor's dog.

Fuck.

Letty climbed up the hill, faster this time. Checking every few feet to make sure the fence held. The frenzy of barking echoed in her ears, broken only by the splintering thwunk of the animal beating itself against the thin planks of wood separating her from it.

The fence bowed again. The barrier was six feet tall and rooted in concrete every three or four feet, so new the lumber was still green in places. And yet it bent in toward her, as if it might give way.

Letty ran the rest of the way to the front stoop, cursing the uphill grade. Slipping on loose pine straw. Fighting her way forward. Every step seeming somehow slower than the one before. She didn't stop until she stood back on Caroline's welcome mat, where she'd started. And even then, she waited for the final crunch of the fence as the animal overran it. For the sharp sting of teeth breaking through the skin of her heel.

The dog went quiet.

Silent but no doubt still there. Somewhere.

Letty waited. Still, except for the heave of her breath. Listening. But there was nothing.

Even Jessa would've pissed herself over that.

Letty hurried through the rest of a scrawled note to Caroline, her hands shaking. "I need to talk to you before I go. It's important." She signed her name and tucked the paper in between the front door and the jamb. Then made herself stop. Even though everything in her screamed to get in the car and lock the fucking doors.

The note didn't feel like enough. Wasn't a half-assed note shoved in the door a cop-out? She'd almost been eaten alive trying to make sure Caroline was okay, couldn't she do better than that?

She dropped her hand to the doorknob. If it was unlocked—

Letty's phone rang again.

She yelped, yanking her hand away.

What was she thinking? She couldn't just walk into Caroline's house. Even if the door was unlocked. Another ring, and she glanced toward the neighbor's fence. Would the noise draw the dog's attention?

Get your shit together, Duquesne.

She jogged the distance back to her car, digging through her bag. Searching for the phone. What if it was Mark again? She found it on the third ring.

Andrew.

Relief and disappointment hit her in equal measure. Letty connected the call as she fell into the driver's seat, an idea taking form. "Hey, what's going on?"

"You okay? You sound out of breath."

She forced her voice steady. "Yeah, I'm good."

"Just wanted to give you a quick Richardson update." Something made a loud thwack in the background. "He's still not talking, but Mary says the DA's decided to go ahead and charge him with stalking. I thought they might go for aggravated, but it doesn't sound like that'd stick." Another thwack. "I'd bet money he's responsible for that body you found in the woods, though. So, my guess is more charges are coming eventually."

Letty grimaced, her gaze still glued to the side of the house, watching for the neighbor's dog to round the corner. "The fact that you think my stalker's also a murderer doesn't make me feel much better."

"Well, don't be too worried. He's not likely to get bail. Not with him already trying to run. And the fact that he won't cooperate or offer any explanations isn't helping his cause." Another thwack. "Shit."

She backed out of the driveway, second-guessing herself. The last thing Andrew needed was more trouble. But he was a big boy, if he didn't want to get involved, he'd have no trouble saying so. "What're you doing right now?"

"Hitting golf balls into the woods behind my apartment."

Letty shook her head. Of course he was. She scanned Caroline's house one last time, but nothing moved. "Any plans for tomorrow?"

Thwack. "Why?"

She flipped the bird in the general vicinity of the neighbor's dog and put the car in drive. "I have another favor to ask."

CHAPTER 30

May 16, 2018

Andrew stepped out of the hospital under a sky heavy with misshapen, jaundiced clouds. He shoved Letty's list of questions for Sue Ellen into his pocket and crossed into the parking lot. None of the faces of the people coming in or out looked familiar. But he put his head down anyway and lengthened his stride. The last thing he needed was to get almost back to the car and have the wrong person see him.

Wouldn't this be fun to explain to Captain Levinson?

And the whole stupid, risky goose chase was because he couldn't keep his mouth shut. He rolled his eyes. One slightly tense conversation with Pete Hendrick when he'd interrupted Letty's date at her hotel, and here he was.

Not that it hadn't been worth it.

Hendrick's expression when Andrew had asked after Sue Ellen was priceless. Because what date wasn't improved by a nice chat about your wife? A smile crept onto Andrew's face. Served the douchebag right. Pete wasn't even divorced yet, and he was already rebounding with someone like Letty? She deserved better, and so did Sue Ellen.

His only real regret was that bringing up Sue Ellen's name had made Letty think he and Sue Ellen were close enough friends that she might agree to see him. He'd known it wouldn't go well. Sue Ellen had hardly even known his name when they were in high school together. She'd been a year older and way out of his league.

And she still was. Andrew rounded the aisle where they'd parked, and the car came into view.

Letty sat hunched in the passenger seat with her eyes closed and a phone pressed to her ear. The light coming through the windshield painted her the same sickly shade of yellow-gray as the sky.

He opened the car door as she finished leaving what sounded like a voicemail.

"…just call me back, okay. Please?" Letty dropped the cell to her lap and looked at him, a spark of hope in her eyes. "Any luck?"

He shook his head. "I told you it was a long shot."

Letty's shoulders drooped. "What happened?"

"'No visitors permitted' was as much as I could get out of the old biddy at the front desk. But I did run into a friend in the lobby. Nurse who used to date one of the SWAT guys I know." Andrew started the car and turned back to Letty, who had sweat darkening the edges of her shirt. He turned up the A/C. "Word's all over the hospital. Sue Ellen came in last night, totally out of control. Knocked a cup of water out of the nurse's hand when they offered it to her. Then she started gagging and retching…" He faded off, hating the image that brought to mind. "She's unconscious now."

Letty looked away. "Hydrophobia."

"What?"

"It's a classic sign of rabies. The patient has an overwhelming fear of water, more like a physical repulsion. It means she has encephalitic rabies, like Randy Bullard. Canning's was the other kind, paralytic." Her voice faded off. "Muscle weakness leads to paralysis, then death."

Andrew flinched. As awful as that sounded, he remembered what Bullard had looked like. And he couldn't imagine Sue Ellen that way. Even in high school, she'd always been so put together. So in control. Nothing like the crazed animal thing Bullard had become at the end. "Can't they do something?"

"Not really." Letty sagged back in the passenger seat. "Rabies travels through the connections the body uses to send electrical impulses into the brain. And, once it's there, the blood brain barrier — the thing that usually keeps the brain safe from infection — does the opposite, locking antiviral medications just out of reach. The damned virus is even shaped like a bullet."

She ran a hand back and forth over her forehead. "I feel terrible for her, but I also can't help thinking about what this means for our chances to stop other people from getting sick." She let out a deep breath. "We just have to hope the CDC got in to talk to her while she was conscious. I mean, it's possible she'll regain lucidity here and there. But if she's already that bad... she'll be gone in a few days."

Gone?

That didn't make sense. He knew rabies could kill you, but... "She was fine just a few days ago."

"With encephalitic rabies, once the symptoms set in, people usually die within a week."

They both went quiet. The car engine an empty hum in the background.

Andrew put his hand on the shifter but didn't put it in gear. There had to be something else they could do. He pulled the crumpled list from his pocket, forcing himself to think like he would if the whole thing was just another case. Not someone he knew lying a hundred yards away, dying a horrible death. "Looks to me like your questions are really getting at two things. Any time Sue Ellen spent working in the lab with samples taken from Canning or Bullard. And any time she spent time in Signal Mountain Park. Is that right?"

Letty looked back to him, her eyes tired. "More or less. Why?"

"The hospital's lab would have cameras, right?"

She sat up straighter in her seat. "I'm sure."

"And is it safe to assume the CDC would know to check them?"

She gave a slow nod. "They'd check to see if she was there. And if there was any indication of an exposure."

"So, if we accept that the CDC has that angle covered. Or as close to covered as it can be under the circumstances, that just means we need to know whether Sue Ellen was at the same park as Canning and Bullard?"

"Yeah, but I don't think there are any cameras there."

"Nope." If there had been, identifying Richardson would've been a hell of a lot easier. Andrew put the car in drive.

Letty reached for her seatbelt. "Where are we going?"

"We aren't going anywhere." He pulled out of the parking lot. "You are."

■ ■ ■

The heavy wooden doors of Chesapeake Hill Baptist Church closed behind Letty with a soft thunk. A dozen stained glass windows lined the walls, each one rendering a familiar biblical scene. Moses parting the Red Sea. Jesus cradling a lamb. Judas with his bag of silver.

Near the front of the church, a tidy woman with a fluff of permed white hair shuffled aisle to aisle, rubbing a cloth along the backs of the pews. She didn't look up.

On the dais behind her, an enlarged photo of Randy Bullard rested on an easel. The place still smelled of funeral flowers, the lingering stink of old roses adding an edge of nausea to Letty's headache. The same smell had hung in the air at Jessa's memorial.

Letty walked down the center aisle under a series of gilded lanterns, her footsteps muted by thick red carpet.

The woman sung something under her breath — a tune Letty couldn't place — and rubbed lemon furniture polish into already shining wood.

Letty cleared her throat. "Ma'am?"

The church lady looked up, adjusting her glasses. "Mornin'. Can I help you?"

"I hope so. I have a few questions I was hoping someone could answer. And I didn't have any luck getting through to the church office."

The woman's lips pinched together. "You with the press?"

"No, ma'am. My name's Letty Duquesne. I'm a disease ecologist with the University of Georgia." It didn't carry quite the weight Andrew's title would've, but it wasn't like he'd be able to walk into Bullard's church and start asking questions.

The old lady's brow furrowed. "You're a what now?"

"I'm a scientist. I've been trying to help figure out how Reverend Bullard and Ms. Canning got sick."

The lady twisted the rag in her hands. "Doris Mahue. Nice to meet you. Wish it were under other circumstances."

"Yes, ma'am. I'm looking for information about a church picnic held in Signal Mountain Community Park this spring."

"The picnic? What's that got to do with anything?" Ms. Mahue frowned but plowed ahead, not waiting for an answer. "I didn't make it this year. I was down in Galveston visiting my sister. Try to make it out there a few times a year. Though I don't always." She turned away, heading to the right of the pulpit. She waved for Letty to follow, the cleaning rag still clutched in her hand. "Sorry I missed your call earlier. Hard for me to hear the phone when I'm out here in the sanctuary. Especially during choir practice." She nodded toward a stack of hymnals sitting in a spot of sunlight near a piano. "They just finished up."

Letty followed Ms. Mahue toward a wooden placard displaying hymns and page numbers. Just beyond it, a door had been inset into the wall. Hidden until she got close enough to see the small brass handle. Ms. Mahue pulled it open to reveal a walk-through closet lined with robes. Mainly dark green, but a few white in varying sizes at the end. The ones they probably used for baptisms.

"Come on this way." Ms. Mahue led Letty past a short set of stairs that led up to a hot tub sized baptismal, then down a narrow hallway, to an office. It held a few chairs, a metal desk, and in a place of honor on the back wall, an oil painting of the Lord's Supper.

Ms. Mahue dug through one of the lower desk drawers, flipping through a series of hanging files. "Ah, here we go." She pulled out a rumpled sheet of lined paper and smoothed it against her leg. "I made 'em use a sign-up sheet this year. For the potluck. Last year, we had three people bring potato salad and only Denise Lewis's is worth eating." She winked and handed Letty the list. "But don't tell anyone I said so."

Letty scanned the names. Sue Ellen's wasn't on it. "This isn't everyone who was there, was it? Just the folks who brought a dish?"

"That's right. So, you can bet there were about twice that many folks there. It's usually only the ladies that sign up."

Which would not explain why Sue Ellen wasn't on it.

Ms. Mahue looked at Letty over the top of her glasses "Does that help?"

"Yes, ma'am." Letty snapped a photo of the list with her phone. Sue Ellen might not be on it. But chances were, someone who was might remember if she'd been there. Letty returned the document to Ms. Mahue, just in case the CDC did come looking.

Ms. Mahue filed it away and led Letty back into the sanctuary.

A round-faced woman in a baggy flowered dress stood behind the piano, gathering papers from the music rack. She looked up, smiling at Ms. Mahue. "Got all the way to the car and realized I forgot my music. Isn't that just the—" She stopped, seeming to notice Letty. "Well, hello. I don't think we've met."

Ms. Mahue turned back. "Letty, this is Evelyn Ford. Our choir director."

Letty smiled a hello, then stopped. The name was familiar. "Did you happen to attend the church's spring picnic this year, Ms. Ford?"

"Evelyn, please." She smiled again. "I sure did. It was hot for that early in the season, but still a beautiful day. Why do you ask?"

"Do you remember if Sue Ellen Hendrick was there?"

The choir director paused, her smile fading. She looked to Ms. Mahue, who gave a soft nod. Ms. Ford continued. "Terrible business. First Pastor Bullard and now Sue Ellen." She looked away, pushing a lock of mouse-brown hair behind her ear. "No, she didn't make it. Had work that day, I think."

Shit.

So much for that idea. Every time Letty seemed to get closer to an answer, it slipped away. "Okay, well thanks for—"

"But Pete was there." The choir director came around the piano, adjusting the embroidered collar of her dress. "That's Sue Ellen's husband."

Letty fought to keep her expression neutral.

"I remember because we'd been missing him at church for a while." Ms. Ford sped up, as though what she'd said had brought back a memory. "And he was so thoughtful. Brought a fan to help with the heat, some extension cords to plug it into the truck, and this fancy mister thing, like they have in all those high-end…"

Letty tried to listen, but her thoughts kept interfering. She'd talked to Pete about the park, but had she ever mentioned the picnic?

She must not have. Or he would have said something.

Letty nodded along, not hearing what Ms. Ford was saying.

What if Pete, Canning, and Bullard had all contracted the disease in the park that day? If, God forbid, she'd been right about asymptomatic transmission, Pete could've passed it to Sue Ellen without ever knowing he'd been sick.

Could've passed it to me.

She swallowed a spike of fear.

Pete could be the connection she'd been searching for. And if he was, if he had it now, the disease would be creeping through his system. The incubation period on some unknown count down. A death sentence about to carry itself out.

CHAPTER 31

Heavy clouds lingered over Signal Mountain but offered no respite from the day's heat. It crackled in the air, a promise of the storm to come. Pete settled next to Letty on the clinic's back stoop, sitting the paper sack with his lunch in it by their feet. Even flushed from the heat and the stress of the day, Letty was beautiful.

She gave him a weak smile. "Sorry for making such a commotion."

"You didn't." He pulled a bottle of water from his lunch bag and held it out. It was barely still cold, but maybe it would help. "I'm sorry I made you worry."

She took the water but didn't open it. "Trish must think I'm nuts."

"She doesn't. And neither do I." He lifted a sandwich wrapped in wax paper from the bag. "Have a late lunch with me?"

She waved him off, pressing her hands to her cheeks. "When I heard you'd been at the picnic, and then I couldn't get through on the phone…"

He put the sandwich in his lap and slid closer, until her leg rested warm against his. "I'm glad you came to make sure I was okay."

"Any other day, I'm sure I would've thought about the fact that you'd have been vaccinated in veterinary school. But with everything as crazy as it's been and—"

"Any other day, someone would've picked up the phone here and saved you the worry."

She smiled at him and shrugged. "I suppose."

"I didn't get out of surgery until noon and, when I walked out, there was a waiting room full of folks panicked about the rabies cases. I've been in with patients since, so Trish stepped out to grab us some food. Which is why no one answered when you called. Sure I can't share?" He held up half of his usual ham and Swiss, mayonnaise dripping onto his palm.

"No, thank you. Really." She scrunched up her nose and looked away, her gaze falling on a flock of starlings. The birds shifted in organized chaos from one side of the clearing surrounding the clinic to the other. Tiny flecks of black against a darkening sky.

He stared at her profile, remembering the feel of her body against his last time they'd been together. He wanted to pull her close. To stop talking and thinking. To get lost in the moment, in each other.

She's not part of your lunch. Stop looking at her like you want to eat her.

He looked away, digging around in the bag until he found a napkin. Sex would be easier than any kind of real intimacy, but the tug of wanting to know Letty and be known by her was strong. "I wish I'd mentioned the picnic earlier. I could've saved you a lot of time and anxiety." He wiped the mayo off his hand. "I'd forgotten all about it." Except that wasn't true. He folded the napkin in half, creasing it down the middle. He wanted to be as honest with her as possible. And if anyone would understand, it'd be Letty. He swallowed hard. "Maybe it was more like I put it out of my mind."

She looked back at him, her head cocked. "What do you mean?"

"Sue Ellen grew up in that church, and for a while, I thought it could be my church family, too." Which had been idiotic. He'd known better. Had known better since he was a child. Churches were all the same. Just a bunch of hypocrites preaching piety while they did whatever they pleased behind closed doors. Appearances were the only thing that mattered.

"No son of mine is gonna go around spreading rumors."

Pete stared off toward the birds, his father's words ringing in his ears. It hadn't mattered that what he'd said was true. Even at eight years old, when he'd stumbled on the pastor and one of the girls from his youth group behind the Fellowship Hall, Pete had known what it meant that the pastor's hand was down her shirt. He'd run to tell his father.

And he could still see the quick shift of emotions on the pastor's face as he turned to go. Fear, anger, denial. Could still hear the sharp bark of the pastor's voice as Pete ran away. "Don't let the devil's venom color your view of the world, Peter. Remember Ephesians 4:29."

"Let no corrupting talk come out of your mouths..."

Only the pastor hadn't needed to worry.

Because no one believed Pete — or maybe they just hadn't wanted to. It was easier to blame him. Call him a liar and pretend nothing had happened.

Letty leaned forward, searching his face. "And something happened to change that?"

"Sorry?" Pete cleared his throat, snapping back to the present.

She tilted her head, her voice soft. "Something changed how you felt about the church?"

He swallowed, his throat dry and scratchy. "When Sue Ellen and I started having problems, she thought it would help to go see Pastor Bullard for counseling." He wrapped the uneaten sandwich in his napkin and tucked it back into the bag. "It was awful. More like a scolding from the principal than anything helpful." He stared up at the birds again. The flock had split in two, the birds whipping themselves left and right across the sky as if driven by some mad, unknowable imperative.

His chest ached at the memory of their first counseling session. Even before Pete had spoken, he could tell it was too late. Bullard couldn't see Sue Ellen as anything other than the little girl who'd been there to hear him preach every Sunday. And, after he'd heard what she had to say, the preacher had never looked at him the same way again. Pete grimaced. "Worse, after we went, it was like everyone at church knew our marriage was in trouble. Thought it was my fault." He finally met Letty's gaze. "You might say Sue Ellen got the church in the divorce."

She put her hand over his. "I'm so sorry."

He squeezed her fingers. "I went to the picnic as a sort of last ditch effort to see if maybe I was wrong. Maybe I could stay a part of the community even after we'd split." How badly he'd wanted that. To be accepted. To be believed. Except church wasn't any different now than it had been when his father's belt taught him the lesson the first time.

Letty leaned her head against his shoulder, her dark hair brushing his cheek. "I'm so sorry. That must've been really—"

The clinic's back door burst open, and they both turned at once.

Trish stepped outside, tears in her eyes, a mascara-streaked wad of Kleenex in one hand. "The hospital just called." She shook her head, mouth crumpling. "They wouldn't give me the details, but... I think Sue Ellen's gone."

■ ■ ■

Letty wanted to pull Pete into her arms and whisper soft loving things until it soothed the pain he must feel. But she stopped herself.

He sat next to her, his eyes squeezed shut, as if to block out the world. No doubt struggling to process the loss. Letty tucked her hands under her legs. He wouldn't want her to hold him, not now. No matter how much bad blood there had been between him and Sue Ellen, she'd been someone he loved. Someone he had shared his life with. And now she was gone. Letty glanced up to Trish, who stood in the clinic's doorway pulling a tissue to shreds.

What must she think?

Pete there with her while his wife lay dying. Letty cringed and pressed a palm against the ache in her temple. But there was no speculation or judgment on his receptionist's face.

Trish stared down at her boss with eyes full of compassion. "Dr. Hendrick? Are you okay?"

Pete gripped the porch rail behind him, his face set in grim determination as he pulled himself to his feet. "I should go back to the hospital." He looked at Letty. His eyes were dry but wide, a muscle in his jaw twitching as he spoke. "They'll probably need me for paperwork or… arrangements."

Trish pushed the door further open. "Alright then. Let's get your calendar cleared for the rest of the afternoon. I can drive you over, if you want. And Kenny can watch the kids tonight, if you need me to stay." Her words came out even and smooth, probably the same tone she used to calm skittish animals they treated. She stepped onto the porch, holding the door open so Pete could go in. "Oh, and your mother called again. She said not to worry about calling back. She and your father will be here in the morning."

Pete sank back to the porch steps. "Thanks, Trish. Would you go get started on dealing with my calendar? I'll be right in. I just… need a minute."

"Take all the time you need. I'll go get things rolling." Trish said, then looked to Letty and cocked her head toward Pete in silent question.

Letty nodded. She'd make sure he was okay, or as close to it as possible under the circumstances. Trish gave a small, sorrowful smile and disappeared inside, her footsteps quick with purpose. The door fell closed behind her, leaving Letty alone with Pete in what became a growing silence.

He slumped against the opposite porch rail, staring off into the forest.

Letty tried to think of something to say. "She's in a better place," or, maybe, "I'm so sorry for your loss." But it all sounded like empty platitudes. She chewed her bottom lip. She had to say something. "Is there anything I can do?"

Pete dropped his head to his knees and curled into himself, his face hidden in his arms. His body shook, but no sound came out. Letty slid closer, pressing a hand to his back. The shaking got worse, and she wrapped her arms around him, trying to absorb some of the pain. To help him bear it.

He lifted his head, his face flushed and inches from hers. He had tears in his eyes.

And he was laughing.

Letty sat back. The tears she could handle, but hysteria?

She had no idea what to do with that.

He scrubbed his hands over his face. "Sorry. I don't know what's wrong with me. This is all just... it's too much."

She found his hand and took it in hers. Of course it was too much. Someone he'd once loved, maybe still loved, had died a horrible death. Probably gone before he'd had a chance to come to terms with the loss of that relationship. Before he'd had a chance to say goodbye. "It's okay." She squeezed his fingers.

Who was she to say what grief should look like? It wasn't like her mourning of Jessa had followed any logical path. "I get it."

He cleared his throat and got back to his feet. "Would you come by my place tonight? Maybe eight? I should be back by then, but I'll text if it's later."

She hesitated. What would people say if they knew he'd had another woman over the night his wife died? It was bad enough they were together right now. Pete's waiting room had been full when she came barging in, and she had been too afraid he was sick to be subtle. People would know.

"Please." He waited by the clinic's back door, his hand on the knob, a vulnerability in his face she hadn't seen before. "I don't want to be alone tonight."

"Okay." She nodded. If he needed her to be there, she would be. "See you at eight."

He gave her a sad smile, then disappeared inside.

Letty waited until the door shut behind him and sunk back against the porch rail, closing her eyes. God, she was tired. Beyond tired, exhausted. Everything was such a mess, and the weight of the things she hadn't done — of everything she'd gotten wrong — pressed down on her.

Fuck that.

She was finished wallowing in the past. Finished obsessing over what she had or hadn't done right. Finished blaming herself for sins she hadn't actually committed.

For Mark.

She still hadn't checked his voicemail. But she would. She owed him that. Owed him better. Thunder rumbled in the distance, and Letty blinked her eyes open. The murmuration of starlings that had been dancing across the sky coalesced into one large group and vanished over the treetops, as if they were escaping a coming disaster.

That's what a sane person would do.

She hadn't checked her phone since she'd gotten to the clinic, but she'd bet she had at least one message from Bill wanting to see if she was on her way. Except she couldn't leave, and not just because of Pete.

It was time she took control of things.

Letty fanned her shirt against her chest, making her own breeze. The most important questions she needed to answer were whether, and how far, the disease had spread beyond the first three cases. Which meant finding Caroline.

She gathered Pete's abandoned lunch, crumpling the bag under her arm. If she confirmed Caroline wasn't infected, she could silence the nagging worry that the virus had somehow become airborne.

Please God, let me be wrong.

Once that was done, either way, she'd take all the data she had to the CDC. Getting them to listen might not be easy, not after what Rafferty had done to her reputation, but she'd find a way. And then she'd deal with Rafferty himself. It was time the public knew what his priorities really were.

Letty got to her feet, and the world shifted. Everything canting sideways, as if it had come loose from its hinges.

She plopped back down on the top step, landing hard on her tailbone.

Her breath whooshed out all at once, and her vision darkened, pinpricks of light floating in and out of view.

What the hell?

When did she eat last? She hadn't been hungry for breakfast. She'd been too busy for lunch, and Pete's sandwich had looked disgusting. She pressed a hand to her forehead, where a headache still sang. The pain a single note, high-pitched and persistent.

Her skin radiated heat.

Not just hot like she'd been sitting in the sun too long. A fever.

Her mouth went dry. She'd handled the sick bat. She'd been face to face with Sue Ellen. She'd thought she was careful, but...

No amount of careful would matter if the disease is airborne.

Her throat tightened. What if she was infected? Pete might be vaccinated, but what about the other people who'd been around her? Trish, the women at the church, Andrew and Mary, the young family she'd chatted with that morning as she grabbed a cup of coffee from the communal urn in the Inn's lobby...

And, if it was rabies, now that Letty had symptoms, there'd be nothing anyone could do to help her. It was only a matter of time before she wound up like Sue Ellen and the others. Nausea gripped her stomach, whatever little was inside it threatening to come out.

She forced her shoulders down from around her ears.

Don't be ridiculous.

She took a long, deep breath. In through her nose, out through her mouth. Then another and another. The fever might be anything, the headache and nausea were because of her hangover. And she felt like shit because she hadn't taken care of herself. That was all it was. All it could be.

She had a job to do.

CHAPTER 32

An army of kids in knee socks and matching purple jerseys trampled across the soccer field, un-mowed grass swishing around their feet. They ran to one goal then back to the other, chasing the ball like greyhounds after a rabbit. Andrew propped his elbows on the empty bleacher behind him and leaned back. "Marcus looks good."

Mary glanced up from the file in her lap. "Can't even tell which one he is from up here."

She wasn't wrong. The kids moved in a pack, and Marcus seemed to stay somewhere in the middle. It didn't help that Andrew had chosen seats near the top of the bleachers. Partly in the hopes he wouldn't be recognized, but mainly so he wouldn't be overheard. "Any news on Richardson?"

She smirked. "I was wondering how long you'd make it before you asked." She closed the file. "He's still not talking, except that he insists he wasn't the one who chased Letty through Signal Mountain Park."

Andrew adjusted the baseball cap he'd taken to wearing any time he was going out in public. "That seems like an odd hill to die on. Why deny that and nothing else?"

She shrugged. "Hard to say, but you were right about Phil. He was on duty the night they brought in Richardson's father. It's possible Richardson saw him then."

"Which could explain Richardson's freak-out. Especially if he bought into all that police-conspiracy bullshit his mother peddled after his dad died." Thunder rumbled in the distance. Above the trees lining the edges of the park, the day's yellow-gray clouds had given way to heavier, darker ones, some almost black at the center. The kids would be lucky to make it through practice before the bottom fell out.

"We tracked down a former girlfriend. She says Richardson told her Chattanooga cops are all..." She made air quotes. "'corrupt fascist pigs,' but she hasn't talked to him since he left Tampa. So, it's hard to say where his head's at now."

"I'm gonna go with up his ass."

"I don't know." Mary tucked the file back into her bag, eyeing the clouds. "Something feels off."

He frowned, not liking where he thought she was headed. "Which part?"

"For starters, I think Richardson's telling the truth about not being in the park."

"What?" Andrew sat up straight, turning to face her. "Why?"

"I checked with the park ranger who was on duty the night Letty says she got chased. He spotted what he thought was a teenage girl trying to tag the bathrooms at approximately nine p.m., but she ran, and he couldn't catch her. The graffiti's been a recurring problem there, so they have a regular patrol go by to keep an eye on things. Anyway, he described the girl as approximately 5'4" with dark hair and a blue or black backpack."

"And you think that was Letty?"

"Maybe. She's on the small side, and I know she sometimes carries her equipment in a backpack. At night, in the dark, she'd be easy to mistake for a high schooler."

Andrew crossed his arms. Mary had a point. "But what about her car? If they'd been there at the same time, wouldn't the ranger have seen Letty's Subaru in the lot?"

"There are two parking areas. One on each side of the park." Mary shrugged. "If I had to guess, I'd say her car was in the other one."

Andrew ran his fingers back and forth across the nicotine patch on his bicep. "Alright, I buy that. But what about the rest?" He picked at the edge of the patch. His skin itched underneath. "You can't think Letty just made the whole stalker thing up. I saw Richardson, too. That first day I went to the park to meet her, he was outside the gate."

"You saw a silver sedan, from a distance." Mary looked down her nose at him. "That's not the same thing, and you know it."

He rolled his eyes. "Right, okay. But—"

"I'm not saying she made it up. We've got three witnesses who confirmed a silver BMW was on Letty's bumper the day of her accident. One of the other drivers even picked Richardson out of a photo line-up." She held Andrew's gaze a long minute before she went on. "So, I'm not saying he wasn't up to something. Just that the pieces aren't fitting together as neatly as I'd like." She nodded down at the file still sticking out of her bag. "I'll keep at it until they do."

He had no doubt she would.

Mary cleared her throat, her voice softer when she spoke again. "What time's your meeting tomorrow?"

Andrew looked away, focusing on the pack of kids moving up and down the field. His meeting with Levinson was the last thing he wanted to talk about. He picked at the patch again. "Supposed to be there at nine."

"Did Levinson say what it was about?"

Andrew snorted. "No, but I can guess well enough." The only reason the captain would ask Andrew to come in now was if the news was so bad Levinson didn't want to break it over the phone. It had to be about the indictment.

A series of short, shrill whistles from the field signaled the end of practice and saved them both from Mary attempting to make him feel better. If that was even possible.

Mary stood. "I need to go talk with the coach before the other parents mob him. I'll be right back." She took off down the bleachers.

Andrew scratched around the edges of the patch on his arm until the skin turned red. Nothing was going to change what was coming. He could see the judgment in people's faces when they recognized him — the neighbors who didn't wave anymore, the clerk at the convenience store, his mouth a flat-line of disapproval as he slid Andrew's change across the counter. As if what Andrew had done had made him untouchable.

The media had as much as convicted him already. It was just a matter of time until a judge made it official.

He ripped off the nicotine patch and rolled it into a ball.

What I need is an actual cigarette.

On the field, Mary pointed at something on the coach's clipboard, and parents gathered their kids' gear while the children downed bottles of water or Gatorade. Marcus stood with two kids Andrew recognized from years of coming to watch Mary's son play. A heavy-set boy who had the coach's same bushy eyebrows and a girl with long blonde pigtails and a smudge of dirt on her forehead. The three of them laughed and rough-housed, same as always.

How long until he couldn't be at any of the kids' soccer games or birthday parties? Until he was locked up with a bunch of assholes he'd help put there? His stomach clenched.

The clang of Mary's footsteps as she climbed back up the bleachers interrupted his thoughts. He refocused his gaze on Marcus and his friends, who were back out on the field, playing something that looked more like hacky sack than soccer.

"You okay?" Mary sat back down.

"I'm fine." He wasn't, but dwelling on the inevitable wasn't going to do anything but make it worse. He needed a change of topic. "Did you hear about Sue Ellen?"

"Yeah, what a shame. She still had so much life in front of her." Mary shook her head. "Nurse from the hospital called it into the station just before I left."

"Why?" From what Letty had said, it didn't sound like anyone expected Sue Ellen to make it more than a few days. There'd be no reason to report it to the police unless they thought someone had sped up the process. Maybe saved her all that suffering. "Was it not the rabies that killed her?"

"Doesn't seem to be any question it was natural causes."

He frowned. "What then?"

"Near the end, Sue Ellen regained consciousness for few minutes. It's not clear how lucid she was, but she claimed Pete tried to kill her." Mary looked up at still darkening clouds, that seemed to answer with a grumble of thunder. "From what I've read that's not uncommon. In the final stages, people lose track of reality, get paranoid. The two of them were mid-divorce, maybe her brain turned all that animosity into something worse."

He hadn't known Sue Ellen well enough to know the state of her marriage, but he'd seen it often enough before. And that kind of hate made him glad he'd never gotten married. "I'm surprised the hospital even reported it."

Except part of him wasn't. He stared down at the soccer field, where a woman meandered through the sea of sweaty kids, passing out baby oranges and bags of goldfish crackers. He'd had a bad feeling about Pete Hendrick since they'd first met. The man had always seemed to be posturing, trying to seem like a good guy more than be one.

"I don't think the nurse who called it in would've bothered, but Sue Ellen wore a scarf to work for a few days a couple of months ago." Another peal of thunder echoed across the field, this one louder. Mary got to her feet and collected her bag. "The nurse noticed bruises underneath. She said it looked like Sue Ellen had been choked."

Andrew's jaw clenched. It was hard to get that kind of bruising any other way. A fat drop of rain plopped on the bleacher beside him. Then another. A nurse would know what strangulation injuries looked like. More lazy, dime-sized splats of water fell around him. Mary started down the bleachers, calling Marcus's name. But Andrew didn't move, even as the drops came faster. The fact that Pete Hendrick was likely a wife-beater didn't feel like a surprise. More like confirmation. That guy was bad news.

Anyone who'd been on the force more than a few years knew what choking meant. Domestic violence victims often reported it, shortly before they were killed.

Bastard just got lucky the rabies killed her first.

Andrew's hands tightened into fists. The fact that Pete hadn't actually been the one to kill Sue Ellen didn't make him feel any better. And it sure didn't make him worry any less for Letty.

He still wanted to drop Pete's battered body into a deep, dark hole.

■　■　■

"I know it's asking a lot, but if there's any chance the information I've gathered may help prevent further cases, I think we have to get it in the right hands." The wipers swished across Letty's windshield, a rhythmic give and take that cleared her view of Pete's house only to have it obliterated by rain again. She sat forward in the driver's seat, ignoring the ache in her lower back. "I wouldn't ask if I didn't have to. But after Rafferty's smear campaign, I'm not sure anyone at the CDC would even agree to see me, and— "

"Okay." The onslaught of rain on the car's roof muffled Bill's words so badly, she could barely hear him.

Letty adjusted the phone against her ear. "Okay?" Relief eased the pounding in her head, and some of the tension lifted from her shoulders. She'd been expecting a no, or at least an argument.

"Of course I'll help. The CDC should have all the data. No question about that, especially now, with Dr. Hendrick's death. And if Rafferty isn't being completely transparent with them, they need to know that, too." Bill's voice held no hesitation. "What exactly are we giving them?"

"Everything. The photos showing the victims' connection, my field notes, the data from our testing and from both of my canvasses of the park. Plus, copies of all my correspondence with Rafferty and the health departments."

"He's not gonna like that."

Sucks for him.

Rafferty was going to like what else she had planned even less. She glanced over at the stack of thick envelopes on her passenger seat. The one on top bore the address of the Chattanooga Times Free Press, written in her blocky print. "It'll be fine. By the time Rafferty knows, I'll be back in Georgia, way outside his jurisdiction. Should be at your place by ten tomorrow."

"I'm afraid to ask what you're doing in the meantime. Whatever it is, be careful."

"I will. I promise." She disconnected the call and let herself melt back against the seat.

The wipers cleared the windshield again. The light from Pete's front windows shone onto the sidewalk, and the reflection simmered in the rain. Beyond her headlights, nothing else broke the night's darkness. The neighbors' houses were either uninhabited or too far away for her to see, hidden behind mature oaks and iron fences. Just as quickly as her view of the house had appeared, raindrops replaced it, smashing fast and hard against the glass. She cut off the car's engine, and the wipers stopped. The outside world lost to the downpour.

She'd been pushing herself hard all afternoon — organizing data, preparing the packages, trying to find Caroline and failing — all while ignoring her body's growing protests. One foot in front of the other, aches and pains be damned. But now that she finally sat still, the exhaustion settled heavy in her bones. Letty closed her eyes.

She'd rest, only for a minute, before she went inside. God knew what state she'd find Pete in. After what he'd been through, he'd need all the support she could give. She remembered what that was like. And she'd be so much more able to help if she could just... have a little break.

A knock cracked against her window.

Letty startled awake, the seatbelt jerking tight against her chest, pinning her in place.

A dark form stood on the other side of the glass.

What the hell?

Her body went cold. She blinked hard, chasing the sleep from her eyes, praying whatever it was would disappear back into her imagination, and—

Pete.

Rain soaked his clothes and plastered his hair to his head. Drops clung to the thick strands drooping over his eyes. "Are you okay?" Even through the window and over the roar of the rain pummeling her roof, he sounded worried.

She undid the seatbelt, trying to make her muddled brain catch up with reality. "Yes, sorry. Hang on." How long had she been out?

Long enough for the car to go cold.

She grabbed her cell from the center console. The face lit as she shoved it into a pocket. She'd been out almost an hour and missed two calls from Pete and one from Andrew. Too far gone to even hear the ringer. What must Pete think? She swung the door open, and rain gusted in, drenching her before she made it outside. "So sorry. I wasn't feeling well, and I thought I'd rest my eyes a minute, and..."

He hunched against the storm. "Don't worry about it, just come inside."

Pete lifted one side of his fleece jacket and tucked her under it. It did little to keep the rain from continuing to pelt her, but his body was warm and solid against hers.

She wrapped an arm around his back. They jogged together up the front walk and stumbled into his foyer, their sneakers squeaking on the hardwood floor. Whether it was the nap or the cold shower, she felt more alert, more herself, than she had all day. "I can't believe I fell asleep, I— "

"It's okay, really." He stripped out of his soggy fleece. "I'm just glad you're here now." He pointed her toward the living room, talking over his shoulder as he disappeared down a hallway. "I'll go grab us both something dry to wear."

Letty hesitated at the edge of the living room. It was pitch black beyond the light bleeding in from the foyer, revealing a long triangle of Persian rug and nothing else. She felt around for the switch, a wet chill finding its way beneath her collar and seeping into her skin. No luck. She tried the other side of the door.

The longer it took for her to find the light switch, the more she felt like she wasn't alone. Like something waited for her in the dark.

Snap out of it.

She was being ridiculous. Still on edge from the scare she'd had in the car. She found the switch and flipped it on. The room was exactly as she remembered it — oil paintings, heavy drapes, a grandfather clock in one corner. A little formal for her taste but nothing sinister. Her phone buzzed in her pocket, and she pulled it out. Another message from Andrew.

Crap.

He was probably responding to the rambling voicemail she'd left him. Had she even made sense?

"Here you go."

Pete appeared in front of her, and she fumbled with the phone, nearly dropping it. "You startled me." She put the phone on the coffee table and gave him a smile, trying to look like he hadn't almost made her pee her pants.

"I could tell. I think that's twice now." He grinned at her and held out a sweatshirt.

"Thanks." She took it. The shirt was several sizes too big, but it was dry.

He turned his back, as if he hadn't already seen her naked. "So what's going on? You're not feeling well?"

The gesture felt old-fashioned, gentlemanly. It was unreasonable how much she liked it. She stripped out of her wet top and pulled the sweatshirt over her head. It smelled like Pete. "I thought it was just a hangover at first. You can turn around. But then it didn't really seem to go away, and…" Did she even want to get into the fact that she'd thought she might have rabies? It seemed so silly now. He would think she was crazy.

He gestured toward the couch. "And what?"

"I almost didn't come over. I didn't want to get you sick, but then I also didn't want to just not show up either. Especially not tonight." She sat beside him. "How are you—"

"I'm glad you're here. And, if I was going to catch whatever cold you've got, I'm sure I have already." His gaze drifted to the spot on the floor where they'd had sex a few days before, and his hand dropped to her knee.

Her body warmed at the memory, at his touch, and a flush rose to her cheeks. But now wasn't the time. Not on the day his wife died. She leaned her head against his shoulder. "Well, either way, I feel like an asshole. With everything you've got going on, the last thing you need is to have me passed out in your driveway." She cleared her throat. "Are you okay? How was today?"

It took him a few seconds to answer. "Not good." He stared off at the grandfather clock, the brass pendulum swinging back and forth in a relentless beat. She let the ticking fill the silence, waiting until he was ready.

His voice was rough when he finally spoke again. "Would you mind if we didn't talk about Sue Ellen right now? I spent all evening with her parents. They're... beside themselves." The muscles clenched in his jaw. "And once mine arrive tomorrow, it'll be worse. My mother hasn't had a family funeral to throw in years."

She raised her eyebrows. What did that mean?

He didn't seem to notice her expression. "I think I need a break from it all for now. If that's okay?"

She nodded. She wouldn't say so, but she was glad for the reprieve. She had no idea what to say or what he needed, except for that he'd asked her to be there. "Of course."

He gave her a small smile. "Maybe tell me about the rest of your day instead."

Letty still wasn't sure she wanted him to know about her freak-out at the clinic, but there didn't seem much use in hiding it. "When I started to feel sick, at the clinic earlier, I panicked a little. I know this is gonna sound ridiculous, but I started thinking, what if I have rabies? I mean, I have the same symptoms as the other victims. Fever, headache, nausea. And I was exposed. To the bat and... this is going to sound even crazier, but to Sue Ellen."

He rubbed a hand over the back of his neck before meeting her eyes. "You don't sound crazy. You sound exhausted. And you don't have rabies." He took her hand. "What you described could be any common cold or flu. Isn't that more likely?" He held her gaze until she nodded, then went on. "Sue Ellen treated those other two victims. You know as well as I do, accidents can happen. A bit of saliva in an open cut, maybe something gets dropped in the lab."

He shrugged. "We might never know. But there's no reason to think you'd have gotten it just by sharing space with her for a few minutes at the bar. And I saw how you were with the bat we sent off for testing. You were gloved and masked and taking every precaution. I don't think for a minute you'd have been careless enough to get it that way."

Letty sank back into the sofa. What he'd said made sense. She was just exhausted, seeing the virus everywhere she looked. Not only in herself, but in Caroline, too. Why had she assumed her friend's illness was rabies? She'd heard hoofbeats and thought zebras. Letty rubbed at her temples. It was so much more likely to be something else. Pete's grandfather clock bonged the hour, one… two… three…

But what if I'm right?

The thought came unbidden and unwanted, quiet but persistent.

It yelled at her in a whisper.

What if the infection is still spreading, and I do nothing?

Four… five… six….

Some risks weren't worth taking.

Seven… eight…

Even if everything logical said the outbreak was over and Caroline's illness was unconnected, she couldn't let it go.

The clock struck nine, and Pete gave her a small smile. "That old thing's so loud, I'm not even sure why I keep it." He pressed a hand to her forehead, sliding it down to cup her cheek. "You feel warm. Would you like some tea? I'll have to dig around for it, but I have some my mother swears by when I'm not feeling well."

She leaned into his touch. "I'd like that."

Pete pulled a cable-knit blanket from the back of the sofa and tucked it around her. "I'll be right back."

Letty nodded and nestled into the blanket as he turned to go. Even assuming she was right about Caroline, about the risk of airborne transmission, what more could she do?

She closed her eyes, listening to Pete move around the kitchen — the clink of a mug on a stone countertop, the clang of a kettle put on the stove. She'd done all she could do. A faint click-click-click of a gas range being lit drifted in from the other room. She'd pass on the information she had and move on.

Her phone dinged a text.

Probably Andrew.

She tossed off the blanket and grabbed her cell from the table.

Caroline.

Finally.

"Got your note. Home sick with flu."

Adrenaline buzzed across Letty's skin. This was her chance. Except, now that she had Caroline's attention, Letty wasn't sure what to say. The symptoms of flu would be identical to the early onset of rabies, but Caroline wouldn't know that. And how could Letty tell her friend she might be dying? That, if she was right, and Caroline had symptomatic rabies, it was too late for anyone to help her.

They needed to talk in person, except that didn't seem possible. Caroline had been avoiding her for days. Letty held her thumbs poised over the phone's keypad.

And what if Pete's right?

She swallowed hard, her throat dry.

Caroline texted again. "CDC says Sue Ellen's rabies was raccoon variant. Wanted to tell you before you saw it on the news."

Letty dropped the phone to her lap.

It wasn't the bats.

All the air left her lungs, the exhaustion she'd felt earlier was nothing compared to the heavy, devastating realization — she'd been wrong.

About everything.

All the time and resources she'd wasted. Her job lost. Her credibility destroyed.

The kettle whistled from the kitchen.

As bad as things had been, now it would be worse. She'd been proven conclusively, and soon publicly, mistaken. It would confirm everything Rafferty had said about her.

The kettle grew louder, the gentle note drawing out to an insistent shriek.

She'd known the variant test would be performed once the CDC got involved. It was a resource they brought to the table beyond the reach of academic labs like hers. But she hadn't expected the results this soon or for them to do anything except confirm her theory.

Fuck.

The kettle's whistle died away. None of that mattered. And none of her data would be useful. She'd noted all the animal activity she'd seen in the park, but she hadn't detected significant evidence of raccoons. Had she been off the mark about the park, too? Did Canning and Bullard have some other commonality? Could the time they'd spent together at the picnic have been nothing more than happenstance?

Maybe.

It was so tempting to fall back into old patterns, to hide under the thorny crown of her mistakes. But that had never gotten her anywhere. This wasn't her fault any more than Jessa's death had been. And she wasn't going to waste more time wallowing in what might have been. The only thing that mattered now was what happened next.

What had she missed? She sat up straight, forcing herself to think everything through again from the beginning — her research online and in the park, the testing, the data, all the interviews she'd done when the investigation began…

The raccoon.

"Pete?" Letty called out.

A cabinet door smacked shut. "Yeah?"

"What happened to the dead raccoon you found?"

A long silence drew out, but he finally answered. "The one that got poisoned? I buried it in the Petersons' backyard, behind the gazebo."

Shit.

"I guess it's too late to test now anyway."

Pete stepped back into the room with a canister of tea in his hand. "What d'you mean?"

"Caroline just messaged me. The rabies in Sue Ellen's system came from a raccoon. I know you thought the one you found at the Petersons' died from poisoning, but couldn't its symptoms have indicated rabies?" The more she thought about it, the more sense it made. She pressed her hands to the sides of her face. "Oh my God, Pete. You need to call Belinda Peterson. Now. She has to get vaccinated."

Pete nodded, slowly, as if he was still processing what Letty'd said. "Right, no that makes sense. I mean, it's a long shot, but..." He tapped the can against his thigh. "Hang on. I'll get my phone." He hurried back to the kitchen.

Letty rubbed her hands over her face. All this time, she'd been focused on Caroline. Following her all over town. While a bomb might be ticking in poor Belinda Peterson's nervous system.

God, please let us not be too late.

Pete's voice drifted out of the kitchen. "Mrs. Peterson, this is Dr. Hendrick from Signal Mountain Veterinary Clinic. Would you give me a call as soon as you get this message? I don't want to alarm you, but..." His voice faded, muffled by the sound of the refrigerator opening and closing.

Letty didn't even care anymore that she'd been wrong about the bats. If she could help even one person, she'd have done what she came to Chattanooga to do.

CHAPTER 33

Andrew pulled to a stop outside Mary's place. A flash of lightning lit the sky, framing the house in a perfect silhouette before it disappeared into darkness. Wind whipped through the trees and sent the rain sideways, pelting into his window.

What would the station be like tonight? With the power already out and the storm still raging, half the force would be responding to drunks in ditches. And the other would be following up on house alarms, where a door had blown open, or a housewife heard something go bump in the dark. Classic, Grade A, pain in the ass grunt work.

And he'd have given anything to be there.

Andrew put the car in park. Nothing good was going to come from thinking like that, especially not tonight. Not when less than twelve hours stood between him and whatever Levinson had to say. He found his phone, sent a quick text to let Mary know he was there, and flipped through the news.

Not even ESPN held his attention.

Fuck it.

He pulled up Letty's voicemail and replayed the end. "— Caroline's office said she was home sick, but my note's still stuck to the door and yesterday's paper is still wedged under one of her tires... I don't know. It doesn't feel right to me. And I.... never mind. I'm heading to Pete's now, but just call me back when you can." Something about her message sounded off. Not what she'd said so much as how she'd sounded.

He put down the phone. Was it the message that bothered him? Or Letty's relationship with Pete Hendrick? Andrew cut off the headlights.

That was an easy answer.

The real question was, what did he do about it? There was no proof Pete had hurt his wife. The nurse could've been mistaken, the injury could have been sustained some other way. Or, even assuming Sue Ellen had been choked, there was nothing to support that the assailant had been her husband.

Except the statistics.

But was that enough reason to assume Pete was dangerous? Andrew tapped his thumbs on the steering wheel. Or was he just searching for something to worry about that wasn't his meeting with Levinson?

Maybe so.

Movement came from Mary's front stoop, a shift in the shadows near her door.

Andrew squinted into the darkness, and a flashlight beam speared him in the eyes. "Son of a bitch." He blocked it with his hand.

The beam shifted to the ground, and he could just make out Mary behind it. She jogged down the front steps, dodging puddles and fighting the wind for possession of an umbrella. One of its ribs had broken, and the thing had all but turned inside out by the time Mary dropped into his passenger seat, dripping and breathless. "Hi." She fought the umbrella closed. "Thanks for coming back." The wind slammed the door behind her.

"No problem." Andrew reached behind his seat and handed her a pair of well-worn Nike high tops, trying not to inhale. How the funk coming off Marcus's sneakers hadn't given away the fact that he'd left them behind was a mystery.

"That kid would lose his head if it wasn't attached." She sat the shoes by her umbrella. "Sorry to bring you back out in the storm. I didn't think the school would appreciate him coming in cleats, and these are the only other shoes he has that still fit."

"I was headed out anyway." Sitting at home watching the clock tick was bad enough when he had TV and a fridge full of beer. Right now, he had neither. "Renee gets off her shift at the truck stop at eleven. I thought I'd head over and keep her company 'til then. They've still got the lights on and the coffee's always hot." Even if it did taste like burnt dirt.

She looked him over, eyes narrowing. No doubt reading him, the way she always could.

Might as well have "I don't want to be alone" tattooed on my forehead.

Mary touched his shoulder. "I know it's a rough night. Why don't you come inside and wait it out here? I've got a bottle of Johnnie Walker and an extra flashlight."

"Nah, don't want to wake the kids." And, even more than that, he didn't want to have the conversation that would follow if he sat down with Mary and a bottle of scotch.

At least with Renee, they wouldn't be talking.

Mary pursed her lips. "You're too hard-headed for your own damn good." Lightning flashed again, freezing the world outside his car in an icy blue-white light before plunging it back into darkness.

One, two—

Thunder cracked.

"You're not gonna believe this." Mary twisted her hair, dripping water out on her jeans. "Richardson's counsel just entered a plea deal."

"I didn't even realize he'd lawyer'd up." Andrew turned off the car. "He admitted the stalking?"

"No. Well, yes, sort of."

"I think that pretty much covers everything but 'maybe.'"

She gave a long-suffering sigh. "He copped to Wilkes's murder but claims it was self-defense."

Andrew frowned. "The murder? Wasn't he only charged with stalking? And how do you dump a body in the woods and then claim self-defense?"

"Take a breath, Andrew." She shifted in the seat. "Richardson says he walked in on Wilkes trying to free the animals, after he'd lit the place on fire. Not real clear why Wilkes didn't wait until all the animals were out to set the blaze, but my guess is he got spooked and rushed the job." Mary pushed her wet hair into place and turned to face him. "Anyway, Richardson says when he got there, he tried to put it out. Wilkes attacked him, the two struggled, and Richardson hit him with the extinguisher. Which jives with the medical examiner's report. Single antemortem blunt trauma to the head."

Andrew's mind flashed to the dented fire extinguisher he'd found lying near the second point of origin. That fit. But even if things had gone down like Richardson said, there were parts of his story that didn't make sense. "Why would Richardson have been there then?" Andrew crossed his arms over his chest and raised an eyebrow. "Does he usually go into work at midnight?"

"Apparently, the facility's alarm system sent an alert to Richardson's phone." She looked off toward the end of the house where the kids slept. "We think Wilkes triggered it when he entered through an unlocked rear window."

It hadn't even occurred to Andrew to check the windows, but then, the front door had been unlocked, so why would he? He shook his head. "So, Richardson gets a notification there's been a break-in at the facility, and he doesn't think to call the police?"

"The system's new, and they'd been having a lot of false alarms." Mary shrugged. "Plus, you know how Richardson feels about local law enforcement."

"Yeah." He knew all right, and the feeling was mutual.

What a dumbass.

"You know, if he'd called us then and his story held, there's a good chance he'd have come out in the clear. Now..." Andrew shook his head. Richardson's life would never be the same. The DA might've agreed that self-defense made Wilkes's death a justifiable homicide, but Richardson was still going to jail. He'd concealed the crime, evaded the police, and—

"I know, but he thinks we're the bad guys. So instead, he hauls Wilkes's body out to his car and dumps it in the first spot he can find."

Which tracked with what Andrew had noticed when he'd plotted out the crime scenes on his map at home. The gulley where they'd found Wilkes's body would have been the best spot — maybe the only spot — to effectively conceal a body between the facility and the edge of town. And it explained why it'd taken Richardson so long to show back up at the facility the night of the fire. He'd have had to go home, shower, and change out of his muddy clothes before he came back.

The only piece that didn't fit was Letty Duquesne.

Andrew scratched under his chin. "I still don't get why he was following Letty."

"He wasn't."

Andrew stopped scratching. "What?"

"He was following you."

■   ■   ■

"Careful, it's hot." Pete turned the glass mug so Letty could take it by the handle. He settled on the couch beside her, shifting throw pillows out of the way. They still smelled like Sue Ellen's perfume, and the scent made his stomach sour.

"Thanks." Letty blew steam from the top of the cup but didn't drink it.

He eyed the cup. Had he gotten the ratios right? The brew wouldn't taste good, no matter what he did to it, but he'd tried to add enough sugar to make it palatable. He picked up the throw blanket from where it had fallen by Letty's feet. "Did you get through to Caroline?"

"Yeah." Letty lifted the mug out of the way while he tucked the blanket back around her. "She agreed to see me tomorrow, so that's a start."

"Good." He'd overheard most of Letty's side of their conversation from the kitchen, but then her voice had gone quiet at the end. Pete picked at the weave of the blanket. "What did you tell her about the raccoon?"

"Just that I might know where an infected animal had been buried." Letty studied his face. "It's not your fault, you know."

"What?"

"Finding that raccoon the way you did, of course you'd assume the bait bricks were what killed it. Anyone would've. And there's a good chance you were right." She smiled at him. "No one's going to blame you for not realizing it could've been something else."

Letty took a sip of the tea, and her smile wilted.

He gave a sympathetic cringe. "It's awful, I know."

"It's not so bad." Letty held the mug between her hands, swirling the murky brown liquid inside. "Just really sweet."

Crap.

She drank again, and, this time, managed to maintain something that almost resembled a smile. Almost.

"You are a terrible liar." Pete crinkled his nose and laughed. "It's pretty bad, I know. I think it's the zinc."

"Maybe." She took another swallow. "It tastes like something else. I can't put my finger on it, but it's almost…. astringent." Letty put the mug on the coffee table, pushing it away like Brussels sprouts on a child's plate. "Anyway, I guess it's kind of late to call Bill. And I don't see any reason to call the health department or the CDC tonight, do you? They already know they're looking for a raccoon, and, even if the one you found was rabid, there's no reason to think there'd be other infected animals in the same area. That was months ago."

He nodded. "Right, and you'd probably just get an answering service."

"Maybe. I feel like the CDC would have someone available." A gust of wind rattled the window in its frame, the rain snapping against the glass like tiny icy stones. She glanced up at the noise, then back at him. "But I don't think there's any rush now that we've reached out to the Petersons."

"Agreed." He picked up the mug and handed it back to her. "Besides, it's not like that raccoon's going anywhere, and you could use a good night's rest. You're not going to be of any use to anyone if you don't get better."

She pulled the blanket tighter around her, as if the wet chill of the storm had seeped in. "You're probably right." Letty held her nose and downed the rest of the tea with an exaggerated shiver. "Yuck. At least that's done." She handed him the empty mug.

He stared down at the grainy dregs coating the bottom.

It wasn't done yet. But it would be soon.

■ ■ ■

Letty rested her head on the arm of the sofa and her feet in Pete's lap. She blinked a few times but still couldn't get the face of the grandfather clock to come into focus. Her eyes had gone dry and sticky. "What time is it?"

Pete checked his phone. "Almost ten."

"I should go." She struggled to sit up. The surge of energy she'd had after falling asleep in the car was gone as quickly as it'd come. Getting off of the couch was going to take every bit of effort she could muster.

"Don't be silly." Pete slid his phone on top of a stack of magazines on the coffee table. "There's no reason for you to go back to the hotel tonight. Not in this storm and especially not with how you're feeling."

The idea of lying back down was almost too appealing to resist. But she couldn't stay over, not with Sue Ellen having just died, not with Pete's parents arriving in the morning. And even if she could...

"My car is still parked out front. We can't leave it there overnight. I don't want..." Her words came out slow. She swallowed, trying to get what felt like cotton balls out of her mouth so she'd be able to finish the sentence. So she could explain that she didn't want to make an already hard situation worse.

People would talk.

"I didn't think about the car." The muscles in his jaw tensed, and he turned to look out into the rainy darkness beyond the window. He patted her leg. "I'll move it around back. And I really would like it if you stayed. Things are easier with you here."

"Are you sure?" She sank back into the sofa. Even knowing all the reasons she shouldn't, she wanted to stay. And if she could make things better for him, what was the harm? "Car keys are my bag. By the front door." Her eyes drifted closed.

He lifted her feet and slid out from underneath.

Letty relaxed into half-sleep, her thoughts floating like ash in still air.

Poor Pete would get soaked again moving the car. When was her next payment on it due? She needed to update her resume. Call her mother. Get an update on Priya. And she'd forgotten to ask Pete about the...

"Pete?"

He stepped in from the foyer. He'd put his wet fleece back on and had her keys in his hand. "Yeah?

Her words came out thick. "Who were the flowers for?"

A line appeared between his brows. "Flowers?"

"You had a..." She struggled to find the word. "Bouquet. In your truck. The day I saw you outside the police station."

He paused, as if deciding something, then gave a short nod. "I took them out to the memorial for Emma Canning. The one the students made for her at UTC."

Of course he had. She nestled deeper into the sofa. That made perfect sense.

Pete's voice drifted in, coming closer, instead of receding toward the door. She tried to open her eyes to look at him, but they were too heavy for her to lift. His words reached her somewhere in the space between sleep and reality. "She wasn't supposed to be there."

What did that mean?

It didn't matter. She could ask him tomorrow. Right now, she was just too tired to bother with it. She cradled a throw pillow under her head. It smelled familiar. Like lilies and bergamot. Like...

Sue Ellen.

Like the perfume Sue Ellen had been wearing when she'd gotten in Letty's face at the bar. When she'd warned Letty away from Pete. Letty forced her eyes open. Pete had perched on the edge of the coffee table and was still talking.

"—I wasn't even sure the mister would work." He had her keys hung from one finger and swung them back and forth as he spoke. "I mean in theory, sure. It'll aerosolize whatever you put in it, but still. I mostly thought it would fail, and I had no idea Emma's parents would bring her along to the picnic." He shook his head.

None of what he was saying made sense. "What?"

"Ah, you're still here." He smiled. "Good. It's important to me that you know Emma was an accident. I didn't mean for anyone innocent to get hurt." He leaned back, tucking the keys in his pocket. "I mean, Sue Ellen was different. She didn't give me any choice. She was trying to take the clinic away. To ruin my reputation." His face hardened. "I had no way out. And then when I found the raccoon, and I realized what I could do with it."

"It was like…" He leaned back, crossing one leg over the other. "Fate. I mean I did worry a bit about not reporting what I'd found, in case there were others. But it all turned out fine."

His words reached her through a fog. What did that mean? What was he—

Letty recoiled from him, recognizing the truth on his face. "You infected your wife."

He lifted his chin, defiance glinting in his eyes, like a toddler refusing to apologize to someone he'd hit with a toy. "She turned on me. Then Bullard's vultures did too. They were no different than the church I grew up in. And they got what they deserved."

The mister.

That's what he'd meant. He'd used it to aerosolize the rabies, turning the raccoon's virus-laden saliva or liquefied tissue into a fine mist that floated into people's eyes, and up their noses, and onto their food. Made it so that the contagion rained down onto their skin, where he knew the virus would search for any small scratch or abrasion that might let it in. Because, of course, all a disease wants is a host.

How many people had he infected? How many lives would be ruined?

And why?

Because he felt like they'd rejected him? Taken Sue Ellen's side?

Letty went rigid. She wasn't just tired or sick. Something much worse was wrong with her. Her words came out thick and clumsy. "And me?"

He leaned closer and tucked a strand of her hair behind her ear, his touch as gentle as it was repulsive. "Don't worry. It'll be quick, painless. Nothing like the others."

No.

She pressed her eyes closed, willing it all to be a nightmare.

But Pete was still there. He kept talking. "I want you to know that I really care about you. And if I'd had any choice…" He sighed. "But you weren't gonna let it go. And this needs to be over."

It couldn't be. Not like this.

Letty forced herself to her feet, lurching forward off the couch. She had to get away.

He stood as she did, hands out, whether to steady or restrain her, she couldn't tell.

It didn't matter.

The world shrank away, her vision tunneling, her skin clammy, as if the oxygen in the few feet above the couch were somehow too thin to breathe. Letty fell forward into the coffee table, knocking her empty mug off the end. It landed with a sharp crack, and a shingled stack of magazines followed, slithering over the edge. Pete's cell phone went with them.

The phone.

And where was hers? Hadn't she had it?

She could call for help.

Letty dropped to her hands and knees, crouched in the narrow space between the couch and table, trying to clear the spots from her eyes. She took slow breaths, in and out, trying to hold on to consciousness. She focused on a single point on the floor, where the mug lay broken in two pieces. Another breath, in and out.

Don't pass out.

When she could see again, she searched the floor for Pete's cell phone, but didn't see it anywhere. Had it fallen under the couch? She swept her hand underneath and took another deep breath in.

Where is it?

"Don't make this harder than it needs to be. I've done everything I can to make sure you don't suffer." Pete loomed over her. "And there's no reason for anyone else to either. When they find your body, if they do, they'll think you just wandered off the trail, that you slipped and fell. Died in a place you loved best here." He reached down, gripping her under her arms. "Isn't it better that your family thinks that, rather than know the truth?" He pulled her to her feet.

Her head lolled to one side.

He made a face she might once have thought was sympathetic. "I know you understand how hard it is to live with something like that. Think about what it will do to your parents to lose another daughter to a violent death."

The coal of anger burning in the middle of her fear flared red, caught her terror like tinder and burned, hot in her chest. Letty dropped her head and pushed off against the ground. She rammed into him, using every ounce of strength she had left to jam the shard of the mug she'd palmed into the side of his neck.

They toppled forward, her on top of him, and hit the ground hard. The shard slicing into her fingers and slipping out of her grasp.

Had she cut him? If not badly enough to kill him, then at least to slow him down?

She couldn't tell. Couldn't even feel the cut on her hand, except for the slippery warmth coating her palm.

She fought past her panic to draw breath, pushing off of him, dragging herself away. Every inch of progress came hard fought and unbearably slow, her palm leaving a bloody crescent on the floor with every lurch forward.

Pete rolled to his side but made no move to stop her. Either because he wasn't able to or because he knew she wouldn't get far.

She'd used up every reserve of energy she had. It didn't matter how hard she screamed at herself to move. Her body no longer responded. She collapsed against the side of the couch, watching him from under heavy eyelids.

He pressed both hands to his neck, but nothing leaked out between his fingers. "You're just like her." He spat the words. No more kindness or remorse lived in his eyes. Just the cold hard resolve of someone with a problem that needed to be solved.

She stared at his hands, willing blood to seep through.

But there was nothing.

Her eyes fell shut, and she slid down until she lay on the floor. The polished hardwood pressed cold against her cheek. It smelled of lemons.

Get up.

Get up!

But she couldn't. She was locked inside a body that wouldn't follow the commands she gave it. She forced her eyes open, one last time.

The rug beyond the coffee table. The clock in the distance.

A pair of soft leather loafers filled by sock-less feet.

A drop of blood landed on the left shoe.

Then another.

Then there was only darkness.

CHAPTER 34

The power flickered. Pete looked up from where he'd been digging through Letty's bag. The can lights dotting the kitchen ceiling dimmed again but stayed on, which was good. It would be hard enough to figure out what he'd missed when he could see. He went back to pawing past breath mints and crumpled post-it notes. He found her cell phone turned off and tucked into an outside pocket.

Of course it was there. He sat back on his heels. That's where he'd put it when she'd fallen asleep.

He knew he was forgetting something. But, if the phone wasn't it, then what?

I can't believe this is happening to me.

Putting the raccoon's saliva into Sue Ellen's eye drops had been nothing short of genius. A simple, perfect solution to a complicated problem. And even so, look where he'd wound up.

It's all so unfair.

He went back to the living room, where Letty lay on the floor. His stomach seized, and the back of his throat burned. She didn't even look like herself. All the fire and vitality that had made her who she was were gone. He swallowed hard. If Bullard and the rest of the church hadn't acted the way they did, none of this would have happened.

He rubbed a hand through his hair. He wasn't sorry for what he'd done to them. They'd deserved it. And those two rabies cases, along with any others who became sick, would muddy the link between him and Sue Ellen's illness, just as he'd hoped.

He only wished he'd realized a bigger outbreak would draw so much attention.

Letty's attention.

His stomach cinched tighter, but he forced himself to keep moving. No one could have expected word of the rabies cases to spread so fast or so far.

Not even him.

Pete lifted Letty's body from the floor. She was small but, mainly muscle, and heavy. The weight of her in his arms pulled against the sutures he'd used to close the wound in his neck, and it burned. Like he'd been lashed with stinging nettle down that side of his body. He hissed in a breath and paused, eyes closed, waiting for the pain to pass.

He couldn't take anything for it now. Not with what he had left to do. He needed to be clear-headed, and he'd already wasted too much time stitching himself up.

He carried her into the kitchen, and the sutures smarted with every step. They weren't his best work. He'd been rushed, knowing her car was still sitting in front of his house while he did it. But he hadn't had a choice. Leaving his DNA behind was one thing — people knew they'd been together — but a trail of his blood in her car or on her body was something different altogether.

He adjusted his grip under Letty's knees. The real trick would be concealing the wound until it healed. Although he could probably say he'd gotten it from an unruly animal at the clinic.

Probably.

He'd have to manage. He didn't have any choice. His mouth twisted into a grimace. He never had any choice. He made it to the back door and braced Letty's weight on the edge of the counter so he could get it open.

Almost there.

The wind ripped the handle from his grasp, and the door banged open. It hit the wall hard enough to rattle its glass panels. But Letty didn't react to the sound, or to the rain that blew in, pelting them both in the face.

What a nightmare.

He shifted her weight from the counter to his chest. He had to keep moving.

Pete left the door standing open, hunched against the weather, and carried Letty into the night. The wind fought against him, slowing every step. It whipped through the trees, a rippling mass of limbs and leaves and darkness. At least no one else would be out in this weather. He slogged his way across the yard to where he'd parked her car, stepping around downed branches and crushing the remains of Sue Ellen's garden under his feet.

He covered the last few yards as quickly as he could, popped the trunk to Letty's car, and lowered Letty inside. Sweat mixed with the rain on his forehead, and his neck throbbed from the effort. He gave himself a minute to breathe. Getting her the rest of the way to the spot he'd picked in the woods was going to be torture. It would mean carrying her a quarter mile from where he parked at the trailhead and then hiking all the way home.

But it had to be done.

He didn't bother to check Letty for a pulse. If she wasn't gone yet, it wouldn't be long. He'd given her enough pentobarbital to put down a Great Dane.

Which should work out perfectly.

If her body was discovered and the authorities found the drug in her system, they'd assume she'd overdosed. Given the type of research Letty's lab did, they'd have the tranquilizer on hand, too. She'd told him she had a habit of hiking alone when she was upset. And with the way her life had been falling apart, and her recent behavior being so erratic... it all fit.

He straightened, and the movement pulled at his stitches. He patted the dressing on his neck. It was soaked with rain, like the rest of him. No way to tell if he was bleeding through the bandages. He needed to go in and check. Pete grabbed the trunk's lid to pull it closed and stopped.

The trunk light in Letty's Subaru was cracked and fogged over. It barely produced enough light for him to tell it was on. But even that was enough for the "UT" on Letty's borrowed sweatshirt to glow a bright orange.

Crap.

That's what he'd forgotten.

It wouldn't be smart to leave her in the woods wearing his shirt.

Pete checked his watch. Quarter to eleven.

He needed to hurry. He reached for the hem of the sweatshirt and stopped, looking down at Letty one last time. She lay curled on her side, her hair a tangled mess. He wanted her to look peaceful, but she didn't. Her skin was too pale, her body too still.

I'm sorry.

Rain slipped under his collar and crawled down his back, but he didn't care. Things with Letty could've been good. He'd really thought she might get it. Might see how badly he'd been treated by the people who were supposed to love him, to accept him, to believe him. He hadn't meant for…

Pete shook his head.

It's not my fault.

And Letty hadn't been what she'd seemed. She'd turned on him, too. If he hadn't figured that out from the hole she'd put in his neck — half a centimeter from one of his jugular veins — the little surprise he'd found on the passenger seat when he'd moved her car made it clear. She hadn't said a word about her plan to go to the media. Who knew what else she'd been hiding from him?

He turned for the house. He'd get her wet shirt and her purse, check his bandage, change into better hiking shoes, and—

A beam of light pinned him in place.

■ ■ ■

Rain assaulted Andrew from all sides. The wind drove it into his eyes and up his nose, howling as it whipped through the trees around him. Apparently loud enough Pete Hendrick hadn't heard him coming.

The man squinted into the beam of Andrew's flashlight. He had a bloodied bandage on the side of his neck and stood hunched, frozen in place. Like a roach caught in the middle of the kitchen floor when the light came on.

Letty's car waited behind him, the rear hatch standing open in the downpour.

Andrew could barely make out the form under the dirty yellow glow of the trunk light. But once he did, there was no mistaking it.

A body.

His eyes narrowed, tension tightening his every muscle. He'd never wished he had a gun more in his life.

Whatever happened next would go a lot easier if his Glock wasn't locked in Levinson's desk, along with his badge.

Fuck.

"Hands where I can see them." Andrew kept the flashlight trained on Pete's face while he peered through the darkness and into the trunk. He fought the urge to shift the light. He needed Pete to stay blind until he knew what the hell was going on. Needed Pete not to realize he was unarmed.

Pete inched his hands skyward. "It's not what it looks like."

Andrew edged closer. Whoever lay crumpled in the back of Letty's car was on the small side, a woman or a teenager. The hair long and dark, like Letty's.

Please don't let it be her.

The thought was irrational, wishful. Who else would it be? Still, he held on to the hope. He might not have known her long, but Letty had become a friend.

I should've warned her.

He'd known Pete was no good and said nothing. The back of his throat burned.

She might be okay.

That might not be her.

Pete shifted a hand in front of his face, blocking the light. "I think she overdosed. I'm trying to take her to the hospital. To get help."

In the trunk?

Andrew's lip curled in disgust, but he ignored the man. There would be time to deal with him later. And he would. Right now, he needed to move faster. Pete's eyes would adjust eventually. Andrew was running out of time. He closed the distance to the car.

It was her.

His stomach roiled, but he forced himself calm. He needed to focus. What looked like blood smeared one of Letty's hands, and she seemed to be unconscious. Maybe dead.

Pete lowered his hand. "Andrew?"

"Back away." He kept the light trained on Pete's face, reaching down with his other hand to shake Letty's shoulder. "Are you okay?" He asked the question, even though he knew the answer. Knew there was no way she'd be able to respond. Not when she looked like that.

She wobbled like a rag doll under his hand. Her mouth falling open. Her eyelids almost, but not quite, closed.

Blood pounded in Andrew's ears. This was his fault. He'd driven by twenty minutes ago, still bothered by Letty's voicemail and hoping not to see her car in Pete's driveway. When he'd spotted her hatchback's distinctive taillights disappearing around the rear of the house, he'd grumbled to himself about women and their piss poor taste in men.

And kept driving.

A leaden weight settled in his chest. He'd gotten all the way to the truck stop before he realized something about what he'd seen didn't sit right. Why would she move her car to the backyard? That late at night. In the middle of a storm. Putting ruts in Pete's otherwise manicured lawn. It didn't make sense.

He should've known. Should've done something sooner. The weight in his chest expanded up through his throat until the guilt nearly choked off his breath.

Get your shit together.

Andrew gripped the flashlight so hard, his knuckles ached. The only thing keeping him from beating Pete to death with it was the fact that Letty needed help. Now.

"On your knees, hands on your head." Andrew's words came out like a growl.

Pete's eyes went wide. He nodded and crouched down, his voice plaintive, almost pleading. "She's been so upset about her job and what happened with Rafferty. I didn't know she'd taken anything until it was too late. We need to get her to the hospital. I can drive." He reached for his jeans pocket.

"I said, hands on your head." Andrew barked out the words, and Pete's hands shot high. He nodded and bent his knees, dropping toward the ground.

Andrew tucked the flashlight under his arm, keeping the beam down so he'd still have ambient light. He patted his jean pockets until he found his cell. What he needed to do — what he should've done already — was call for help. God, he wished Mary was there.

The lights in the house blinked out. And Andrew glanced up.

A sudden flash of movement, a blur in his periphery.

Pete's shoulder collided with his thigh.

The tackle caught Andrew off-guard. It threw him backward, lifting him from his feet, knocking the flashlight God knew where. He might've had fifty pounds on Pete, but that didn't mean a damn thing once he was airborne.

Andrew hit the ground hard. The air whooshed out of his lungs, and his head smacked back into something that felt like concrete. His cell phone flew from his hand, landing somewhere in a dense thicket of Camellia bushes lining the back of Pete's house. Pain radiated out from the back of his skull.

Pete leapt up, backing away. He looked toward the car, then the house, as if weighing his options.

Andrew tried to push himself up. Whichever direction Pete chose to go, Andrew was going to make damn sure he didn't get far. He lifted onto an elbow and stars danced in his eyes.

He probably had a concussion. But there was no time to worry about that now. Andrew blinked, trying to get his vision clear.

Pete looked down at him, his face hardening. Andrew knew the look. He'd seen it before — in the traffic stops that went sideways or domestic calls that ended in the abuser trying for suicide by cop. Pete was out of options that didn't end in jail.

Pete rushed forward, drawing his foot back like a kicker on the thirty-five yard line, aiming for Andrew's head.

Everything slowed. The cold resolve on Pete's face. The ugly gray-black sky behind him. The smell of wet leaves. The knowledge that if Pete's kick connected, Andrew was as good as dead.

Andrew grabbed Pete's foot in mid-air and twisted, pulling him off balance.

The man fell with a grunt but didn't stay down. He turned on Andrew again, like an animal backed into a corner and gone feral. Pete straddled Andrew at the waist, punching at his head and chest with blind abandon. Most of the blows glanced off, thrown wild and with more force than discipline.

Andrew deflected as many as he could, but a few landed. His reflexes slowed by the steady ringing in his ears, the pain in the back of his head a steady throb. One of Pete's blows split his lower lip, and he tasted copper.

Andrew forced himself out of the mental fog. He slammed his fist into Pete's side.

Pete jerked sideways, the blood stain on his bandage blooming larger. He coughed out a curse, and his hand flew to his neck.

Andrew twisted, trying to get off his back. He pushed against the ground, but his palm hit the rough edge of what felt like a paver behind him and slipped.

Pete came at him again.

Andrew gripped the paver and swung it up.

It connected into Pete's face with a sickening crunch.

Pete fell to the ground beside Andrew, boneless and unmoving. The bandage on his neck now an unbroken crimson.

Andrew left him there. Not caring if he was dead or dying. He ran to Letty, stumbling at first. Then righted himself, shaking his head, as if he could sling off the persistent radiating pain in his skull. Andrew closed the distance. He pressed his fingers to her neck, searching for a pulse.

Please, please.

Nothing.

He adjusted the position of his hand and tried again.

No sign of life.

Fuck.

He tried her wrist, even though he knew a pulse would be harder to find there than at the neck. But he had to try.

He had to do something.

He touched his fingers to her skin and prayed. Not breathing for fear he'd miss it. Wishing his own heartbeat would be silent so he could stop mistaking it for hers.

Why didn't I stop?

I knew something was off. And I didn't stop.

A tiny jump of the skin under his fingers.

Then another.

She was alive. Barely.

Thank God.

He could start CPR, but if help wasn't coming, what good was that? And who knew how long it'd take to find his cell phone. He scanned the dense bushes where he thought it'd gone.

Lost cause.

Andrew patted Letty's pockets but found nothing. Her cell was probably still somewhere inside. He looked toward the darkened house.

The windows stared back at him, empty and black.

His chances of finding her phone or Pete's in the dark, in an unfamiliar house, were slim to none. He might be able to find a land line, assuming Pete had one. But the odds of that were fifty-fifty at best. And unless it was the old-fashioned corded kind, it wouldn't do him any good with the power out.

Shit.

He prodded the cut on his lip with his tongue, ignoring the sting. There was only one option left. He needed to get Letty to a hospital himself. He scooped her up and carried her to his car, trying not to pay attention to how pale she was or how waxy her skin had become. He buckled her in the passenger seat and ran around to his side of the car, stabbing the key into the ignition.

Click, click, click.

God damned, mother-fucking, son of a...

The starter again.

He scrambled back out of the car, lifting Letty from the passenger seat. Pete's SUV was probably in the garage, or he could take Letty's car. But that would only work if he found the keys.

He ran back up the driveway, his sneakers slipping on the rain soaked pavement. His balance had been off since he'd hit his head, and Letty's weight in his arms made it worse. He listed side to side but pressed her tight to his chest and kept going.

The wet slap of his shoes against the pavement landed in time with the pounding in his head. He needed to go quicker. Every second he wasted could be the difference between her making it and not. Andrew rounded the back of the house.

Pete lay where Andrew had left him, his face and neck a bloody mess, his nose clearly broken. Pete's chest moved up and down, but he showed no other signs of life.

Andrew ran for the back door. It gaped open, black as the windows. Maybe darker. Keys or a phone, he'd find one or the other. He stumbled to a stop.

Pete had been reaching for a pocket when he'd said he was taking Letty to the hospital.

It had to be keys.

He ran toward Pete, praying with every step forward.

Hang on, Letty.

CHAPTER 35

May 17, 2018

Andrew chewed two antacids and chased them with a piece of nicotine gum. None of it calmed the nauseating mix of anxiety and vending machine coffee in the pit of his stomach. He stepped onto the precinct's ancient elevator and punched the button for Levinson's floor.

He'd been up all night, sitting in the hard plastic chair beside Letty's hospital bed, and he felt every minute of it. His eyes half-stuck to their lids, his body ten times heavier than it should be. And sleep wasn't coming any time soon.

He needed to get back to the hospital before Letty woke up, and Levinson was expecting him. Andrew's stomach burbled a protest.

Two rookies he recognized but couldn't name stepped into the elevator car and moved to stand behind him. Both were over-muscled and thick around the neck, like they'd done a little too much CrossFit. They stood in silence as the doors rattled closed, although he could feel the mouthed conversation probably taking place behind his back.

"Is that him?"

"Think so."

"Poor bastard."

Andrew kept his gaze glued to the numbers on the elevator's control panel and rubbed the knot on the back of his head. He just had to get through the meeting. That was all.

The elevator display lit for floor two, and the uniforms stepped off. The shorter of the two gave him a nod on the way out.

Like you'd do for a man on his way to the firing squad.

Andrew returned the gesture, doing his best to look unworried. Or, at least, he did until the door rattled closed again.

Whatever happened now, he'd know what was coming. He could make peace with it. Couldn't he?

Life as a mall cop.

Or somebody's cell block girlfriend.

Maybe not.

The elevator dinged his arrival. Andrew swallowed hard as he stepped onto the building's top level. The noise on the brass's floor was decidedly lower than in the squad room, and it bore little resemblance to where he spent his workdays. Ivory tile polished until the scratches almost didn't show, potted plants, the city's seal on the wall.

Andrew took a deep breath and turned toward Levinson's office. He walked past a row of photographs memorializing each of Chattanooga's past Chiefs of Police and through a maze of offices with actual doors instead of cubicle walls.

I'm in high cotton now.

Andrew rounded a corner. Captain Levinson stood outside his door, hunched over a file with the deputy chief. Both men looked grim.

Shit.

They glanced up at his approach. Levinson's steady brown eyes met his, and the deputy chief's cold battleship gray ones did the same. But Andrew couldn't read either of them. The deputy chief turned on his heel and strode down the hall without a look back.

That can't be good.

Levinson gestured for Andrew to follow him into the office, but the captain waited until he'd closed the door to speak. "Heard you had quite a night."

Here it comes.

No helping it now.

Andrew took a seat opposite Levinson's desk. One of his legs bounced up and down, nervous energy finding a needed outlet. "Yes, sir."

Levinson didn't sit. He went to the window, hooking a stubby finger into the blinds and pulling down a slat. He stared out onto the street below. Likely looking at the same place Andrew had been when he'd imagined the captain doing just that a few days before. The same place where Mary sat waiting for him now.

The older man cleared his throat. "When I told you to stay home and lie low, I assumed you knew that meant not to try and kill anyone else?" Levinson let go of the blinds, and they bounced back into place with a metallic thwack. Like a trap springing closed.

Fuck.

"Yes, sir."

Levinson's forehead crumpled up like one of those ugly, wrinkle-face dogs rich people seemed to like. "You may be the first officer in the history of police work to smash a civilian's face in with a brick while the DA is in the middle of deciding whether to convene a grand jury against him."

"It was a paver, sir." Andrew regretted the words the moment he spoke them.

Levinson's head snapped around. He stared at Andrew over the top of his glasses. A shaking started at the bottom of his not-insubstantial belly and worked its way up until a laugh erupted out of him. "Damn right, it was." Levinson rode out the laugh, finishing with a slow shake of his head and a long sigh. "How's your friend?"

"In the hospital. She hasn't woken up yet, but the doctor says chances are good she will." Andrew swallowed. "Eventually." Although that didn't mean Letty would be herself when she did. God knew what the drugs in her system had done to her. Andrew tried to swallow again, but it got stuck halfway.

"Right. Well, you'll let me know."

Andrew flinched. "I will."

Levinson dropped into a well-worn chair behind his desk. "And Hendrick?"

"He won't be winning any beauty contests anytime soon, but the doctors say he'll be fine. Lost a lot of blood." Courtesy of a neck wound Andrew suspected Letty had given him. "But they don't think there's permanent damage. Should be able to release him into custody in a few days. Although, as of right now, we've still got no real idea what happened before I got there last night. He's not talking and..."

Letty can't.

The knot in his throat swelled again. He fought it away, but it came right back.

Levinson shook his head. "Damnedest thing I ever heard..." He tapped the desk, his thick gold wedding band clunking against the wood. "Well, I don't want to draw this out any more than I have to."

The knot grew twice as big, cutting off Andrew's ability to breathe. He stared at the captain's hands instead, each like a fistful of sausages covered in the coarse black hair that crawled from his rolled-up shirtsleeves all the way down to his second knuckles.

"As you know, I called you in because I finally heard something official from DA Nguyen." Levinson leaned back, the chair protesting with a leathery squeak. "She's not going to move forward."

Andrew's leg stopped shaking. "What?"

"I assume you've seen the video?" Levinson rested clasped hands over the widest part of his belly. "Hard to miss it."

Andrew nodded. The damn thing was everywhere.

"Turns out the girl who recorded it had more footage than she posted. Claims she was trying to be respectful of the preacher's family, didn't want them to see him get shot." He crossed his arms over his chest. "Although, if she was trying to be respectful, it seems like she'd have turned the thing over to us, rather than blasting it all over the internet. But what're you gonna do? I can tell you from raising two of them that teenagers are as irrational as— "

"I don't understand." Andrew worried the cut on his lip until he tasted blood.

"When the girl got word she'd be called in for questioning, I guess she fessed up to her parents." Levinson shrugged. "They must've realized the severity of what she'd done. Known that by not turning the whole thing over to police, she'd tampered with evidence. Maybe even tainted the jury pool. That's why they wouldn't let her sit down with IA without counsel."

Andrew's mouth went dry.

Son of a bitch.

The whole thing might be over.

"Nguyen's deciding now whether to prosecute the girl, but you're off the hook. She says, given what's on the rest of the video, there's no reason to impanel a jury. You did what you had to do. Pure and simple." Levinson pulled open one of his bottom desk drawers.

He put Andrew's gun and badge on the desk. "Dr. Cisneros cleared you for duty, the internal investigation came back clean. This was the last step. Welcome back, son."

■   ■   ■

A steady, persistent beep nagged at the edge of Letty's consciousness. She tried to ignore it, fought to hold on to the soft numbing darkness tucked in around her. It kept her safe. Kept her away from whatever waited if she—

"Ms. Duquesne?"

More beeping.

Letty forced one eye open, but nothing made sense. Beige walls, scratchy sheets, that damn relentless noise. "Where am I?" Her mouth was dust bin dry, and her words came out thick. They sounded like someone else's. Someone drunk or half-dead.

Pete.

Letty jerked up, and her head spun. She needed to go slow, and she needed water. Her throat ached, parched and raw. She lay back down.

"Ah, good. You're awake." A man she didn't know spoke from the foot of the bed. He had a stethoscope around his neck, turquoise scrubs, and the look of someone who'd worked more hours than he'd slept the night before. "My name's Dr. Miller. I'll be your attending physician this morning." He came around to the table beside her bed and poured a glass of water from a worn plastic pitcher. "You were intubated. Your throat'll be sore for a while."

She took the glass with a nod of thanks, propped herself on an elbow, and gulped the whole thing down despite his admonition to "go slowly."

The water tasted like plastic and old pipes, but she was too thirsty to care. She handed back the empty cup. "Thank you." She took a deep breath, trying to pull herself together. "I need my phone. I have to tell the police what happened."

"I'm sure they'll be back soon. I understand an officer brought you in last night."

An officer?

Letty's brow furrowed as the doctor adjusted the bed for her, raising the head so she was sitting. She couldn't remember anything after she'd passed out in Pete's living room. Letty wrapped her arms around her chest but couldn't get comfortable, not with one hand bandaged and the other trailing an IV. She winced, not wanting to look at the needle embedded in her skin.

What the hell happened to me?

The doctor sat on a short stool and rolled it closer, pulling a pen light from the breast pocket of his scrubs. "Let's get you checked out. With the amount of pentobarbital they found in your system, I'm surprised to see you so alert so soon." He clicked on the light and leaned closer, bringing a faint whiff of halitosis with him.

She stopped his hand with hers. "Pentobarbital?" That didn't make any sense.

Dr. Miller gave a short nod, his eyes assessing. "Pretty hefty dose according to your blood work." He sat back on the stool, pen light still on but now resting in his lap. "Why don't you tell me what you remember?"

Letty's words came out in a jumble. "Pete Hendrick tried to kill me. He must've put the pentobarbital in the tea he gave me. And he killed his wife. And he may have infected the people who attended the Chesapeake Hill Baptist Church's spring picnic with rabies. We have to let all those people know they might be sick, before they develop symptoms. They need the vaccine. I've been sick for days, and I think maybe he gave me rabies, too. Or I got it from Sue Ellen, I'm not sure."

The doctor nodded along as she spoke, but he wore the neutral face of a clinician who'd had more than his share of irrational, day-after conversations with overdose patients. "Maybe let's focus on what's going on with you for now. Start from when you first felt sick."

Letty took a deep breath. She needed to stop sounding crazy. She needed him to listen. Her stomach burbled, threatening to return the water she'd gulped down. "I spoke with Sue Ellen Hendrick the night she was admitted for treatment. And I woke up with a headache and nausea the next day, realized I had a fever not long after that, and I've been headachy, dizzy, and exhausted ever since."

He pursed his lips. "It's unlikely you have rabies."

"But you don't understand, I also handled a sick bat not long before and—"

His eyebrows went up, and he raised his pointer finger in a "just one minute" gesture. "We'll test you for rabies given your contact with the bat, but the symptoms you've described sound more like the flu. And I don't think you could've contracted rabies from Dr. Hendrick. For one thing, that would put your incubation period at something like twelve hours. That's way too short."

Shit.

He was right.

If she'd had any time to process what had happened, she'd have realized the virus's unusual spread had been Pete's doing. Not because of some new rabies variant she contracted from Sue Ellen. "What if I was already infected with rabies before that?"

He gave her a small smile that was probably meant to be reassuring. "Have you been around anyone sick?"

Frustration grew hot under Letty's skin. The doctor wouldn't listen, and she didn't have time to convince him. Pete was still out there. And—

Kaylie.

The day Mary had given Letty a ride to the police station to make her statement, Mary'd had Kaylie with her. The little girl had been home from school with a snotty nose and a fever. They'd dropped her off at her grandmother's house on their way. "Yeah, I guess I have. A friend's daughter, but—"

"I see." He adjusted the stethoscope hanging around his neck. "How about we get this examination done? Then I'll go order the rabies test. Just in case."

She nodded, finally letting him shine the light in her eyes and listen to her breathe. He'd been nothing but polite, but he also wasn't rushing off to report what she'd told him to the authorities. And she couldn't think of a damn thing to say that might convince him there were people's lives were at risk.

A knock came from the door, and it swung open.

Andrew strode in, exchanging a quick nod with the doctor before he looked back to her. "You're awake." He grinned. "Still got all your marbles?"

She scowled at him. But he had bags under his eyes, and something told her he'd been there with her — for her — when she was unconscious. A sweat-stained Braves cap she thought was his lay forgotten in the chair by her room's window, and paper coffee cups lined the windowsill. Letty returned the grin. "Most are cracked. But yeah, I think so."

Dr. Miller patted her arm. "Everything looks good, considering. I'll go order that test." He gave Andrew another nod and slipped out of the room.

Andrew plopped down on the doctor's stool. "Want to tell me what happened?"

She ran through everything she remembered. About the night before, what Pete had said, and the doctor's apparent disbelief. Not that she blamed him. It did sound crazy. "I think Pete dosed the tea with pentobarbital he took from the clinic. If I had to guess, I'm only alive because he didn't account for how much more he'd have to administer giving it by mouth instead of injection." She shifted in the bed, trying again to get comfortable and failing.

"I don't remember anything after I passed out on Pete's floor." Flashes from the moments before came back to her — the sickening taste of the tea, the resolve in Pete's eyes, her body going numb and useless. Trapping her inside.

Letty's chest tightened, and the beep from the monitor picked up speed.

Andrew looked at the bouncing lines on the display. "When I got to Pete's last night, he had you in the trunk of your car and had a big gash on his neck. I couldn't tell what the hell had gone on, just that you needed help. You were out cold. And by the time I got you here, I wasn't sure…"

"I know." Her voice came out rough. She swallowed hard, her throat still thick and painful. When she'd blacked out, she hadn't expected to wake up.

If Andrew hadn't been there, she probably wouldn't have.

She put a hand to her throat, tears threatening her eyes. "Thank you."

His cheeks colored, and he shook his head. "I just wish I'd been there sooner." He looked away. "You should know that Hendrick's here, too."

She stiffened. "What?"

"I sent an ambulance back for him after I brought you to the ER. Even though I seriously considered just letting him bleed out in the rain."

All the air went out of the room. She kicked off the blankets and eyed the IV. Could she pull it out? She had to go. What would stop Pete from coming to finish what he'd—

Andrew covered her bandaged hand with his. "He's not gonna be a danger to you or anyone else for a long while. You really did a number on his neck. And he's under guard on a different floor."

He smiled, but it faded fast. "I'm just sorry you missed his voice box. He's telling anyone who'll listen you overdosed on purpose. Says he was trying to get you to the hospital when I arrived. That I attacked him before he was able to explain what happened. And, of course, I couldn't say for sure what'd gone on before I got there, and—"

"That son of a bitch." She kicked the blankets off the rest of the way. That's why the doctor hadn't believed her.

Andrew raised a hand, as if to calm her. "I only told you so it wouldn't come as a surprise. Not because you need to worry about it. The crime scene folks are at Hendrick's house this morning, and Mary's in talking with him now." Amusement glinted in Andrew's eyes. "Won't be long, he'll break."

She slumped back, cheap hospital pillows crinkling behind her. If anyone could get Pete to tell the truth, it was Mary. And unless he'd done a damn good job cleaning up, there'd be plenty of evidence for the police to collect.

The mug would be covered in her blood and his, with trace amounts of the pentobarbital he'd used in the bottom. Even he couldn't explain that away.

Still.

She'd put herself in that situation.

How had she not known? Not realized what a monster he was? She rubbed her hands over her face, the bandage rough against her skin. "Do I attract crazy men? Pete, Richardson... I don't get it. What am I doing wrong?"

"Actually..." Andrew hissed a breath between his teeth. "I don't think Richardson had anything to do with you."

She looked at him from between her fingers. "What?"

Andrew grimaced. "He was trying to turn himself in. But the dumb ass is convinced that the entire Chattanooga PD is corrupt. So he'd been alternating between driving past the police station and following me around, trying to get up the nerve. When he saw us together, he convinced himself you might be law enforcement, too."

She shook her head, lowering her hands to her lap. "Why would he think that?"

"He heard about the Bullard shooting on the radio and then saw us having what he said looked like a heated discussion outside the hospital. Thought you might be my boss." Andrew rolled his eyes, as if the idea was preposterous.

Letty chose to ignore it, and Andrew went on. "Then, the next day, he drove by the place he'd dumped Wilbur's body, and he saw you again. Talking to another cop. You were probably giving your statement, but, in his mind, that sealed it."

She shook her head. "Still, he was at my hotel. Wouldn't that've clued him in that I'm not with the police?"

"That seems to have been why he kept following you, instead of forcing himself to go into the station." Andrew shrugged. "He assumed you were staying at the Inn because you were outside law enforcement. FBI, I guess. Probably thought you'd be more likely to give him a fair shake."

"So he followed me." She pulled the blankets back up over her legs. The gown they'd put her in was two sizes too big and provided plenty of coverage, but it was too thin to keep her warm. "Until I ran from him and into an intersection."

"Bingo." Andrew nodded. "That's when he realized his mistake. He came to your hotel to make sure you were okay, and, once he saw you come in, he made a run for it."

The cigarette smoke.

She picked at the edge of the bandage. Richardson must've been smoking while he waited, probably in one of the alcoves off the Inn's upstairs hallway.

"If he hadn't killed somebody, I'd almost feel bad for him." She smoothed her bandage back in place and stared out the window, where the day was clear and bright. Yesterday's storm had wiped the world clean, not even leaving a cloud behind to mar a sky of perfect cerulean blue.

Except not everything was cleaned up.

Not yet.

"Do you know where my phone is? I need to call the health department. We've got to make sure they warn everyone who went to Bullard's picnic."

"I'll take care of it." Andrew stood. "And I'll make sure they listen. Once Pete confesses, and he will, they won't have much choice." He had the same bulldog-tenacity look on his face he'd had when they first met.

Her shoulders relaxed, and she settled deeper into the pillows. The burst of adrenaline that had powered her since she'd come to had all but evaporated. "Thanks, Andrew. I still need my phone, though. I need to call Bill and my parents and…"

"I didn't have your parents' number, and your phone is probably in an evidence bag somewhere. But Bill's on his way. Should be here any minute." Andrew collected his hat from the chair by the window. "I called Chris, too. He'd be here already, but he's at the airport." Andrew smiled at her. "Had to go pick up your friend, Priya."

"What?" Her breath caught in her throat. She hadn't heard any news about Priya in days, and she'd assumed the worst. But if they'd allowed her to fly home…

Andrew's smile widened. "Bill says she's gonna be fine."

"Thank God." A warmth spread through Letty's chest, gratitude and relief and something she hadn't felt in so long she barely recognized it.

Hope.

CHAPTER 36

May 27, 2018

"You know you didn't have to come up." Letty glanced over her shoulder. "All I need to do is drop this stuff off and change clothes."

Andrew stopped halfway up the apartment stairs, her suitcase resting on his shoulder. His breath came heavy, and red splotches crept up his cheeks. "If I don't help, we'll never get to the bar on time."

"I promise they won't drink all the beer before we get there." Although she'd seen Chris try before. And tonight, he had good reason. Priya's parents might not have stopped the engagement, but they couldn't be too happy about the couple's plan to marry within the month.

The night promised to be awkward.

"Bill said they'd be there at four, so we've got at least an hour." Plenty of time for her to toss on a dress, read over her speech, and make it to the Flying Dawg before the engagement party started. "Besides, you're only here because Bill promised to take you to the Braves game tomorrow. What d'you care if we're late?"

"I care." Andrew huffed up the last of the steps. "Chris is good people. And besides, I gotta be back at work on Tuesday. This is my last hurrah."

She shook her head. He'd been not-so-quietly chomping at the bit to go back to work since Levinson had given him the good news.

Letty unlocked her apartment's door and swung it open. The alarm beeped its displeasure, and the air inside hung still and stale. Everything just as she'd left it. Even so, the space felt like something out of the distant past. A place that belonged to someone else.

Maybe it had.

She stepped inside, and her foot slid on something left on the floor. A folded piece of paper lay just beyond the threshold, as if someone had tucked it beneath the door. It had her name scrawled on the front.

In Mark's handwriting.

The alarm's beeping changed tone and quickened, keeping time with her heartbeat. She forced herself to punch in the code, but her skin hummed with anticipation and her breath came shallow.

Andrew bumbled into the apartment behind her, dropping the suitcase in the hallway floor with a loud thunk. "I gotta use the head."

She pointed him in the right direction, her gaze never leaving the paper. Why would Mark have come to her apartment? And what would he possibly have to say to her? After so long. After she'd treated him the way she had. She swallowed hard.

Letty waited until she heard the bathroom door close to unfold the paper. The first page was a handwritten note. The second looked like some kind of press release, "Stafford Oil and Gas Announces its Launch of the Jessa Duquesne Foundation."

Holy shit.

She sped through the press release. Lots of nonsense about Mark's company being a leader at the forefront of sustainable energy. Its commitment to finding balance between fossil fuels and a healthy environment. She found the part that mattered two paragraphs in. The foundation would seek to explore whether man-made environmental causes could be contributing to the world-wide increase in zoonotic spillover and abnormal animal activity — like the aberrant smack of box jellyfish that had killed her sister.

A familiar lump rose in her throat. She shifted to the letter, written in Mark's messy scrawl. "Sorry to stop by unannounced. I tried your phone but couldn't reach you. My connecting flight through Atlanta is delayed until eleven. Call me if you get this before then."

He'd written the date on the top right corner of the page, but she knew when he'd called. She still hadn't checked the message he'd left her that day outside Caroline's house. She'd been too afraid of what he might say.

What he might know.

Never in her wildest imagination had she thought this might be why he was calling.

She made herself refocus on the letter. "I don't know if your parents told you about the foundation, but I'd love to talk with you about what we've got planned. Maybe even see if I can coax you into helping. I can't think of anyone better suited for the work. Call me." He'd signed it, "Love, Mark."

The distant splash of water running from a tap came from down the hall.

She dropped the letter. What happened in Chattanooga might've been orchestrated by Pete, but it didn't change the fact that, all over the world, something was wrong on a much greater scale. Her mouth went dry.

A month ago, Mark's note would've put her into a tailspin. She would never have considered calling him. Much less jumping into something like what he'd proposed. But she wasn't that person anymore. She could make a difference. And there was nothing holding her back.

Jessa would tell her to live the life she wanted.

Andrew walked out of the bathroom, wiping his hands on his jeans. He slowed as he got closer. "Everything okay?"

Letty smiled at him with tears in her eyes. "Yeah, I think it will be."

THE END

ACKNOWLEDGEMENTS

Thank you to my husband for supporting me as I took the crazy leap from big firm lawyer to first-time author. It's been a wild ride, and I wouldn't change a thing.

Thank you to my writer friends. You are my village. E. Ardell, Janice Rocke, Spencer Lipori, Jason Jurinsky, Sarah Pruitt, Joshua Naylor, Paula Scott, Melissa Bowers, Carolyn Rogers, Brandt Hill, Austin Roy, Amy Cluck, Barb Dill-Varga, Dorothy Vriend, Margie Hamilton, Jean Grabow, Liz Thompson, Joshua Bruce, Will Wraxell, and Penny Righthand — thank you for your friendship, your support, and the use of your editorial pens.

To Heather Lazare, who is chiefly responsible for editing out all the bumpy bits and to C.S. Lakin, who taught me how to make less of them.

Finally, a huge thank you to Heart Dominguez, who answered an unreasonable number of veterinary questions, usually late at night and in a flurry of emails. His help was invaluable, and any errors or omissions are my own.

ABOUT THE AUTHOR

Brooke L. French is a recovering lawyer who now writes full time. She lives between Atlanta and Carmel, California with her husband and sons.

NOTE FROM THE AUTHOR

Word-of-mouth is crucial for any author to succeed. If you enjoyed *Inhuman Acts*, please leave a review online—anywhere you are able. Even if it's just a sentence or two. It would make all the difference and would be very much appreciated.

Thanks!
Brooke L. French

NOTE FROM THE AUTHOR

We hope you enjoyed reading this title from:

BLACK ROSE
writing™

www.blackrosewriting.com

Subscribe to our mailing list – *The Rosevine* – and receive **FREE** books, daily deals, and stay current with news about upcoming
releases and our hottest authors.
Scan the QR code below to sign up.

Already a subscriber? Please accept a sincere thank you for being a fan of Black Rose Writing authors.

View other Black Rose Writing titles at
www.blackrosewriting.com/books and use promo code
PRINT to receive a **20% discount** when purchasing.

Printed in the USA
CPSIA information can be obtained
at www.ICGtesting.com
LVHW030801240823
756118LV00049BA/1337